Rules of Falling

Leslie Tall Manning

ISBN: (Paperback) 978-0-9600177-5-1
ISBN: (Digital) 978-0-9600177-2-0
ISBN: (Audio) 978-0-9600177-6-8

Original cover photo provided by Morristowne Photography © 2008.
Cover design by J. Kenton Manning Design, Inc. Copyright © 2021.
Interior formatting by Polgarus Studio.

Available at Amazon.com and other online and traditional bookstores.

Other books by Leslie Tall Manning

Upside Down in a Laura Ingalls Town
i am Elephant, i am Butterfly
Gaga
Maggie's Dream
Knock on Wood

Rules of Falling discussion questions can be found at the end of the book followed by an excerpt of the award-winning novel *Upside Down in a Laura Ingalls Town.*

To learn more about Leslie, visit her website:
www.leslietallmanning.com

This book is dedicated to S.V.
Your true story became the inspiration for this fictional one.
Thank you for being my unsuspecting muse.

No one saves us but ourselves.

~ ***Buddha***

Syncope (**sing**-kuh-pee): loss of consciousness resulting from insufficient blood flow to the brain.

Chapter One

The harsh smell of Formaldehyde attacked my sinuses, trying to gag me. The lights hit me next, the flicker from the fluorescent lamps overhead causing my half-closed eyelids to twitch. My tongue pressed hard against the roof of my mouth. My scalp tingled. I was the star in a sci-fi movie, floating inside an alien's spaceship, immobile.

I always felt this way when I came to.

Familiar thighs cushioned the back of my head. A gentle hand pushed the hair from my eyes. A girl's whisper: "Erica…" Thin fingers pressed lightly against my wrist.

Feel for a pulse.

Count the seconds.

"You dropped so fast, I almost didn't catch you in time," Lindsay said, her dark, silky ponytail falling forward, nearly touching my chin, the scent of lilac deodorant filling the space between us.

I stretched my neck and felt it pop. I tasted sweat above my upper lip.

"Sheep's eyes, Erica, remember?" Lindsay said. "We're dissecting today. You're not the only one who felt like fainting, trust me. Half the kids in this class are green."

Squatting with her hands pressed firmly against my back, Lindsay helped me sit up. I moved my head in circles.

"She all right?" Mr. Baines our AP Physiology teacher asked. I couldn't see him, but I could picture him, standing next to the white board with that I-can't-wait-to-retire-from-this-high-school-crap look on his scruffy-bearded face.

"You good?" Lindsay asked.

"Good," I answered, so quiet I could hardly hear the word. Even though I was never out for more than a few minutes, it always took time for my throat muscles to return to normal. First I smelled, then I saw, then I spoke, then I could feel my hands and feet again. That was the order of things.

"She's fine," Lindsay announced, to the whole universe it seemed.

One of the girls on the other side of the room let out a loud shriek. "Ew! Michael, that's disgusting!"

"Mr. Johnson!" Mr. Baines called out. "Please refrain from playing with the *vitreous humor*."

"The *what*?" Michael asked.

Mr. Baines did not respond.

Still sitting on the floor, I spotted pairs of Adidas, New Balance, and Converse, along with a smattering of heels and dress flats next to the tall counters where lab partners were engrossed in—or grossed out by—the slimy eyeballs staring up from their dissecting pans.

It's funny how my classmates were no longer aware of when

I went down, or when I woke up, for that matter. They had adapted to my situation, like white noise spilling out of an old radio. At first the noise is irritating and intrusive. But after a while, it just blends in with the backdrop.

"I'm sorry," I whispered.

"No worries," Lindsay said. Then, after a moment, "Let me know when you're ready to stand."

She breathed loudly in my ear, slowly, methodically, through her nose, until my own breath matched hers. My head finally stopped spinning. My hands and feet came back to life.

"How many fingers?" she asked, splaying them out.

"Fifty," I said. When Lindsay didn't respond to my wit, I said, "Three."

She helped me to my feet. I leaned against her for support.

"Want to see the nurse?" she asked.

I shook my head.

She pulled the salty-sweet power bar out of my backpack, undid the wrapper, and placed the snack in my hand. I was never hungry when I first came to, but my Pavlovian mother had conditioned me to suck down a little salt immediately after an episode. As the other kids poked and prodded their sheep's eyes, I sat at my desk and tried not to gag on the crumbly power bar.

Lindsay handed me my yellow Gatorade. "Electrolytes," she said as she unscrewed the lid.

I wanted to say, *No shit, Sherlock.* But, of course, I did not.

Back in middle school, Lindsay and I were like a nerdy pair of bookends. We joined and quit Girl Scouts at the same time; painted our bedrooms a matching shade of Pepto-Bismol pink; braided each others' hair on Friday nights; and got to school early to hang out with the librarian. As high school seniors, we still did just about everything together, only now it was because we were attached by an invisible, almost mythical, umbilical cord. If it weren't for Lindsay, I might not have been standing in a physiology room, digging into some poor sheep's cornea. I probably would have been sitting at home instead, dissecting a cartoon frog on an interactive home-school website.

"Thanks," I told her.

Lindsay slid her goggles back in place, took the forceps, poked at the eye in our own pan, and hurriedly jotted down notes.

"Bell in five," Mr. Baines said. "Start putting your things away. Don't forget to wipe down your tables. And Mr. Johnson, please leave your lab coat behind this time, much as you'd like to start a fashion trend."

Some kids giggled. I downed the rest of my Gatorade.

After class, as Lindsay and I hiked through the bustling hallway to second period, she asked me, "Did you eat breakfast today?"

"Yup."

"Take your medication?"

"Like a junkie."

Lindsay's backpack slapped against her back. Mine wasn't as heavy since I had two sets of textbooks: One stayed on the teacher's desk in each of my classes, and the other remained at home. The only items I carried during school were pens and pencils, a divided binder, and my homemade lunch which included a thermos of soy milk.

"What are you going to do during gym?" Lindsay asked.

I shrugged. "It's too cold outside to watch you all run the

loop. Guess I'll hang out inside and read our book for lit class. I'm more than halfway through."

"You're way ahead of me. That book is confusing."

"Don't worry," I told her. "I'll help you with it."

We pushed our way down the crowded stairwell in the direction of the gym.

Adam Carchelli and his entourage stampeded up the steps, fresh from the locker room showers. The three boys looked nearly identical in their Volunteer Fireman T-shirts and faded jeans. The only thing that set them apart was the color of their hair.

"I'll catch up," Adam told his buddies.

He pushed his damp brown curls from his forehead, skipped steps until he stood on the one below Lindsay, and kissed her on the lips.

I glanced down at my Uggs.

"You smell weird," Adam told Lindsay, scrunching up his nose.

"It's her new perfume," I said. "It's called *Ewe de Vitreous Humor.*"

The deliberate misspelling of *e-a-u* was only in my head, but Adam laughed.

"Hey, Erica," he said.

"Hey."

Lindsay placed a hand against Adam's cheek. "It's dissection day. Blah." They leaned in for another kiss.

It was strange to see Lindsay so gaga over someone. Up until the end of our junior year, she'd spent her free time devouring fantasy books like *The Hunger Games, Harry Potter,* or *The*

Spiderwick Chronicles, writing fan letters to her favorite movie stars, and digging potato chip bits out of her braces. Then, this past July, after she came back from her yearly trip to her grandmother's in the Appalachians, her braces were removed. Things happened really fast after that: Her complexion cleared up, leaving behind velvety Cherokee skin; she fell out of her training bra; and boys who hadn't known she was alive the year before were suddenly sniffing her out. Lindsay chose Adam, a non-jock, straight-B student, over all the other boys who asked her out, including our high school's number-one, very sexy golfer.

"Gotta get a move on," Lindsay told Adam.

"Okay," he said. "See you in guitar class. You, too, Erica."

I nodded as he continued up the steps.

As Lindsay and I entered the gym, she said, "I'm making Adam wear a tux to Winter Formal."

"How's he handling it?" I asked.

"Mister John Deere? Not so good. But he'll learn to deal."

We reached the girls' locker room entrance.

"See you after," Lindsay said. "I'll tell Mrs. King you're here."

Her ponytail swung back and forth as she disappeared beyond the double doors.

I sat on the bottom bleacher, readjusted my cloth headband, and opened *Uncle Tom's Cabin*. I tried to focus on the horrific things that were happening to Tom in his slave-ridden world, but my mind kept drifting.

Winter Formal was to be held in the main gym. In two months, the space would be magically transformed by Glee Club and the Girls Athletic Board from a stinky basketball court into a palace ballroom. I pictured myself in a silver sparkly dress, with my mother's real diamond earrings to match, and my hair in one of those up-do's from Queen of Curls Hair Salon. I would leave my uncomfortable compression stockings buried in my underwear drawer. My shoes would be from Belk, black velvet, open-toed heels, carrying me into the pale blue light on the dance floor. There'd be a band no one had ever heard of playing songs the teachers liked more than the students. The punch would probably be spiked before the band's first break and, even if it wasn't, bottles of Jack or lemon vodka would make the rounds, and all the girls would float like visions in their way-too-sexy gowns, wrist corsages, and body glitter.

I pictured Lindsay and me going to the dance together, getting into double-trouble without dealing with the pressures of the boys. We'd whisper-gossip about whose dress was prettiest or whose dress looked like it was yanked off the mannequin at the old lady's shop. She'd point out how one of the female chaperones was stuck in the seventies, and I'd mention how hot the boy's basketball coach looked in a suit. Lindsay would get us some punch, hers high-octane, mine unleaded.

Breaking me out of my thoughts, a female student dashed through the gym to make it out to the field before the gym teacher freaked. She disappeared through the locker room doors, leaving a swish of air behind.

In reality, Lindsay would go to the dance with Adam, and most of the other girls had dates as well. No one was going to ask me to the formal. I was too much of a risk. Add those sexy heels to my five-foot-five frame and there's a recipe for disaster. Hitting the floor from that altitude, I could sprain an ankle or pop a knee. Or worse yet, crack my head open on whatever stopped my fall. Maybe end up with someone's tiara jabbed through my skull. That's why I owned only four types of footwear: Ugg boots and slip-ons for fall and winter, tennis shoes and flip-flops for spring and summer. There would be no high heels. No up-do's. No Winter Formal. No Spring Fling. No Senior Prom.

Whatever. It was my goal to disappear into the woodwork rather than be the center of attention, and I was definitely an overachiever when it came to goal setting.

I sank down among the wooden bleachers and refocused on *Uncle Tom's Cabin*. I read for the next forty minutes until the bell rang, and Lindsay and her ponytail once again bounced alongside me on our way to guitar class.

The guitar teacher, Mr. Shimmel, leaned back in his chair, his outlet-mall Reeboks up on his desk, reading an old copy of *Rolling Stone*.

"Let's go freestyle today," he told the class, never taking his eye off the magazine article, not bothering to take roll.

Freestyle meant we didn't have to do any workbook lessons; that we could play whatever we wanted. It also meant Mr. Shimmel would get a free period.

Only seven of us made up the class: two rockers who were in bands and only took guitar class to get their elective credits, and two wannabe Goths who played the same eighties retro punk music my mother listened to when she housecleaned. And, of course, there were Adam and Lindsay, who spent a large portion of class time giving each other goo-goo eyes and making up their own slow songs. As the odd-girl out, I sat alone, working on some new Taylor Swift and vintage Joan Baez tunes.

After class, Lindsay and I moved upstream to AP Psych.

"Crap," she said.

"What's the matter?"

"I hate this class."

"You do?"

"I think Freud was a—" She pulled her lips together, thinking. "What do you call a guy who hates women?"

"A misogynist," I said.

"Right. And I think Carl Jung—"

"It's pronounced *Yung...*"

"Whatever," Lindsay said. "I think he had a screw loose. All that *anima* and *animus* bullshit."

We arrived at our classroom which was filled with some of the brainiest kids at Grayson High.

Lindsay stopped outside the doorway. "Look at them. It's a geekazoid frenzy."

"Hey, watch it," I told her. "I'm a geekazoid."

"Yeah," she said, laughing, "but you're at the top of the geekazoidal food chain."

Lindsay and I shared the same fall schedule: AP Physiology, Gym, Guitar for Beginners, AP Psych, Statistics, and AP Lit. Our science teacher would have called our relationship *symbiotic:* Lindsay needed my help with the difficult concepts in our AP classes, and if I kept my grades up, I had a shot at valedictorian. As a bonus, my mother had stopped harassing the poor school nurse, and Lindsay's mom was hopeful her daughter would receive a community service scholarship for helping me out.

After school, we walked across the parking lot to Lindsay's truck, an old white Ford F-150. The vehicle was a clunker, but

Lindsay didn't seem to care. I think it reminded her of her dad, who had deserted the Bennett family when we were freshmen. That piece of tin was pretty much the only thing he'd left behind.

After Lindsay finally got the truck started, she said, "I have to babysit tonight."

"On a school night?"

"I can use the money."

I knew how true this was. Over the years, I'd given Lindsay dozens of hand-me-down sweaters, coats, even shoes, until her feet grew to a size larger than mine. It made me happy to give her my clothes, but it probably made her happier to shop for her own things.

Ten minutes later, she dropped me off at my house only a few blocks from hers.

"Who are you babysitting for?" I asked as I grabbed my backpack.

"The Taggert family," she said. "Over on Whaling Road. Adam hooked me up."

"Adam?"

"He knows Mr. Taggert from the fire department. Three-year-old twins. One boy, one girl."

"Yikes."

"Nah," Lindsay said. "I'll watch their *Sesame Street* DVD's and get paid to be a couch potato. Babysitting isn't so bad."

We stayed silent for a moment, the word 'babysitting' dangling between us like a rusty bridge.

"Well," I finally said, "have fun watching Elmo."

I shut the door and stood on the curb as Lindsay drove away, thinking that even watching a pair of three-year-olds would be better than hanging out alone.

Chapter Two

My mother stood at the kitchen counter dumping powdered protein mix into the blender. Her skinny tattooed arms stuck out from the sleeves of one of my dad's old Billabong T-shirts. Her jeans had more holes than my rattiest pair.

"Strawberry smoothie," she said.

"Does it taste like salt?" I asked.

"I did my best to make it taste like strawberries."

I tossed my backpack onto the floor slid out one of the tall stools next to the counter.

"Table, please," she said by rote as she pressed the button on the blender.

I went to the table and sat down on one of the low wooden chairs.

She poured the smoothie into a glass and brought it and a box of organic whole wheat crackers to the table.

"What'd you do to your hair?" I asked, sipping the smoothie that tasted like seawater with strawberries thrown in as an afterthought.

"Added dark blue sheen to my roots," she said. "The gray hairs were driving me nuts."

"Oh."

"How was school?"

I dug a cracker out of the box and popped it into my mouth. "Fine."

"Erica?"

"What?"

She narrowed her eyes. "When?"

I may as well have had a microchip in my brain.

"Physiology. In the middle of stabbing an eyeball. Mary's little lamb will never look at me the same way again."

My mother reached into the drawer for the log book I'd started the summer after ninth grade. A lot of *Syncopians*—aka chronic fainters—kept journals, so I figured, why not? Some shared their logbooks on the Internet, but I kept mine to myself. Witches and vampires were popular topics at the time, so I had named the ledger, *Erica's Book of Spells*. I'd even decorated the cover with yellow and purple glitter glue.

"Why didn't the nurse call me?" my mother asked as she jotted with a pen in the book. "She's supposed to notify me every time you faint."

"I didn't see her."

"Erica…"

"Don't make a federal case out of it, Mom. Anyway, Lindsay was there."

My mother sipped her smoothie and toyed with one of the three tiny hoops in her ear lobe. When she set the glass back down, she said, "I meant to tell you…I saw Lindsay with a boy."

I didn't respond.

"Last weekend," she went on. "They were holding hands in front of the movie theater."

"They've been going out since September."

"Oh," she said. "Is he a nice boy?"

"Lindsay seems to think so."

"She's really blossomed this year, huh?"

"I guess…."

Pause.

"Did you eat your lunch today?" she asked.

"Yes."

"Did you hurt anything? During your spell?"

I shook my head.

My mother put the log book back in the drawer. "We have to talk about next year, you know. Open up that can of worms."

"What worms?"

"When your dad comes down from his office. We'll have a family meeting."

"Mom…"

"I think it's time we discussed what we're going to do about college," she said.

"It's not *we*," I told her, irritated.

"Yes, honey, it is."

"No, Mother, it's not."

She picked up my empty glass from the table and placed it in the sink. "Your father will be at his computer for another hour or so, and then we'll have an early dinner and talk about things."

I grabbed my backpack and headed to my bedroom down the hallway. I used to sleep upstairs, but my mother had convinced my dad to trade my room for his office, so I wouldn't have to go up and down the steps, even though I did it all day long at school. I sat at my desk studying *Uncle Tom's Cabin* vocabulary words and AP Physiology terms until my room turned from bright yellow to dim autumn orange, and my dad called me for dinner.

***

After we finished our baked chicken and quinoa and the dishes were washed—one of the only chores I *wasn't* forbidden from doing, as long as I didn't bend over to put them in the dishwasher—the three of us sat at the kitchen table.

My mother didn't waste any time.

"It's because of me," she said.

Dad shook his head. "Ruthie, don't start."

"Marcus, there's no argument that what we do to our bodies early on can affect us later in life, and can affect our offspring. God knows I've proven that."

My mother was referring to a baby she'd lost a few years before I was born. The baby died an hour after the delivery, and even though my mother didn't mention it too often, whenever she got emotional over something family related, the topic seeped into the conversation.

"This isn't the time to watch you self-flagellate," Dad said. Then he turned to me. "Your mother tells me that Lindsay has a boyfriend."

"What does Lindsay Bennett's personal life have to do with anything?" I asked.

"Nothing," my mother said. "It's just that…"

A lone tear rolled down her cheek.

Dad patted her arm.

"What the hell's going on?" I asked.

"Erica," Dad said, "we need to figure out the details of college. Your mother, no matter how dramatic she gets, has a point."

"I've applied to three schools, Dad. I've aced all of my Honors and AP courses. My SAT and ACT scores are great."

Dad said, "The question isn't whether you'll get in, but what happens when you do."

My mother said between sniffles, "What if…what if Lindsay doesn't go to the same school as you?"

"So?"

My mother looked to Dad for support, but he stared at his folded hands.

"Is that what you both planned on?" I asked. "Having Lindsay follow me to college? That's ludicrous."

"Honey," Dad said, "you may find it in your best interest to have an assistant in college, just like you do in high school."

My mother burst out, "I want you to do it online."

"Do what online?" I asked.

"Ruth," Dad said, "not now…"

"Wait," I said. "You want me to attend four years of college on the Internet? Are you crazy? I'm not a freaking invalid—"

"Of course you're not," my mother said. "But there are so many gray areas; I don't think they all occurred to us until now. Until I saw Lindsay with that boy."

Heat rose to my ears. "*That boy's* name is Adam. And you're acting like Lindsay's robbing liquor stores or hooking on the corner. It's a stupid boyfriend. She's a senior. She's entitled to one."

"It's just that seeing her with that—Adam—made me realize she has a life of her own, and that next year, if she—" My mother cut herself off.

"If she what?" I said, standing up. "Gets knocked up and moves to a trailer park? Joins the army? Mops floors at the Piggly Wiggly?"

My mouth dried up. I licked my lips but couldn't feel them. My clammy hands gripped the back of the chair for support. I stood on a swaying limb, up high in the wind.

"Erica," Dad said, moving toward me faster than a soccer player at the net. "CLIFF."

CLIFF was our family's acronym for "Cross legs. Lie down. Feet up," even though it only used the *C*, the *L*, and one *F*. In reality, it meant that if I was too late to cross my legs, then I would aim to do the last two. And if I didn't do any of them, there was a good chance I would topple *over* the cliff.

"Since ninth grade I've had to deal with this," I said, ignoring my dad's coaching and the sudden fire that filled my veins. "Not *you*. It's *my* thing. *Mine*. So stop telling me—"

Dad repeated, "CLIFF, Erica…CLIFF…"

The blood vessels behind my eyes throbbed. Fog entered my brain. Then my eyelids fluttered and the world went black.

***

The comforting smell of aftershave. Cushions beneath me. Head throbbing. Fingers rubbing my temples. Hands rubbing my feet.

"She's back," my mother's voice said.

My eyes opened a crack. I squinted under the recessed lighting in the kitchen ceiling.

"Crap," I whispered. "I'm sorry."

Dad stroked my hair. "It's okay, baby."

My parents helped me sit up then waited as I regained my composure and my voice came back to me.

"Hands and feet?" Dad asked.

I shook my hands. "Here."

"Headache?"

Fatigue filled my joints and my eyes still throbbed, both I was used to and could handle.

So I lied.

"Head hurts. Bed. Please."

Together they helped me walk into the dark room. I lay down on my bed and rolled away from them, toward the wall. Within a moment, I heard the door click shut and my parents' voices as they floated down the hallway toward the kitchen.

I snuck out of bed, went to my door, opened it a crack, and listened.

"Every time you blame yourself, we get off track," Dad was saying. His voice was firm, but his patience never grew thin, with my mother or with me.

"You know what kind of wild woman I used to be, Marcus," my mother said. "All the partying. It's a miracle I didn't end up dead, hanging out with those freaks."

"It was the nineties," Dad reminded her.

"Try using that excuse for the baby we lost."

"God, Ruthie...you were young and grunge and stupid. Just like half the population."

"You weren't stupid," my mother said. "You were my voice of reason."

"I was plenty stupid. You were blinded by my tats."

My mother's voice softened. "Not all of them. Just the one on your ass." She let out a tired giggle.

"Ruth," Dad said, "what we did decades ago is null and void."

"Null and void," she repeated.

I pictured her staring intensely at my dad, her dark hazel eyes matching my own.

"Marcus," she said, "do you remember in the ninth grade, when Erica first fainted? She was singing in the Christmas chorus: 'Chestnuts Roasting on an Open Fire.' Such a silly detail to remember, as if the song means anything. Do you know I've gone over every second leading up to that moment? Did I feed her too many Big Macs? Not enough protein? She'd had a tetanus shot a few weeks earlier, remember? For that awful cut she got while playing in that rusty pile of junk near the park..."

What my parents *didn't* know was that I'd fainted two months *before* that front-page-news Christmas pageant.

The incident occurred at the North Carolina Fair. Lindsay had come along, and my parents let us run off by ourselves for an hour. I'd known from messing around on the monkey bars and doing cartwheels that I got dizzy when I went upside down—or, I should say, when I came back up—but I, being the braver between the two of us back then, convinced Lindsay we should take on the biggest roller coaster at the fair. Soon, we were soaring through the sky, rolling up and down the steep tracks, whipping around and upside down. Then the final loop came, and the world disappeared, and when I came to, I was being dragged off the ride by Lindsay and a toothless carnie.

"You'll be fine," the carnie said as he headed back to the controls. "Go suck down a Pepsi."

Lindsay helped me to a bench.

I had begged her, like a kleptomaniac or a closet pothead, "Please don't tell my parents."

"Okay."

And that was that. The beginning of the trust between Lindsay and me.

"Syncope isn't caused by a tetanus shot," Dad told my mother now.

"What if we've overlooked something?" she asked.

"You've spoken with dozens of specialists," Dad said. "You've researched more websites than a professional hacker. Erica is living a pretty normal life, all things considered, and that's because you're here for her, twenty-four-seven. Whenever she needs you."

My mother whispered then, and I wasn't sure I'd heard her correctly, but it sounded like, "She doesn't seem to need me these days."

"She's a senior," Dad said. "Give her some space. She'll let you know when she needs you. I promise."

The tinkling of a spoon against china traveled up the hall to my room, and I imagined my mother sipping a cup of Jasmine tea.

"Tell me you forgive me, Marcus," she said. "Tell me you don't blame me."

"For the billionth time, I don't blame you, Ruth, so there's no reason to forgive you. You need to forgive yourself. Stop being neurotic. It's not good for anyone. Stop talking about the past, since no one can change that, and let's move on to what the future holds for our daughter…"

Their voices disappeared from the kitchen into the den, and I could no longer hear them.

I shut my door, took off my compression stockings, got into my pajamas, and crawled into my adjustable bed. With the remote control, I moved the head of my bed into an upright position and continued reading *Uncle Tom's Cabin* by the mini-light clipped to the book. Before too long, I fell into a troubled sleep. I dreamt that Uncle Tom suffered from syncope, and each time he fainted, whether in a cotton field, or a stable, or out on a dirt road, a mean overseer would come up behind him and try to whip him awake.

But the whipping never worked.

Chapter Three

Lindsay was late picking me up for school on Friday morning.

"Sorry," she said as I climbed into her truck. Her long brown hair was out of its usual ponytail, with pretty waves along the edges.

"Late night babysitting?" I asked.

"The Taggerts didn't get home until after midnight." She pulled onto the street. "But it was still a good night."

"Money-wise?"

"Uh-huh. And other things."

"You like the kids?" I asked.

"What? Yeah. Sure. But that's not why it was a good night."

"What do you mean?"

Her face turned bright pink. She glanced over at me and whispered, "Mr. Taggert is a freaking hottie."

"Really? What does he look like?"

"Brown eyes. Thick, dark hair. About six feet tall."

"Like Adam?"

"Oh, no, not at all. He's way more…" She shook her head. Again, the rosy color filled her cheeks.

I helped her out. "Way more *old?*"

"Well, yeah. But not like *old* old. A *young* old."

"Anyone who has two kids is *old* old."

We drove in silence until we passed a pumpkin farm a few blocks from school.

Lindsay said, "Larry wants me to be their permanent babysitter."

"Larry?"

"Mr. Taggert," Lindsay explained. "His real name is Lawrence. But he told me to call him Larry."

The names Lawrence and Larry *both* sounded old to me, but I didn't tell her so.

Lindsay pulled into the school parking lot. "Anyway, he's nothing like the boys that go here."

"That's because he's not a *boy.*"

"He definitely is not," she agreed. "*Definitely.*"

She parked in one of the last open spots and turned to me. Her words spilled out in a warm rushing stream. "He drove me home, and he went the long way, you know, out past the old shopping center, and he told me things, like how exciting it is to be a fireman—he became one almost fifteen years ago—and how he's hoping to become chief—"

"*Fifteen years?*" I said, silently doing the math in my head.

"And he's so sweet," Lindsay went on. "He loves going to the beach to look for sand dollars, and listening to modern music, not that old shit. Maybe I'll make him a playlist…."

She turned her head in the direction of the building, where large silver letters spelled out GRAYSON HIGH SCHOOL. Beneath the sign, kids were streaming in through the two sets of double doors.

Lindsay said, "Larry said his wife is a total biatch."

"Whoa," I said. "That's brutal."

"What? Oh, no. I mean, she's really nice to me, but like my mom always says, you can never judge a book by its cover, and sometimes what goes on behind closed doors is totally different than what you might expect."

"I guess so."

"Anyway," she said, "Mr. Taggert—I mean, Larry—told me he's super sad about his marriage right now. And confused. That he could really use a friend. I feel sorry for him."

The first of two homeroom bells rang out across the parking lot.

Lindsay jumped out of the driver's side and grabbed her backpack from behind the seat. I did the same. Together we walked to our shared homeroom, even though my last name is O'Donnell and hers is Bennett. Alphabetical order didn't matter when it came to Lindsay and me.

We made our way through our classes, learning about the human brain, discussing the plight of slavery. The day was "uneventful," which was good, because that meant no fainting spells.

Later, on our way home from school, Lindsay said, "What are you up to this weekend?"

"Not too much. You?"

"Adam and I are going to a picnic," she said. "Something the fire station does for the volunteers every few months."

"Oh."

"They'll probably have a terrible shag band and lots of screaming kids around…"

"Then why go?" I asked.

"I don't know. Thought it might fun to mingle."

"Won't you be with Adam?"

"Yeah," she said, "but that doesn't mean I'm dead. A girl has the right to keep her eyes open, doesn't she?"

I wasn't sure if she wanted an answer, so I didn't give her one.

"Wanna come with?" she asked.

Lindsay hardly ever asked me to go to events that weren't school related. And I didn't care if the band only played Down East shag music, or if there were screaming kids everywhere. A picnic sounded wonderful.

"You sure?" I asked.

"Why not? There'll be tons of guys there. From other counties and everything."

"When is it?"

"Tomorrow afternoon," she said. "It'll be catered by Barbeque Baron."

"I'll have to pass it by the commandant."

A few minutes later, I entered the kitchen where my mother stood like a sentry at her after-school post.

"How was your day?" she asked.

"Uneventful."

"Awesome."

A bowl of extra salty popcorn sat on the table. She poured a glass of soy milk and handed it to me.

"Lindsay asked me to do something with her tomorrow," I said, setting the milk on the placemat and grabbing a handful of popcorn.

"Oh?" she asked. "What kind of something?"

"A fireman's picnic."

"She's going with her mother?"

"With Adam," I told her.

"Where will it be?"

"I don't know."

"Well, Erica, how can I say yes if you don't even know where it is?"

"It's not on the moon in the month of June. It's not on a float. Or on a boat. Or on a goat…"

"Sarcastic poetry," she said. "Nice skill. They teach you that in your lit class?"

"What difference does it make where it is?" I asked, trying not to show my annoyance.

"What if we have plans tomorrow?"

"What plans?"

She didn't answer as she sat at the table across from me.

"Please," I said. "Lindsay asked me. I want to tell her yes."

My mother tapped her foot against the leg of the chair. I don't think she realized she was doing it.

"You don't want to go shopping for winter clothes?" she asked.

I sometimes wished my mother had remained loyal to her pop-punk days, like when I was little and she'd hire a babysitter so she and Dad could go see an underground band in an old warehouse. Except for the tats and belly ring and shiny blue roots, she had slowly morphed into a television mommy, cooking casseroles, clipping coupons, shopping for winter clothes in early autumn.

"We can go shopping anytime," I told her.

"Your father won't be back from his trade show until Sunday night."

"Dad would let me go."

My mother paused, her foot still tapping. "Get me the info," she said after a moment.

"Really? Okay."

"But before you call Lindsay," my mother said, "I have a surprise."

I glanced around the kitchen, a small fraction of my heart hoping there was a puppy hiding in the pantry. For years I had printed out Internet photos of dogs and taped them inside the pantry door, hoping my mother would eventually give in. I even tried to convince her to let me get a service dog. But pets were a no-go in my house. Dander could cause allergies, and that could be a trigger. There could also be fleas. Maybe flea bites were the culprit. Then there was the barking. Maybe it was loud noises that dropped me to the floor.

According to my doctor, heat and stress were the likely triggers.

According to my mother, *anything* could cause a spell, so better to have *nothing*.

"Check it out," my mother said. She stood up, turned around, and lifted up the back of her shirt.

I squinted, trying to make out the blue-green writing above her waistband.

"Chinese characters," she said. "Is it swollen?"

"Totally. What does it say?"

"'Forgiveness equals happiness.'"

"Oh."

She pulled her shirt back down. "You don't like it?"

"Yeah. Sure."

"You have my permission to get one, whenever you're ready," she said. "I can go with you. Help you pick one out."

How could it be okay to have a needle squirt ink through layers of my skin, but it wasn't okay to have a puppy? I had given up a long time ago trying to make sense of what my mother thought was logic.

"No, thanks," I said.

"No, you don't want me to go with you?"

"No, I don't want a tattoo."

"Oh."

"I should probably call Lindsay before she thinks I can't go," I said, gulping down the last of the soy milk and grabbing my backpack.

"Take this with you."

My mother handed me the bowl of popcorn and I headed up the hallway toward my bedroom. As I left her in the kitchen with her new Chinese tattoo, my stomach rolled happily at the thought of going to a picnic; of spending time somewhere besides home or Grayson High, with people other than my mother or the school nurse.

Chapter Four

To celebrate the warm fall day—a mid-sixties breeze rustled through the copper-colored leaves—I wore my cute red flip-flops with the fake daisies on top, a red and pink mini-dress, and a cropped pink sweater. Obviously, my compression stockings would not be part of the ensemble. I spent the entire morning after breakfast curling my hair with my extra fat curling iron and putting on my Aubrey Organics makeup. I didn't leave my bedroom until I heard Adam's Dodge Ram pull up to the curb.

"What if you faint in that thing?" my mother asked as I stepped into the kitchen. She was referring to my short dress.

"Wow," I said sarcastically. "Can I have your autograph, Erica? 'Cause you sure look like a movie star."

"I'm sorry. You do look adorable—"

The doorbell rang. I grabbed my pocketbook. As I walked up the hallway, I could tell by the extra weight that my mother had thrown in at least one Gatorade.

I opened the door. "Hey, Adam," I said as he stepped into our foyer.

"Introduce us, Erica," my mother said.

"Mother, this is Adam. Adam, this is my mother."

She shook his hand. "I'm Ruth O'Donnell. Erica's told me so much about you."

"Okay," I said, pushing Adam out the door. "Time to go."

"Nice to meet you, Mrs. O'Donnell," Adam said as I hurried him down the porch steps.

"What time will you be home?" my mother said way too loudly.

"When the picnic's over," I answered over my shoulder.

Lindsay shimmied to the center of the seat and Adam helped me into the truck.

"Gatorade and sunscreen in your bag!" my mother called from the front porch.

I gave her a thumbs-up.

"And keep your cell phone on in case—"

The slam of the passenger door cut her off.

Adam got into the driver's seat and put on his seatbelt. Lindsay and I did the same. Within seconds my house was no longer in view. I was tempted to open the window and hang my head out in the wind like a liberated dog. But there was no way in hell I was going to mess up this fine hair. Not today.

**

There were already a few dozen people at the park when we pulled into the gravelly lot. Adam came around to our side of the truck and opened the door.

"Thanks," I said as he helped me and then Lindsay out of the truck. I grabbed my pocketbook and slung it over a shoulder.

"Smell that barbeque," Lindsay said.

"Amazing," Adam said.

The word *amazing* was exactly how I felt. Amazingly independent. Amazingly happy. Amazingly normal…

The three of us walked up a narrow path through clusters of Cypress trees to the clearing beyond. The park was bordered by the river, the edge lined with reeds and cattails. A flock of geese flew overhead, squawking.

"Look!" Lindsay pointed across the lawn. "A bouncy-bounce!"

The colorful bouncer was a blow-up version of a castle. Inside, little kids jumped frantically like microwave popcorn.

We made our way to the middle of the crowd. The three of us said hello to a few of the volunteer firefighters we knew from school, and Adam introduced us to some we didn't know. Each time we met a new boy, Lindsay elbowed me in the side.

I whispered in her ear, "What did my ribs ever do to you?"

She laughed, and we continued our way around the grounds. Covered serving trays filled with all kinds of picnic goodies lined the tables. Lindsay and Adam each grabbed a bottle of Pepsi from one of several large coolers as I pulled the blue Gatorade out of my bag. We eyed the countless bowls of chips and potato salad and macaroni salad, and headed over to the bouncer filled with face-painted kids. Tigers and zebras and bumble bees flew through the air like fairy tale characters. Near the bouncer, a clown with wild orange hair shook out a parachute. He fanned it out on the ground and called to the children. In a matter of seconds, a dozen or more kids sat cross-legged in front of him.

"He's a little creepy," Adam whispered.

"I don't like clowns either," I agreed.

"This is so boring," Lindsay said, sighing loudly. "I need some Doritos or it won't feel like a picnic."

"Why don't you two go find a table?" Adam said. "I'll be right back."

As Adam headed in the direction of the port-a-potties, Lindsay and I walked toward the food. We strolled by the bowls of chips and Lindsay grabbed a handful of Doritos. Behind the food tables, in a clearing beneath the trees, the band was setting up at one end of a portable dance floor. To the right of the dance floor people nabbed chairs or spots on picnic benches.

"Oh, she's here," Lindsay mumbled, nodding toward one of the picnic tables.

"Who?"

"Larry's wife."

I followed Lindsay over to the table where a woman in her mid-thirties sat sipping a Solo cup of iced tea through a straw. Lindsay introduced me to Mrs. Taggert, then walked around the table and sat on her right.

"Nice to meet you, Mrs. Taggert," I said, shaking her hand and sitting across from her.

"Call me Josephine," she said in a pretty Southern drawl. She gave me a warm smile.

I smiled back.

Josephine Taggert was beautiful. She had the kind of skin that famous actresses have, smooth and clear, probably perfect even without makeup. Her hair was honey-brown like mine, but she had highlights of auburn that sparkled when the sun hit them just-so.

"Y'all are so dressed up," Josephine said. She was wearing a pair of beige shorts filled with too many pockets, a simple white top, and brown sandals. "I used to love wearing high heels to a picnic. But after having twins…"

She looked toward the clown where I assumed her kids were hanging out.

I wanted to tell Josephine that she could wear a burlap sack and still look pretty, but I wasn't all that good at talking to older women. They sort of made me nervous.

Lindsay said, "I adore your kids, Josephine."

"They like you, too, Lindsay. Which is good. Y'all don't want to be on their bad side. They have definitely reached an age where they want to test me. I can't wait until they start kindergarten."

We sat quietly for a moment, watching people come and go, grabbing handfuls of chips or cans of soda, waiting for the real food to be uncovered. Adam found us at the table and sat next to me, directly across from Lindsay.

Josephine said, "Hey, Adam."

"Hey, Miss Josephine."

"Things going okay for y'all down at the station?"

"Yes, ma'am."

"That's good," Josephine said, looking around. Our table was now surrounded by a mob of people as a line started to form, leading to the large pans of barbequed pork. "Has anyone seen my husband?" she asked.

Adam said, "He's talking to Chief Miller."

"Shop talk," Josephine said, dramatically rolling her eyes. "I should have guessed."

Two toddlers came up behind her and pushed against her back.

"Mama! Mama!" they squealed in a high-pitched frenzy. Their words tumbled over one another's as they told Josephine in their excited baby-talk all about the clown.

Josephine laughed, her straight white teeth matching her bleached white shirt. "Erica, this is Willie, and this is Samantha."

They were very cute children, dressed in matching dark blue shorts and light blue T-shirts. They both had curly brown hair, but Willie's was short and Samantha's fell down to her shoulders.

Willie climbed onto his mother's lap, and Samantha onto Lindsay's. I swear Lindsay beamed.

A man wearing a Carolina Panthers T-shirt and a pair of beige shorts that matched Josephine's came up to the table.

"Daddy!" Willie screamed. His sister did the same.

Lindsay pulled a tube of lip gloss from the pocket of her tight jeans. She spread the sparkly pink across her lips.

"Erica, this is my husband," Josephine said. "Larry Taggert. He's First Assistant under Chief Miller."

"Nice to meet you, Mr. Taggert," I said, shaking his hand.

"Call me Larry."

Larry didn't have a Southern dialect like his wife. The word "call" sounded like "cawl."

He sat on Josephine's left, and Samantha jumped off Lindsay's lap, walked behind Josephine, and climbed up next to her daddy. While Larry listened intently as his children competed to describe the clown, I checked him out, trying to decipher what Lindsay had meant when she'd labeled him a hottie. He had plain brown hair and plain brown eyes and a plain round face. Curly brown hairs poked out of the top of his T-shirt like they were trying to escape. His hands were large and raw, his nails short and clean. He looked like any average dad who lives in any average town. *Comme ci, comme ca*, as I'd learned back in French I.

Lindsay stared at Larry, too, while wrapping a chunk of her hair around a finger. Her face was red and glowing. Her super-shiny lips were pressed tightly together, like she was afraid if she pulled them apart, she'd say something she shouldn't.

I looked to see if Josephine noticed Lindsay's face, but she was wrapped up in what her babies were saying.

"I don't know about you all," Adam said, standing up, "but I plan to get me some pig before it disappears."

I stood up next, and we waited for Lindsay.

"You coming?" Adam asked.

"What?" Lindsay said, like she suddenly remembered we were there. "Oh. Yes. Me, too." She stood up. "See you later, Josephine." She looked at Larry. "Bye, Larry."

Larry looked up from his children and gave Lindsay a small smile.

The extra pink in her cheeks didn't fade until our plates were piled high with food.

***

Adam had brought a large blanket for us to picnic on. After lunch, he sat with his legs straight out and his back against a big old oak tree. Lindsay lay on her back with her head in his lap. I sat across from them with my legs stretched out like Adam's, my ankles crossed and my toes wiggling in a stream of sunshine. My flip-flops sat beside me.

"My stomach is so full," Lindsay said, "I can barely breathe."

Adam laughed. "If there was an emergency right now, I'd never save a soul."

"Have you ever had to fight a real fire?" I asked.

"A few."

I found it intriguing that a boy my own age had the guts to go into a burning building. I didn't even have the guts to wear a pair of heels.

"He doesn't only fight fires," Lindsay said. "Adam, tell Erica how you saved that old man who had a heart attack."

Adam ran his hand across her head. "She doesn't want to hear about that, Linds."

I asked, "Do you plan to do it for a living?"

"Yes," Adam said. "But I want to go to college before I enter the Academy. Want to work for the FBI one day. Or Homeland Security. You know, figure out what caused a fire. Or a bombing. Stuff like that."

"Like on *CSI*?" I asked.

"Sort of," Adam laughed. "But it usually takes a little longer in real life to solve a mystery."

We sat under the tree relaxing, listening to the band as it played shag music. On the dance floor, a few brave couples twirled each other around.

After a while, Lindsay said, "Let's take a walk, Adam. You don't mind, do you, Erica?"

"Go for it."

Adam helped Lindsay up from the blanket.

As they wandered off, I heard Lindsay say, "Can I have the keys to the truck?"

"What for?"

"I want to check my makeup."

"You look fine."

"Adam…keys…"

Their voices floated away.

From where I lay on my back, I could see up into the large oak tree. Above me, a squirrel sat on a branch, gnawing on a large nut. I closed my eyes, my full belly making me sleepy.

A boy's voice interrupted my happy snooze.

"This seat taken?"

I opened my eyes and shaded them. Looking down at me was one of the boys Adam had introduced me to earlier. I'd forgotten his name.

"Uh…no," I said, sitting up and shimmying my dress down over my thighs.

He sat beside me on the blanket. "Jack," he said, reaching his hand out to shake mine.

"Erica."

"You here with anyone?" he asked.

"I'm with Adam and Lindsay."

He smiled, and I realized he meant, here with *anyone*, as in *date*.

"Oh. No."

Jack was sandy blond with pearly white teeth. He was tall and super skinny. Sort of cute, once you got past the skinny thing. At least there weren't any wild hairs poking out of his shirt.

"Want to grab an ice cream?" he asked.

I was so stuffed from lunch there was no way I could squeeze one more ounce of anything into my stomach. But I wasn't about to say no to the first boy in forever who gave me a second look.

"Okay."

I put on my flip-flops and walked with him to the ice cream stand. Jack towered over me like a sunflower.

"What flavor do you want?" he asked.

"Interracial."

He laughed and ordered us two swirled chocolate and vanilla cones.

"You seen the river today?" he asked. "There's jumping fish all over the place."

"Awesome."

We headed across the autumn grass toward the water, licking our cones. A few couples hung out on the docks, some cozying up to one another as their feet dangled in the water, others taking selfies or trying to snap pictures each time a fish flew into the air.

"You go to Grayson?" Jack asked.

I nodded. "How about you?"

"Kemper."

We stood near the edge of the dock. A turtle slid off a log and made a plunk into the water.

"You like fishing?" Jack asked.

"It's okay."

"How about tubing?"

Tubing was as popular in our Southern river town as NASCAR.

"I haven't done it since middle school," I told him.

"Maybe I could take you sometime," he said. "My dad owns a Skiff. We've got two tubes."

"Cool."

"You like boogie boarding?"

"In the ocean?" I asked. "Not really. I mean, I like it, it's just that—well, I haven't done it in a while."

"What about bike riding? I know a couple of great paths out in the county."

"I don't have a bike."

My mother had donated it to Goodwill.

"What do you like to do?" Jack asked. "You know, when you're not in school?"

"I like to read."

"I said, when you're *not* in school?"

The sun shone down on my head, making me sweat. My ice cream cone was starting to melt. A dribble of vanilla streamed down my hand. I licked my wrist.

"I still like to read when I'm not in school," I told him. "And I like music. I listen to music all the time, when I'm not doing other stuff."

"What kind of stuff? What is it that you like to do?"

What do I like to do, or what am I allowed to do? I want to play the flute. I want to go bungee jumping. I want to drive a car. I want to go to a live concert and stand in the crowd as close to the stage as possible...

Instead of answering his questions, I said, "I'm starting to simmer."

"You want to hang out in the shade?"

I barely heard his question as I went down the list in my head.

Gatorade: check. Lunch: check. Cute boy to create a diversion: check.

Still, I could feel myself swaying, so I quickly crossed one leg in front of the other. It looked funny, like I had to pee, but sometimes it was the only thing keeping me vertical.

"What're you doing?" Jack asked, gaping at me like I was a dorko.

But the look on his face didn't matter, because I had crossed my legs too late. And I never gave Jack an answer, because the world had disappeared.

Chapter Five

The smell of Barbeque Baron's spicy sauce was so pungent, I could taste it. I tried to rub my tongue along my teeth, but it wouldn't obey. A familiar softness cushioned my head. My eyes fluttered open to the smooth underside of Lindsay's olive-colored chin. I could feel the presence of others surrounding me, could hear the murmurs of the curious crowd.

Lindsay said something over her shoulder. Two male faces appeared: Adam Carchelli's and Larry Taggert's. I felt like Dorothy in the *Wizard of Oz* when she wakes up to see the relieved faces of the Lion, Tin Man, and Scarecrow, but it turns out they're only a bunch of plain old farmhands.

"Just relax, Erica," Adam said softly, crouching down next to my hip.

Larry knelt beside Lindsay. "You'll be fine, sweetheart," he whispered into my face. He grabbed my wrist and placed his fingers against the vein.

"Please tell these people to give her some room," Lindsay said.

"Give her some room!" Larry commanded.

The invisible pressure of the crowd lessened.

My jaw came back to life. Some type of liquid filled my mouth. I imagined swirls of vanilla and chocolate ice cream smeared all over my face. I rolled over on my side with my cheek against the dock and spit.

"Oh!" a woman declared. "She's bleeding."

I wondered what part of my face had split open. Would I need stitches? Would I have a scar?

Adam produced a damp towel and placed it against my mouth.

A young boy asked, "Did she have a seizure?"

Another stranger answered, "Maybe she's got epilepsy."

Lindsay defended me: "She does not have epilepsy."

"It's okay, sweetheart," Larry whispered again, his face so close to mine I could see the tiny pores dotting his nose. His breath smelled like potato chips. "Did you drink any alcohol today?"

"Erica doesn't drink," Lindsay said. Then, like she was reading from a textbook: "She suffers from syncope."

As if he'd invented the definition, Larry announced to the crowd, "That means she faints."

Lindsay nodded. "Right."

"How often?" Larry asked.

"It all depends," she told him. "Once a month. Once a week. One time she fainted twice during study hall…"

Lindsay continued to explain my condition to Larry, smiling like she was talking about world peace at a beauty pageant and not the fact that I was flat on the dock with a bloody towel against my lips.

Larry returned her goofy grin. "Your friend's heart rate is a little fast, but it's strong and steady." Then to me, "You'll be fine, sweetheart."

I worked to find my voice and whispered, "Why issare blood?"

Something was wrong with my speech. My words were slurred. Maybe I had been drinking after all. Maybe someone had spiked my Gatorade.

"Don't worry about it," Lindsay said. "Let me know when you're ready to sit up."

"Now," I said.

I wasn't ready, not quite. My head had a hard time staying above my shoulders and my limbs were weak. But I wanted to know where in the hell the blood was coming from. Slowly, Lindsay helped me into a seated position. The towel fell from my mouth.

"Oh my God," someone said.

Fingers pointed toward my face.

And then I knew.

My hand flew to my mouth. Jagged edges snagged my fingers. I looked between the feet standing around me on the dock.

"My teef!" I screamed.

"Don't worry," Lindsay said. "A dentist can totally—"

"How many?"

"Two, I think. I can't tell…"

"Don't panic, Erica," Adam said softly.

Tears streamed down my face. I sat with both hands against my swollen lips, hiding my gypsy teeth. Lindsay put an arm around me. After a moment, she and Larry helped me stand. As we slowly made our way up the dock, I spotted the ambulance, parked on the grass, back doors open wide.

"Wussat for?" I asked with my new cartoon dialect.

Lindsay said, "With all these EMT's and firemen around...please, Erica, just get in. They'll take you to the ER, have you fill out some paperwork, and before you know it, you'll be back home."

"My mudder..."

"We've already called her."

"No! Why?"

"You knocked out your teeth, sweetheart," Larry said. And then, as if it was any of his business, "Your parents have the right to know."

"You don undersand..."

They tried to make me lie on the gurney, but I refused. Lindsay stepped into the ambulance and held out her hand. The crowd followed close behind. Out of the corner of my eye I saw Lindsay's Adam, skinny Jack, pretty Josephine, and other picnickers; could feel my mini-dress hike up as I took Lindsay's hand and stepped into the vehicle.

But I didn't care. I was actually praying that the last memory these people had of me was of my behind, and not my hillbilly mouth.

Chapter Six

"You can't even tell the difference," Lindsay said the following Tuesday in the cafeteria. I had skipped school on Monday to get temporary caps. Two hours in the dentist's chair. Minus the high of laughing gas, which most non-Syncopians get to enjoy.

"Thanks," I said through puffy lips. "The real ones will be done on Friday. It feels like I have pebbles in my mouth."

"Just be thankful you don't wear braces," Lindsay said.

I tore off tiny pieces of hormone-free turkey from my sandwich and chewed gently.

Later, on the way to AP Stats, Lindsay said, "Larry called me a superwoman."

"What for?"

"He said I handled you with a cool head."

"*Handled* me?"

"Oh, you know what he means," she said. "Did you know that while you were in the ER waiting for your mom, Larry offered to give me a ride home? How sweet is that?"

"You let him drive you home?" I asked.

"Mmm-hmm. We talked for almost an hour."

"An hour?" I asked, doing the calculation in my head. "The hospital's only a ten-minute drive from your house."

"We went to the hospital cafeteria for an iced coffee before he drove me home. We both love iced coffee."

"Does his wife know?" I asked.

"God, Erica. It was only coffee. It's not like we did anything wrong."

"Then why are you getting defensive?"

"I'm not," Lindsay said. "Anyhow, Josephine doesn't exactly make herself presentable for her husband. I think a woman should try to be sexy all the time, whether she's at a picnic or sitting in a hospital cafeteria."

Less than a year before, Lindsay wore yellow Crocs with rainbow charms and homemade skirts that fell below the knee. Bragged about the great deals she found at the Salvation Army. Complained that lip gloss felt like Smucker's strawberry jam. Poked fun at packs of girls in the mall who giggled when older boys tossed them a sideways glance.

I was frustrated by the stupid conversation we were having, so I changed the subject as we made our way up the hallway.

"That guy Jack I met at the picnic," I said. "Do you think you could give him my number? I didn't get a chance...you know...with all the stuff that happened. I want to apologize."

"Your number?"

"Yeah. He seems pretty cool."

Lindsay didn't say anything.

"Don't you think so?" I asked.

"He's fine."

"What's the matter with him?"

"He's just not that great, that's all," Lindsay said.

Maybe she knew something I didn't. Maybe he liked computers more than girls. Maybe he had really bad breath. Or super creepy toenails, the kind that grew under.

We reached the classroom. I stood in the doorway and blocked her from going in.

"What's the matter with him?" I asked again.

Lindsay's shoulders slumped, and I knew what she was going to say before she said it. It was written all over her face. A face I'd seen plenty of times before, on other people, not only Lindsay's. A face that said, "I am so sorry…"

"He doesn't like me, does he?"

"Erica…" She gave an enthusiastic hello to a couple of girls as they passed by, then turned back to me. "He thinks you're pretty and everything…but…"

I knew what came next. I didn't need Lindsay to tell me. It was simple. And classic. He wasn't into me. Into what I had *going on*.

"There are so many great guys out there," Lindsay went on. "Too many to count. And most of them *don't* go to this school, if you know what I'm saying."

"Adam goes to this school," I reminded her.

"FYI," Lindsay said. "I didn't hook up with Adam on purpose."

"How do you hook up with a person on accident?"

"I just mean we have a silent understanding," she said. "We both know there's an end to us sooner or later."

She looked over my shoulder into the classroom where our

teacher was yet to arrive. There were only twelve students in our statistics class, eight of them boys. We watched as a couple of seniors tossed a Nerf football back and forth across the rectangular room.

Lindsay shook her head. "Cavemen."

She pushed past me, not meanly, but with purpose. I followed her into the room. Before long, Skinny Jack's face disappeared from my mind as I became engrossed in managing the pretend stocks I'd bought that were plummeting to the ground.

Chapter Seven

Who cares about some random guy? Not every boy is into every girl, and vice-versa. That's the way the Bojangles biscuit crumbles.

But still, it would have been nice if Jack had at *least* asked for my number, or asked to see if I was okay after I took a bite out of the dock. Maybe he was afraid he'd pick me up for a date and I'd get into his car with a snaggletooth smile.

I had three tests coming up the following week, so I planned to concentrate on those instead of boys. Lindsay asked me to come with her to the River Queen Café on Sunday afternoon to study.

"I don't know how you always ace these stats tests," she said as she parked the truck. "But if a little good juju rubs off on me…"

We walked into the café with our backpacks slung over our shoulders. As I hung mine on the back of a chair, my cell phone played the creepy theme song from *Halloween*.

I pressed the button. "Yes, Mother."

"I wanted to make sure you made it there all right."

"You're kidding, right? I've been gone, like, five minutes."

"Ten. But I wanted to—"

"I don't plan on knocking out my brand new teeth that you keep reminding me cost an arm and a leg."

"You don't need to get snippy, Erica."

"Not snippy. Focused. We're getting ready to study. So my cell is going to be on silent for a while. Okay? So, bye."

I joined Lindsay in line and we ordered cappuccinos—hers with caffeine, mine without—and pumpkin muffins.

At the table, we pulled out our binders. The first hour we worked really hard, crunching numbers like a couple of accountants. But everyone knows how studying goes. After a while, it's easy to drift onto other topics, ones that have little or nothing to do with school.

Lindsay folded her arms across her stack of books. "Larry helped me study Friday night while I was babysitting."

"Why was Larry there if you were babysitting?"

"His plans got cancelled, so he ended up staying home. I helped him get the kids ready for bed. Women are so much better at that kind of stuff."

"Where was Josephine?" I asked.

"Her mother's sick and lives all the way out in Feltonville. Sometimes she goes out there to give her a hand."

"Oh."

She leaned over her folded arms. "Do you think Larry's cute?"

"He's okay," I said. "Not movie star material or anything."

"Yeah, well, you and I have different tastes in men anyway."

"Point of reference, please."

"What does that mean?" she asked.

"How do you know what my taste is?"

Lindsay said, "I assumed we liked different kinds of guys, that's all."

I thought a moment. "I think Adam is cute," I told her. "Don't you?"

Adam wasn't a rock star or anything, but he did have a nice smile, and he never treated me like I was a host to some foreign bacteria. That special quality made him extra cute. Not to mention he treated Lindsay like a queen.

"Cute isn't the same as *hot*," Lindsay said.

"You don't think your own boyfriend is hot?"

She picked up her empty coffee cup, stared into the bottom, and chewed the inside of her cheek for a moment. "I broke up with him."

"What?" I said, unbelieving. "When?"

"Last night," she said. "Over the phone. Actually, I texted him."

"You broke up with Adam by text? That reeks, Linds."

I pictured the two of them, holding hands by the river that day at the picnic, playing songs for one another in guitar class, waiting for each other in the school stairwells so they could sneak a kiss.

"I thought you were totally into him," I said.

"I thought I was, too," she said. "He seems so immature all of a sudden."

"What about Winter Formal?"

"It's not like he's already rented the tux."

While I was sadly surprised, I was also curious, so I said, in a quiet sing-songy voice, like I wasn't judging her at all, even though I was, "Someone's crushing on a married man."

Lindsay giggled and bit her bottom lip with her perfectly straight top teeth. Pink blotches rose to her tan cheeks. "Oh, shit, Erica," she breathed. "You're right. I am so crushing on this guy. Just to hear him talk about all the stuff he's done. He used to be a lifeguard up in New Jersey. In three years, he saved twenty-nine people from drowning. Isn't that incredible? And since becoming a fireman, he's saved so many lives, he's lost count. He said that in the beginning, when he and Josephine first got married, she was totally into the whole fireman thing. She even helped him study for tests. But now, it's like he's going to work in an office cubicle or something. She doesn't even care about the fact that he puts his life on the line every day."

"Every day?" I asked.

"Well, not every day," Lindsay said. "But every time there's an emergency. He said that in the summertime, there are boating accidents up and down the river, and most people never hear about them. He's seen more car accident fatalities than anyone he knows. What's really cool is that he talks about it like it's something everyone in the world does, saving people."

"Adam saves people, too," I reminded her.

"Adam isn't a real fireman."

"He fights real fires."

"Anyway, Larry told me so many things…" Her voice grew so quiet, I barely heard the words: "He thinks I'm beautiful."

I studied Lindsay as she brushed the bangs from her forehead. Her tan face seemed more exotic than last year, her thin nose perfectly centered, her dark hair like fur attached to the collar of an expensive coat. She was taller than me by an inch, and because she'd walked part of the Appalachian Trail last summer, her calves had become sculpted.

I could put up with Lindsay's sudden transformation, the same way she put up with my never-ending spells. And it made perfect sense that I would focus on getting us good grades, while Lindsay did all the extracurricular work, like introducing me to eligible boys.

So there we sat, in a cute little café, with church-dressed families, weekend joggers, and Sunday strollers, nodding their Southern hellos or saying, "Hey" like everyone else in River Town. Here we sat, sucking down cappuccinos, discussing High School Lindsay and Married Larry like it was the most ordinary thing in the world.

"Hey, Linds?" I said.

"Yeah?"

"Has Larry actually…you know…hit on you?"

"He definitely flirts with me," she said. "But he's a total gentleman. He'd never take advantage of me."

"How do you know?"

"I can tell. We have…a…connection. You know what I mean?"

I nodded, even though I had no clue what she was talking about.

"Doesn't it bother you that he's married?" I asked.

"I don't really think about it, to tell you the truth."

A JC Penney family entered the coffee house: a mom and dad with their three little girls about a year apart. They strolled up to the counter, the three daughters wearing the same pink crocheted hats, holding each other's hand. They giggled as they peeked into the glass cabinet, pointing to the muffins and scones, and politely told their parents what they wanted. The mother bent down, picked up the littlest one, and placed her on a hip. Then the dad kissed his wife on the cheek.

It embarrassed me, watching their intimate activities, like I was peeking into their living room without their knowledge. And even though I was the only one who knew, it embarrassed me that Lindsay liked a married man. A man with a beautiful wife and two adorable kids.

I turned back to Lindsay. "We should get back to studying."

I pulled out my physiology notes and put them in a pile on the table.

She pouted as she opened her binder, obviously sad that our chat about her crush was over. But I couldn't worry about that. During school hours, Lindsay was the tether keeping me bound to earth. But time spent together *after* school was up to me to keep us focused.

I suppose everyone has a job to do when it comes to friendship.

Chapter Eight

It was ten-thirty at night. I had just crawled into bed, the tiny LED light clipped to the edge of my physiology book, when my cell phone rang: *Caller Unknown.*

"Hello?" I whispered.

"Erica?"

A boy.

"Who is this?" I asked.

Pause.

"Adam."

"Hey. How did you get my number?"

"Lindsay gave it to me. In case of emergency."

"Oh."

"Has she said anything to you?" he asked.

"About…"

"About dumping my ass?"

"Yeah, she told me. Sorry, Adam. That totally sucks."

His breaths fell heavily into the phone. "What else did she say?"

"Nothing, really," I told him. "Just that you both knew from the beginning you were a temporary thing—"

"*Temporary*? She said that?"

"What? Oh, no, not exactly. I guess that's what I took from the conversation."

"Did she tell you she did a text breakup?" Adam asked. "How freaking lame is that?"

"Pretty lame…"

"It's totally effed-up is what it is."

I'd never had my heart broken before. Little crushes in middle school that fizzled out. One time it was me, the next time it was him. Tit for tat. And every once in a while, I'd wish a certain boy would ask me to a dance, or to a movie on a Friday night. But I'd never given my heart away, only to have it stomped on and thrown back in my face.

"Maybe I'll write her a letter," Adam said. "I could give it to you, and you could give it to her. Would you mind, Erica? I don't think I can look her in the eye right now."

"What about guitar class?" I asked.

"Crap. I forgot about that." He paused. "Maybe I'll blow it off for a few days. Shimmel hardly ever takes roll anyway."

I wondered if that meant I'd have to play duets with Lindsay instead of jamming on my own tunes.

Adam said, "I'll come by your house tomorrow morning to drop off the letter."

"Lindsay picks me up at 7:40."

"I'll come by at 7:20. Does that work?"

"Okay."

"Thanks, Erica. I really appreciate this."

We hung up, and by the time I got my brain to refocus on chapter five's concepts regarding the human body's circulatory system, it was nearly eleven.

I saved Adam's number in my phone, turned off the tiny light, and fell fast asleep.

***

The doorbell rang at 7:20 on the dot.

"Who is that so early?" my dad asked as he spread margarine on his toast.

I put my small backpack on a chair at the table. "A friend from school."

The doorbell rang a second time.

As I headed to the door, my mother called from upstairs, "Can someone get that?"

"Got it!" I called back.

I opened the door. Adam stood before me, an envelope in one hand, a tiny bouquet of daisies in the other, the stems tucked inside a damp paper towel and wound in plastic wrap. He wore a John Deere baseball cap and, for the first time, I noticed the dark stubble along his firm jaw line.

"Nabbed 'em from the vase in our kitchen," he said, stepping into the foyer. He held them out.

Not including the occasional pizza delivery guy, Adam was the first boy to walk across our threshold. I took the flowers, pretending for a moment they were for me. Then he handed me the envelope.

Dad appeared in the hallway.

"Hello," he said, shaking Adam's hand. "Marcus O'Donnell. Erica's father."

"Adam Carchelli."

"You a fireman?" Dad asked, nodding toward the fire department logo on his T-shirt.

"Volunteer."

"Dad," I said, "he has to go."

Lindsay would be arriving in a few minutes, and I didn't want my job as messenger ruined before I actually got the chance to perform the duties.

Adam said, "Nice to meet you, Mr. O'Donnell."

"Same to you, Adam."

Adam offered me a wilted smile. "Thanks a lot, Erica." Then he turned and trotted up the sidewalk as I shut the door.

Dad followed me back into the kitchen and resumed his breakfast.

"Nice boy," he said.

"Super nice."

I put the letter and flowers in the vented pouch on the side of my backpack and grabbed a blueberry yogurt from the fridge.

My mother came into the kitchen dressed for the day. She had already been on her morning run, eaten breakfast, and taken a shower.

"Who was at the door?" she asked.

"A young man for Erica," Dad said.

"Not for me, Dad. For Lindsay."

"Was it Adam?" my mother asked.

I nodded as I licked my yogurt spoon.

"Why did he come here to see Lindsay?" she asked. She went to the sink and filled the tea pot with water.

"He didn't," I said. "He just wanted me to give her something."

"Oh?" she asked. "What's that?"

"A letter," I said.

"And flowers," Dad added.

My mother turned on the burner and leaned against the counter. "Why can't he give them to her himself?"

"He has to miss school today," I said a little too quickly. "He's got an appointment somewhere."

"Well," Dad said, "that's nice of you to act as a go-between."

I nodded and thought, *If you only knew.*

Chapter Nine

"From Adam," I said, excitedly handing Lindsay the letter and flowers the second I got into her truck.

"I can't read while I'm driving," she said, placing both on the seat between us before pulling away from the curb.

A shiny key chain clanked against the steering column.

"Where'd you get that?" I asked, pointing to the charm.

"Larry gave it to me. It's got the County Fire Department design on it."

"Oh."

As she rounded the first corner, she said, "Well?"

"Well, what?"

"Read me Adam's letter."

"Lindsay, I don't think—"

"Just get it over with, Erica."

She kept her eyes on the road as I opened the envelope and pulled out the letter. I nearly put it to my nose, suddenly tempted to smell it, but I refrained as I unfolded the paper.

"'Dear Lindsay: I know you don't want to talk to me right

now, and if it's space you need, then I'll give it to you. Please let me know when you want to talk in person. I am here, waiting for you to tell me what I can do to make things work.'"

"Make what things work?" Lindsay said, scrunching up her face.

"He just wants an explanation."

"He's a child," she said. "How's that for an explanation?"

"You didn't feel that way when you were dating."

"Well, I feel that way now. What else did he say?"

"That's it," I said. "Just his signature and a smiley face with hearts for eyes." I looked inside the envelope. "Oh, there's a picture here of the two of you."

I held it up, but she didn't even glance at it. I gently folded the letter and put it and the photo back inside the envelope. Lindsay took it from my hand and tossed it onto the floorboard where it landed on top of a pile of used notebook paper.

After parking in the school lot, she tilted the rearview mirror toward her face. As she touched up her lip gloss and checked her hair, she said, "I can't be bothered by Adam or his high school drama. I have way too much to think about right now."

"You mean, like college?"

"Yeah, right," Lindsay said, batting her eyes at her reflection. "Like *that's* the most important thing in the world."

"You've changed your mind about college?" I couldn't imagine working so hard for so long and then *not* going to college.

Lindsay righted the mirror and faced me. "My mom never went beyond high school and she does fine."

"Your mother had to get a second job after your dad left."

"That's because my dad's a loser who doesn't give a crap about his family."

"That's exactly why you shouldn't rely on a man to begin with," I told her. "*Any* man. No matter *who* he is."

"Well, Erica," she said, talking to me like I was in kindergarten, "that's because you've never been in love. Real love makes a girl think in a different way."

She got out of the truck and shut her door. I grabbed the flowers and tucked them back in the little mesh pocket on the side of my backpack before getting out.

After Lindsay locked the doors, she came around to my side, dropping the new key chain into her purse. She said, slowly, like she'd just taken valium, "I feel like my whole world is changing before my eyes. Like…I'm in a dream. It's sort of freaking me out. But in a good way. Do you know what I mean?"

I didn't say yes, but my nod told a lie.

As we wormed our way into the rushing horde of students, I thought, *What I wouldn't give to understand what Lindsay is talking about. What I wouldn't give for a little change in my own world.* And, just as quickly, the next thought popped into my head, nearly, but not quite, erasing the others: *Be careful what you wish for.*

***

I found myself missing the brief encounters with Adam, even though they had always been because of Lindsay. He never showed up again in Shimmel's guitar class. We didn't run into him in the stairwells, or near the weight room with his buddies at the end of the day. Lindsay seemed relieved, but I wondered if he was skipping school altogether, a broken heart as justifiable as a doctor's note.

I forced away Adam's sad face and drank up an otherwise awesome day: three tests, three *A*'s.

Lindsay didn't do badly with two B's and one C. The C she got on the AP Physiology test, but that wasn't so terrible. Some kids did way worse.

"Thank God that's over," Lindsay said as we walked to her truck after the final bell.

"I love Scantron tests."

"Only you could love Scantrons, Erica."

"I like knowing my grades right away."

On our way home from school, the firehouse siren went off. This tends to happen when a tornado is spotted, or if volunteers are called in for an emergency. Lindsay and I, like most everyone else in our town, were trained to turn on the radio. She moved the dial around, but the blaring beep-beep-beep wasn't on the local stations, so that meant it wasn't a tornado. It was either a car wreck or a fire.

"I wonder if Larry is there," Lindsay said.

I wondered if Adam was, if only because Lindsay didn't.

Lindsay said, "Firemen have crazy schedules, did you know that? One day on, one day off. They do that for three days, then they get three days off in a row. Larry says he likes sleeping at the firehouse with the guys."

I looked out the window at the dead brown grass. It had been a very dry summer, and autumn wasn't any better. Everything seemed parched. This year's cotton season was reportedly a bad one. The leaves on the deciduous trees had barely turned gold before they fell to the ground during some high winds. And trash fires, part of life out in the countryside, were forbidden until further notice. But there was always some idiot who thought he could get away with it without setting the Croatan Forest on fire.

As we drove toward our Great Pines neighborhood, black smoke rose into the sky behind the clusters of churches and business offices near the river.

"Let's go check it out," Lindsay said.

She headed over the short bridge, drove beside River Park, up one narrow street and down another, and past one of the oldest AME churches in town. Behind the ancient graveyard, one street shy of the railroad depot, dense smoke filled the air.

"Might be a crack house," Lindsay said as she pulled the truck over to the side and put it in park. "Then again, the whole building probably would have exploded if it was a crack house."

"How do you know that?" I asked.

"Larry told me. He also said that a crack house is one of the scariest fires."

"Because it could explode?"

"Because there might be dealers with guns inside."

She got out of the truck and held up her cell phone.

"What are you doing?" I asked, coming around to her side of the truck. We stood about a hundred yards from the flashing red lights.

"Taking pics."

"What for?"

"For Larry," she said. "I'm babysitting tonight. I think the pictures will make him happy, knowing *someone* is interested in what he does for a living."

A dozen or so vehicles were lined up on the same side of the street as Lindsay and me, their drivers clicking photos, sharing the news instantly on social media. I didn't see what the big deal was. The houses that lined the street looked abandoned, their windows boarded up and yards filled with trash.

"You're babysitting a lot during the week," I told Lindsay as we watched from a distance as the firemen battled the flames.

"Making some good money, too," she said. "Not that I wouldn't go over there for free. The other night, Larry got home an hour before Josephine and helped me with the physiology terms. I think he's the reason I got a *C* on today's test."

"I thought *I* was the reason," I said, half joking and half not. I had worked my butt off tutoring Lindsay the ins and outs of the human circulatory system.

With her phone, she zoomed in on the flames.

"Linds?" I said.

"Hm?"

"Can I ask you something personal?"

"Uh-huh."

"Do you plan to—you know—do more than just *hang out* with Larry?"

She lowered her phone.

I expected her to say, *OMG, of course not, Erica. What do you think I am, a flipping home-wrecker?*

Instead, she replied, "It all depends."

"On what?"

"On Larry."

She turned back to the fire and continued clicking.

***

On the way to homeroom the next morning, Lindsay read to me from a newspaper clipping: "'First Assistant Chief Lawrence Taggert of fire station number thirty-two was one of six firefighters who battled the blaze at 624 Renton Avenue yesterday afternoon. Taggert told reporters the fire started in the rear of the abandoned house. By three o'clock, the flames had gutted the building. The house is considered a total loss. Fire Chief Antoine Miller says the fire may have ignited near the kitchen stove, but further investigation is needed.'" Lindsay beamed. "How cool is that?"

"Thank God there weren't any people in it," I said.

"What? Oh, right. That's always a good thing. Though seeing Larry save someone in person would be pretty awesome, too."

Chapter Ten

"Larry says I'm his muse," Lindsay said as she took off her winter gloves to pick up her fork.

We were eating lunch in the school cafeteria in sweaters and scarves. The heating system was having problems, and even though it was only the end of October, the school felt like the inside of an icebox.

"A muse is someone who inspires another person," Lindsay explained like I'd never heard the word before. "Like a model inspires an artist."

I tied my scarf into a knot at my neck and poured soy milk from my thermos to the cup. "I thought maybe you weren't hanging out with Larry anymore."

"Why would you think that?" Lindsay asked.

"You haven't talked about him since that newspaper article."

"Remember, his schedule is funky," she explained. "Seeing him depends on when he's home and if they need a babysitter. And don't forget, he still has to do the daddy thing. He still has to act like he loves his wife."

"He doesn't love her?" I asked, shocked. "Did he tell you that?"

She whispered, "In his own way."

As I sipped my chicken soup, I spotted Adam in the cafeteria line, a few yards behind where Lindsay sat.

"You haven't said one word to him," I said.

"Who?"

"Adam."

"He'll get over it," she said.

"You never even responded to his letter."

I had taken Adam's flowers and put them in a vase in my room. It wasn't the daisies' fault Lindsay didn't want them. They had lasted an entire week.

"He's a big boy," Lindsay said.

Adam looked in my direction. He gave a quick wave, turned back to the food choices, and put something on his tray. After paying at the register, he headed to the other side of the room to sit with his friends.

"Linds," I said, "I know you're crushing on Larry and all, but you should at least say something to Adam. It's really hard to watch."

"As if you ever see him," she said. "He's not even in guitar class anymore."

Adam had switched his elective to an art class.

"He didn't drop off the planet," I said. "I think he's lonely."

Lindsay shrugged. As she prepared to dip a piece of bread into her soup, she rolled up the edge of her sweater sleeve. A pretty bracelet dangled. Miniature gold-colored leaves made jingling noises.

"Is that new?" I asked.

"Larry."

"He gave it to you?"

"Yup." She shook the gold bracelet like she was modeling it for a cable shopping channel and dipped the bread in the soup. "But this isn't the only present." She shoved the bread into her mouth, pulled back her hair, and showed off a pair of tiny diamond earrings.

"Are those real?" I asked.

She swallowed and wiped her mouth with a paper napkin. "As real as it gets."

Only one boy had ever given me jewelry, and that was the summer before eighth grade when Nicolas, a kid two years younger than me, gave me a gold ring that turned my finger green. I wondered if getting real diamonds made a girl feel like a princess.

"What if Josephine finds out?" I asked.

"That'll never happen," Lindsay said. "She doesn't notice anything but her kids." She pushed her tray to the side and leaned forward, nodding for me to do the same. In a tiny voice, she said, "I'm crazy about him, Erica. I know it's probably wrong, but I can't help it. He makes me feel…special."

"Adam didn't make you feel special?"

"Would you quit asking me about Adam? He's out of the picture. Done. Anyway, things are really bad…" She lowered her voice again. "…between Larry and Jo."

"Jo?"

"That's what we call Josephine when we talk about her."

"You talk behind her back?"

"Only when Larry needs to vent," Lindsay said. "I like being a shoulder for him to lean on. And he definitely needs one. Things on the home front are super awful. And, honestly, I don't see them getting any better."

The bell rang. Lindsay stood up, put her gloves in her jacket pocket, and grabbed her tray. She waited for me as I stood, and together we dumped our trash.

***

After school, Lindsay and I sat in front of my house with the Ford truck's engine idling.

"You babysitting this week?" I asked.

"Tomorrow night," Lindsay said. "Larry has a few days off, so we'll be able to spend time together when he drives me home."

"Where do Larry and Josephine go all the time?"

"They don't go out *all* the time. But when they do, it's usually to dinner. Or to the movies. Larry loves movies."

I thought a moment, trying to understand the whole cheating concept. "If their marriage is in trouble," I said, "why do they go out at all?"

"FDN, Larry calls it. Fake Date Night. He says he's just trying to keep the peace. Jo is totally unsupportive. Did I tell you that Larry bought a really cool convertible last year, and she made him take it back? Can you imagine? Taking back a car? How embarrassing is that?"

"Why didn't she like it?" I asked.

"Something about it being too small for a family of four," Lindsay said. "That she wouldn't be able to put two child seats in it, let alone one. She told Larry it was a selfish purchase. He told her it was a gift for her, not the kids. That he bought it so the two of them could take drives out in the countryside. Guess she wasn't up for that, because she made him return it. Larry lost money on it. He says it really hurt his feelings; that he was trying to do something romantic. Well, I didn't keep it a secret that *I* love drives out in the country. We have so much in common." Lindsay paused. She stared through the truck's windshield. "He's also a freaking awesome kisser."

She pressed her lips together like the confession had popped out by mistake, and then she let out a snicker that sounded like a hiccup.

"Larry kissed you?" I shouldn't have been surprised. After all, I figured that at some point they would kiss. But still, when she said it, and I pictured it in my mind, it stunned me. I could not imagine kissing someone nearly my dad's age. I pictured the middle-aged men he played golf with and tried not to let the revulsion show on my face.

But even if I'd made a face, Lindsay wouldn't have noticed.

"Erica," she whispered, still staring through the windshield. "I have never…not in my entire life…I mean, Adam was nice and all, but this…" She shook her head in awe like the Virgin Mary was standing in front of the truck. "This is *real*." She turned and faced me. "*Real*, Erica."

Not sure what to say, I asked, "Where did you kiss?"

"In his foyer."

"In their *house*? Are you insane?"

"I know, right?" She let out a small snarky laugh. "The kids were already in bed when Larry and Josephine came back from Fake Date Night, and Larry said he would drive me home. Josephine paid me, and then she went upstairs to check on the babies. Larry helped me with my jacket, and when I turned around again, he pulled me to him and kissed me. Just like that."

"Did he…you know…was it a *romantic* kiss?"

"Um…yeah!" She let out another quirky guffaw. "Please please please don't tell anyone. You are the only person in the whole wide world who knows about this, besides me and Larry. I made a solemn oath I would never kiss and tell."

Lindsay was my only girlfriend, so I couldn't imagine who I would share this information with. I nodded my head and held up a hand like I was taking the stand in court. "I promise."

"Erica," Lindsay said. "I'm falling. Hard…"

Suddenly, the left side of my analytical brain kicked in, taking over. I didn't plan to share Lindsay's secret, but what she'd just told me was bonkers. Nothing made sense about what she was saying or doing. I knew my thoughts were a total buzz kill, but they made their way out of my mouth all the same.

"Have you really thought this whole thing through?"

"It's all I think about," she said.

"No, Lindsay. I mean Josephine. What if she finds out?"

Lindsay nodded. Her face turned serious. "Larry and I have already talked about it. That kiss in the hallway was totally stupid, so we're going to be more careful from now on."

"What if he's…?" I wanted to say, "using you." Instead I said, "What if he's just going through a phase?"

Lindsay explained, "He said when he first met me it was totally a physical thing, being attracted to me and all, a natural part of being a man and everything. But now that he's gotten to know me, his feelings have grown stronger."

"How do you know he hasn't done this before?" I asked.

"That he isn't saying stuff to you he's already said to a million other girls?"

She frowned. "That's just mean, Erica."

"Oh. No. I wasn't trying to sound mean, Linds. I swear."

"Okay," she said. "Because it feels really good to tell someone I can trust."

I thought about the North Carolina Fair. About Lindsay keeping that first fainting spell a secret.

"You can totally trust me," I said.

She touched my arm. "And not judge me."

Lindsay had saved me more times than I could count. For years she had been there for me, so I would be there for her. It felt empowering to hold a secret in my hands; to know that she could count on me.

"I won't judge you," I told her. "I swear. You can tell me anything, anytime."

She smiled and breathed a quick "Thank you."

As I stepped out of the truck, I reiterated, "Anything and everything."

I shut the door and stood on the curb as she drove away.

Chapter Eleven

The firehouse siren screamed through my skull, waking me from a deep sleep. I squinted at my cell phone: 4:40 A.M.

I crawled out of bed, threw a hooded sweatshirt over my pajamas, and met my mother in the hallway. When Dad was at a trade show, my mother went jogging extra early so she could be back before I woke up at six-thirty. But this was crazy early, even by her standards.

"Let me throw on my sweats," she said.

I waited for her on the porch. The breeze was strong and swirled my hair around my face. The mild scent of something burning filled my sinuses.

"It's close," my mother said as she joined me outside, sniffing the air like a threatened wolf.

"Is it a wildfire?" I asked.

"Don't know."

We walked to the end of the driveway. The sun illuminated the eastern horizon beneath the dark blue sky. Some of our neighbors stood at the end of their driveways like us, others stood in the street. Gathering under the streams of yellow lamplight, we looked like clusters of movie zombies.

"Where is it?" my mother asked our next-door neighbor, Mrs. Phillips.

Mrs. Phillips' short white hair was flat on one side. She held her tiny Chihuahua in her arms.

"Over on Wilshire Court," she said. "Someone said it's a house fire."

A middle-school boy in his pajamas zoomed past us on his bike, a mini-cam attached to the front of his helmet.

Mrs. Phillips hugged her dog to her chest. "I hope it's not anyone we know."

I pictured the firemen as they worked to put out the flames. Had Adam been called to service? Did he have to leave an awesome dream to hold the large hose for the firefighters? Would he have to break glass, crawl inside a building, and fight off flames to save someone?

My hands grew clammy thinking about it.

"Let's put on the news," my mother said. "We can drink chamomile tea, maybe have an early breakfast."

"I want to see it in person," I said.

"It might be too upsetting, honey."

"I'd want neighbors checking on us if something happened to our house."

She chewed on her cheek for a second, watching as a handful of people headed north. "Let me lock the front door." A minute later she joined me with the house keys in one hand and a canned pineapple juice in the other.

"Drink this," she said.

I did as she asked and tossed the can into the recycling bin. Together we shuffled along with the others toward the north side of the neighborhood.

The red flashing lights grew brighter with each step. By the time we'd walked the six blocks, the street was water soaked and yellow tape prevented anyone from getting too close to the scene. Leftover swirls of gray-white smoke rose into the air. Firemen scurried about, hosing the charred pile of rubble.

The house was obliterated. All that remained were some black posts and a brick fireplace. Something that looked like part of a chandelier shimmered under the street lamp.

"Whose house was that?" I asked.

"Not sure," my mother said. "There's a FOR SALE sign. Let's hope the family had already moved out." She nodded toward the house to the left of the rubble. "Looks like the Taylors' house got some damage."

The side of the Taylors' house was black, the vinyl siding melted and hanging like the subject of a Salvador Dali painting. Two of their tall Cypress trees had burned, their naked branches looming like spooky fairy tale trees.

We had known the Taylors since our family moved from River Park to Great Pines the summer before tenth grade. The three Taylor boys were all in college now.

There must have been fifty people standing with us along the curb. In the dark yard, firemen continued to work, dragging hoses and using giant rakes to sift through the wet charred debris.

My mother nodded toward a nearby pecan tree with a gathering of folding chairs beneath the branches. Mrs. Taylor was sitting on one of the chairs, and Mr. Taylor stood next to her. A policeman was questioning them, taking down notes. A female officer stood nearby with a thermos. She poured liquid into a cup and handed it to Mrs. Taylor.

We made our way to the outer edge of the crowd.

"I'm not worried about a little smoke damage," Mrs. Taylor was saying. "But our sweet Billy Jack. We have a doggie door. He must've gone wandering. He used to love going next door when the Adkins family lived there. Maybe he thought they were still there. He was nearly blind, you know. We got him when the boys were little. They'll be devastated."

She put her hands to her face as Mr. Taylor put a hand on her shoulder. He stared beyond the yellow tape at the pile of wet black timber that used to be their neighbor's home.

My mother whispered, "I'm going to see if they need anything."

She walked to the pecan tree and knelt down next to Mrs. Taylor.

A girl's voice called me from behind.

"Erica!"

I turned around. "Lindsay?"

She wore a pretty sundress, even though it was in the low fifties, and her hair was wavy like she'd taken the time to style it, even though school didn't start for another three hours.

I pulled my pajama hoodie over my sleepy rat's nest.

"This is crazy," Lindsay said, approaching me, her voice laced with excitement. "Our houses are only a few blocks away."

"I know."

Then she whispered, "Do you see him?"

"Who?"

"Duh."

I looked at the men hidden beneath their fire hats and jackets, moving around like giant orange and yellow ants.

Lindsay let out an exaggerated sigh. "Over there, next to the ambulance. In the orange coat."

"Oh. I see him now."

The ambulance driver shut the back doors of the empty vehicle and got into the driver's side. Larry Taggert said something to the man before another EMT got into the passenger's side and the ambulance drove away.

"The Taylors lost their dog in the fire," I informed Lindsay.

Lindsay glanced at the older couple and then turned back to the scene.

"He looks so professional in that suit," she said. "Ugh. So freaking adorable."

Then I spotted Adam. I only recognized him because he took off his helmet and pushed back his hair as he came around the side of the fire truck. He pulled a tank from his back and dropped it to the ground and said something to one of the other firefighters.

"Oh, Crimony," Lindsay said, like she'd just remembered she had a pile of math homework. "There's Adam. Catch you later, Erica. I'm going to wander around the other side of the property. Just in case Larry wants to sneak a quick hello."

She bounced away like she was off to mingle at a tailgate party.

People were leaving now, robes and pajamas disappearing around corners. As the crowd thinned, I felt myself moving closer to the scene. Adam stood a few feet away.

"Adam," I said. He didn't respond. I inched closer to the yellow tape. "Hey, Adam."

He turned around. "Erica."

Adam's face was black with soot and shiny with sweat. He looked like a real fireman, the kind on a magazine cover, a child slung over a shoulder, flames in the background reaching into the air. He stepped up to the curb in his long yellow coat and tall black boots.

I nodded to the burned property. "Pretty crazy, huh?"

"For sure," he said. "It was a nice house."

"Do they know what started it?" I asked.

"Not yet."

"The Taylors lost their dog."

"They found him in the basement," Adam said, frowning. He glanced toward the crowd gathered under the tree. "I know Shane Taylor pretty well. He's going to be bummed." He shook out his hair and stuck his helmet back on his head. "I'd better get back to it. Clean up's going to take a while."

"Okay."

"See you later." He readjusted his coat and started walking toward the mess.

"Adam!"

He turned to face me again.

"I'm really proud of you."

He smiled then, his teeth glowing bright white in sharp contrast to his sooty skin. "Thanks, Erica. I appreciate that."

He stepped into the pile of ash. I watched him work until my mother collected me and we walked home together, each wrapped up in our own thoughts. She was probably thinking what every mother in the neighborhood was thinking: *How lucky that it wasn't our house.* I was thinking that a little myself.

But mostly, I was thinking about Adam.

Chapter Twelve

On Friday evening, Lindsay called. "You want to babysit with me tonight?"

She'd never asked me to babysit with her before, and I didn't ask her why the sudden change of heart, because I knew: She wanted me to see Larry; wanted to show him off like the pretty bracelet or diamond earrings. But I didn't care about the reason, only that she'd asked.

"Let me run it by the *Gestapo*," I told her. "I'll call you right back."

I went into the den where my mother sat with her back to me at her pine desk in the corner. She had started a *Mothers of Children with Syncope* blog a few years back and was on the computer emailing another mommy from some faraway city.

"Mom?"

"Hm?" she asked, her fingers tapping the keys.

"Lindsay wants to know if I can babysit with her."

Her fingers stopped clicking. She rotated her swivel chair to face me. "Tonight?"

"Uh-huh."

"Where?"

"A few blocks from here," I said super casually. "Larry and Josephine Taggert."

"Have I met them before?"

"I don't think so. But they're super nice. They have twins. Can I go?"

"Do they have a land line?" she asked.

"I'm sure they do. But I'll bring my cell. And Lindsay has hers."

"Do they have smoke detectors?"

I laughed. "I hope so. Mr. Taggert is a fireman."

"Oh. Okay…I suppose…as long as Lindsay's there…"

I headed up the hallway.

"What time?" she called.

"I'll get the info!"

In my bedroom, I called Lindsay back.

"I'm in."

"Awesome," Lindsay said. "They're leaving for Fake Date Night at seven. I'll come by at six-thirty."

"Why so early?"

"Because I'm walking to your house to pick you up."

"Why not bring the truck?" I asked.

"This way Larry will have to drive me home. Trust me. He doesn't mind."

"Doesn't your mom wonder why you aren't driving yourself?"

"She's gone twelve hours at a time," Lindsay said. "Even if she asks, I'll just tell her I'm saving money on gas."

***

The doorbell rang while I was looking for my tan suede jacket buried somewhere in my closet. I found it and stopped in my bedroom doorway, listening.

Lindsay's voice drifted up the hall. "Hey, Miss Ruth."

My mother started in before the front door was even closed. "Fill me in on the Taggert family."

Lindsay said, very professionally, not at all like the girl who gushed every time she mentioned Larry's name, "They live over on Whaling Road. He's a fireman and she's a stay-at-home. They have adorable three-year-old twins. A boy and a girl."

"Have you babysat for them before?" my mother asked.

"Yes, ma'am. Lots of times."

"Why do you want Erica to sit with you tonight?"

"I thought we could get ahead on our stats stuff," Lindsay told her. "Big test next week."

"Didn't you just have a test?"

I took the cue and quickly grabbed the textbook from my desk.

"We have tests all the time," I said, marching up the hallway to the foyer. "That's how AP classes work."

"Well," my mother said, "I'm glad to see you girls working so hard. Statistics was never my thing, that's for sure."

"Here's the hat you asked to borrow," Lindsay said as she handed me her navy blue wool hat. She'd bought it at the Farmer's Market a month earlier, and I had coveted it since.

"Thanks." I put the hat on my head and turned from side to side.

"It owns you," Lindsay said.

I smiled and opened the door.

My mother stared at the empty curb. "Where's your truck?"

"My mom needs it tonight," Lindsay said, never missing a beat. "Her car's in the shop and my little sister has a ballet thing. It'll be nice to walk."

"What time will you be finished?"

"Around nine-thirty," Lindsay said. "Is that okay?"

"That's fine," my mother said. She said to me, "Text me when the Taggerts get home, and I'll come get you both."

"Oh, no, that's okay," Lindsay interjected. "Mr. or Mrs. Taggert will drive us home. They don't mind."

"Well then," my mother told Lindsay. "Erica's already eaten supper. But if you could make sure she eats the snack I packed for her—"

I grabbed the brown bag from my mother's hand. "I can handle my own feedings, thank you, Mother."

She gave me the stink-eye which I totally ignored as Lindsay and I made our way out the door. Heading across the dusky autumn neighborhood, I felt like we were a couple of trick-or-treaters, even though Halloween wasn't for a few days, and it wasn't candy Lindsay was looking forward to.

***

After Josephine and Lindsay reacquainted me with the twins, Lindsay and Larry stayed in the family room while Josephine had me follow her into the kitchen. I hung my coat on the back of a chair and put Lindsay's hat on the table.

"Love that hat," she said in her charming Southern drawl.

"Thanks."

Josephine looked even prettier than when we'd met at the

picnic. She wore a pair of black slacks with a low-cut black top. Her hair was fluffed up and her makeup looked professionally done. While she introduced me to the snack-filled pantry, I heard one of the twins giggle in the other room.

"They usually go down at seven," Josephine said, "but when we get a babysitter, we let them stay up until seven-thirty. Then it's lights out, no matter what. They'll try to whimper their way into your heart, but don't let them fool you. If y'all don't see real tears, then they're playing you."

She smiled, and my heart suddenly ached. Lindsay and Larry were probably making goo-goo eyes at one another over the playpen, while Josephine and I stood in the kitchen talking baby junk.

I spotted a dozen white roses in a Mason jar on the kitchen nook table. The sweet scent drifted over to where we stood.

"You sure y'all are up to this?" she asked.

"Babysitting? Sure. Why?"

"Well, after what happened at the picnic…"

She tapped her top teeth with a finger as if I needed reminding of what had happened that day.

"I only faint at inconvenient times," I explained. "Like when I'm on a roller coaster. Or in the middle of dissecting a sheep's eye."

"You dissected a sheep's eye? In high school? I didn't do that until college."

"AP Physiology."

"Good for you," she said. "Chemistry was my thing. But that was a lifetime ago."

"I plan to major in biology," I told her. "Research."

"That's wonderful. I was an O.R. nurse. Back in the old days, before robotic surgeries and online pharmacies."

Larry called from the family room, "Joey…"

Josephine glanced at the clock on the microwave.

"So," she said, "you're sure about tonight then?"

"Lindsay's with me," I said. "I'm in good hands. And so are your kids."

And so is your husband, I nearly blurted.

Josephine gave me her toothpaste-commercial smile. "Alrighty then."

I followed her into the family room.

Larry told Josephine, "We'd better scoot."

As she wrapped a pink scarf around her neck, she eyed us girls. "I was a babysitter when I was your age, and the temptation to get into mischief was way stronger when I had a girlfriend with me." She wagged a finger. "No funny stuff. Agreed?"

"Yes, ma'am," we said at the same time.

"Joey, let them be," Larry said. "Kids today are way more mature than we were." He leaned into the playpen and kissed each of his toddlers on the head. Josephine did the same.

"Okay," Josephine said as Larry helped her into a velvety black jacket and opened the front door. "Lindsay, y'all have my cell number, so give a holler if anything comes up. We'll be at the Duck Creek Inn for supper and then home right after."

As soon as we shut the door behind them, Lindsay leaned dramatically against it.

"Oh. My. God. I can't stand it."

I wasn't sure if she meant she couldn't stand how much she liked Larry, or how nicely Larry treated Josephine. But then

Lindsay smiled, and I realized it had never crossed her mind that Larry was being nice to his wife. A wife he had bought pretty roses for. A wife he supposedly didn't like so much.

I followed Lindsay into the family room. For the next thirty minutes, we played with Willie and Samantha and their sticky Playskool toys. At seven-thirty, we put them to bed without any hassle. For the next half hour, Lindsay and I ate popcorn while surfing crappy cable television and Netflix shows we'd already seen.

A few minutes into a B-movie starring some old-school actor who wasn't very funny but probably thought he was, Lindsay abruptly turned off the television.

"This is boring," she said. She stood up and stretched. "Wanna see something?" she asked.

"What?"

"Come. I'll show you."

I got up off the couch and followed Lindsay away from the family room and down the hallway. We passed a formal living room, a bathroom, and a closet. At the end of the hall, she opened a door.

"What do you think?" she asked, turning on the overhead light.

The room was filled with coffee-colored furniture and outdated lamps, like in a private library. Only this room wasn't a library. It was a shrine.

"Larry's room," Lindsay said, beaming.

I walked toward the other side of the study. The wall was covered with a dozen or more newspaper articles, all of them expensively framed. Some of the dates went back to the previous year, but most were from that summer and fall. Each article mentioned a local fire: a barn out near the Croatan; a tool shed in Brinson; an abandoned restaurant in Cloverdale. All of them referred to fire station number thirty-two: Larry's station.

I felt like we'd broken into a church.

"I've spent a lot of time in here," Lindsay whispered, moving to the antique desk in the middle of the office. She opened the narrow center drawer, pulled on a tab inside, and a loud click spilled into the room. She leaned down and opened the bottom of two side drawers.

"What are you doing?" I asked.

"It took me five babysitting sessions to figure out how to open this thing," she said proudly. "I knew there'd be something awesome in here. Otherwise, why would anyone bother to lock it?"

She pulled a leather-bound book out of the bottom drawer and placed it on the desk. When she opened it, I saw that it was a ledger, the kind an old-fashioned accountant might use. Each page had four columns. From left to right and written in ink were a date, a person's name, an address, and a number.

I swiveled the book so I could see it better. "What's it for?"

"They're the names of all the people he's saved," Lindsay explained. "Car accidents, fires—"

"Larry keeps a record?"

"Erica, when you put your life in danger, and everyone sort of clumps you in with the other firemen, like the ones who are still on the list but are too old to fight fires, or the volunteers who make doughnut runs...well, you have to remind yourself that what you're doing is important."

I didn't think Adam made doughnut runs, but I said nothing

as I turned away from the creepy ledger and checked out the books that lined the mahogany shelves. Some were firefighting manuals, others were books with fire as the central theme, a few novels, some memoirs. A bunch of chemistry books were stacked in neat piles next to the others.

"Anyway," Lindsay said, "I think this room is cool. It makes me feel like…" She paused, thinking.

"Like what?"

"Like I'm closer to him."

She put the notebook back in the bottom drawer and shut it, then slid the desk's middle drawer closed. This time the clicking locked it back in place.

From the desk, Lindsay picked up one of three small framed photos.

"This is Larry when he first became a fireman. Look how cute he was."

In the faded photo, Larry stood in front of a firehouse with two older people I assumed were his parents. He had a disco-thick moustache, and he wore a pair of jeans with a black T-shirt. He was actually very handsome when he was younger, even with the moustache. Maybe, when Lindsay looked at Larry, this was what she saw instead of the real-life old guy he'd turned into.

"Not bad," I said.

"Totally hot." She put the picture back on the desk and turned it to its original position. "You know, I've always wanted to snoop through the rest of the house, but I never have."

"What do you want to snoop for?" I asked.

"Maybe Larry has a secret diary hidden somewhere with *my* name in it."

She laughed like she was joking, but I could tell by the way she bit her bottom lip that she believed this was a possibility.

"I don't know, Linds…"

"Come on, Erica. Don't you want a little excitement in your life?"

Without waiting for an answer, Lindsay turned off the light. I stepped into the foyer as she shut the office door. Suddenly, she raced up the hallway and ran up the stairs. I was programmed not to move that quickly, ever. *Walk* up the street, not run. *Sit* on a chair, not flop. *Squat slowly* to pick something up. *Never, ever bend over.* And when snooping in someone else's house, *do not storm up the steps.*

She stood waiting in the upstairs hallway. We checked on the twins, sound asleep in their summery yellow bedroom. A gobo night light cast stars across the walls and ceiling. Samantha and Willie slept in separate big-kid beds, with side railings to prevent them from falling out, and built-in drawers underneath. Both lay on their backs, sucking their thumbs with a tiny hand cupped around their noses. Willie hugged a stuffed animal rabbit, and Sammy held onto a worn blanket.

The room next to the twins' had been painted sky blue. Boxes lined one wall, but there was no furniture.

"This is going to be Willie's room when the twins get a little bigger," Lindsay explained.

A Jack-and-Jill bathroom sat between the blue room and theirs. A guestroom also took up space on the second floor. It looked like it had hardly been used, the white bedspread super smooth, vacuum tracks crisscrossing the plush tan carpet.

Then there was the room at the end of the hall.

"I've looked inside before, but I've never had the guts to go in," Lindsay said as she opened the door. "You make it easier."

I didn't want the pat on the back. I wanted to go back downstairs and sink into the couch while watching super bad television. But my feet took me through the bedroom door, right behind Lindsay.

The master bedroom walls were painted sage green, and the tapestries and curtains were satiny maroon. A large wooden headboard crowned the king-sized bed. Lindsay skipped over to the bed, sat on it, and bounced up and down.

"I knew Larry was a firm-mattress guy."

She picked up a photo of Larry and Josephine from the end table, scrutinized it, and put it back down.

"She's so fake," Lindsay said.

"Fake how?" I asked.

"Oh, mah," she said, fanning her face with her hand. "Ah just kaint get ovah how southernly wonduhful everything is, y'all."

Lindsay had a Southern dialect of her own, and even though she had Josephine's thicker accent down pat, I stared at the high tray ceiling, ignoring her childish imitation.

She suddenly hopped up from the bed and flew past me. "Look at this freaking tub," she called from the other room.

I entered the master bathroom just as Lindsay stepped into the tub.

"It's a Jacuzzi!" She plunked down with her legs straight out and leaned against the back. "Now this is heaven."

"Get out of there."

She laughed. "Rub-a-dub-dub, I could use a scrub." She stood up and climbed back out.

I peeked through the glass door to the large shower. "This is a nice bathroom," I said, not giving in to Lindsay's silliness, but trying to be a good sport.

In between the double sinks, Lindsay opened a vanity drawer and moved some things around.

"Hey, Linds," I said, "don't do that."

"What do you think snooping is all about?" she said as she rummaged. "Anyway, people don't hide anything in their bathroom drawers. The kids might find their stuff."

"What kind of stuff?" I asked.

"I don't know. Whatever grownups hide from their kids."

Lindsay closed the drawer, opened the medicine cabinet, checked out the labels on a few bottles, and grabbed a container of men's deodorant. She popped off the cap and took a whiff. "Larry," she breathed, rubbing the stick against her wrist.

She put the deodorant back in the cabinet and left the bathroom. I followed. She stood in the middle of the master bedroom, hands on her hips. After a moment, she opened the door to a large walk-in closet and disappeared inside. I could hear the clinking of hangers and the rustling of dry-cleaning plastic. She was in there for a while. I wondered if she was trying on shoes.

Her voice sounded muffled. "You should see her clothes. All tan or black."

"That's because it's fall," I reminded her.

Lindsay came out of the closet and shut the door. "You can still wear pink or red now and then."

"I thought she looked pretty tonight," I said.

"She's as boring as plain old grits," Lindsay responded. "Even Larry thinks so."

She walked over to an end table next to the large bed and slid open the drawer. Then she went to the other and did the same. "Not a freaking thing."

I stayed put in the center of the room as Lindsay stood in front of the tall, six-drawer dresser in the corner. She opened the top drawer, grabbed a ball of black socks, unrolled and rolled them again, and tossed them back. She reached inside and pulled out a pair of tighty-whities.

"Gross," I said. "He doesn't wear boxers."

Lindsay put the underwear back and pulled out a pair of shorts with little bears all over them.

"*Les boxers*," she said, holding them up and laughing. She closed the drawer but still held the shorts in her hand.

"Didn't you forget something?" I asked.

"He won't know they're missing," she said. "And if he does, he'll figure one of the twins took them."

Larry's sock and underwear drawer was at the very top of the dresser. There was no way a three-year-old could reach that high, let alone slide out the drawer.

"What are you going to do with them?" I asked.

Without answering, Lindsay rolled the shorts into a wad and tucked them beneath the waistband of her jeans. She wore a long shirt, so no one would be able to tell that she had a pair of men's boxers hidden underneath.

She opened and shut the rest of the drawers, sighing each time. I wasn't sure what she was looking for, but I figured a pair of boxers would be enough to quench her thirst. If that was all she needed to get through this night, then so be it.

I headed to the doorway, believing her joy ride was over; hoping it was.

But Lindsay wasn't finished. She went to the other dresser, this one low with a beveled mirror and four long drawers. Perfume bottles sat on top of a pretty lace runner, along with a large jewelry box.

Josephine's dresser.

I suddenly wanted to defend the woman who had trusted us to watch over her children. I was betraying her, even though it wasn't me going through her stuff. But now I was an accomplice, and that can be just as bad, if not worse, being the one who knows that what her friend is doing is wrong, yet still allowing it to happen.

I threw on a smile. "Come on, Linds," I tried. "Let's go back downstairs. There're still gobs of bad movies to make fun of."

But Lindsay either ignored me or didn't hear me over the crazy voices in her head. She started with the bottom drawer, moving her hands around inside. "Told you so," she said, shutting the drawer. "B-O-R-I-N-G." She opened up the next, and the next, and when she opened the top drawer, she said, "What the fuck?"

I'd only heard Lindsay use that word once or twice, and it frightened me. I didn't want to see what she was seeing; we'd gone far enough already, hadn't we? Hadn't *she*?

Lindsay held up a flimsy piece of lingerie, the kind the Victoria's Secret models wear. Then she held up another. And another. The whole top drawer was filled with lace bras and panties, fine sheer black or red teddies and thigh-high stockings.

"Why does Josephine have all this stuff?" Lindsay said, pinching a pair of red panties with two fingers like they were tainted with nuclear waste.

"Because they're married—"

"What's *this*?" she asked, tossing the panties back into the drawer and pulling out a pile of envelopes. A heavy-duty rubber band bound them together.

"Linds...don't..."

Lindsay's attitude climbing from silliness to disappointment to anger, all in the span of five minutes, made me anxious. My palms sweated. The warmth moved from my hands up my arms and around my neck like an invisible python. I was high up in a tree. A tree I'd climbed many times before. I could see myself in the doorway, far below. Could see the top of my head...

Lindsay slipped off the rubber band and opened the top envelope.

"It's a letter," she said, smirking. "From *Lare-bear* to *Joey*."

She read the letter to herself...or maybe she was reading out loud and I couldn't hear her over the blood flooding my eardrums. The swaying branch was under my feet, threatening to catapult me into oblivion. My fingers stayed glued to the frame as I crossed my legs and leaned against the doorway for support.

CLIFF, Erica, CLIFF...

Lindsay's eyes moved rapidly down the piece of paper. When she looked up again, her face took on a "You've-got-to-be-kidding-me" expression. She tossed the letters onto the dresser and came to me, throwing an arm around my waist. Tunnel vision crept in. My legs turned to mush. As she led me toward the staircase and her face grew hazy like an overexposed photo, Lindsay's impatient voice followed me down the darkening hole: "God, Erica, your timing really sucks..."

Chapter Thirteen

The sweet smell of powder made me think of freshly bathed babies. With my eyes squinted, I traced the crown molding that ran the perimeter of the ceiling. Then I saw the stubby legs of a couch, just next to my head.

Someone stood beside me. I could see the scuffed tips on a pair of black high-heeled boots. Lindsay's boots.

"My head," I told the shoes. "It hurts."

"I'll get you an aspirin," her voice said. But the boots didn't leave.

I wiggled my feet and my hands. I tried to sit up. Why wasn't she helping me?

"Linds?"

No response.

"Can you help me, please?"

Then she was kneeling down, pushing me into a seated position.

"There," Lindsay said. "You're up."

"I'm sorry," I said, fighting back tears. Sorry I had interrupted whatever it was she'd been doing. Sorry she had a tone in her voice that plainly accused me of being a burden.

Still on the floor and leaning against the front of the sofa, my neck cracked as I looked around the room. I rubbed the back of my head. A tender knot at the base of my skull pulsated as bits and pieces floated back to me: We had been upstairs. In the master bath. Then the master bedroom. There were drawers. There was lingerie. And then Lindsay's face had grown fuzzy...

My throat muscles worked hard to speak. "How did I get down here?"

"I dragged you," she said bluntly.

"Down the steps?"

A heavy pause fell between us as though the room itself had gained gravitational weight.

Lindsay spoke again. "Those letters are old anyway."

"Letters..."

I wiped drool from my chin with the back of a hand and gazed up at Lindsay. Even though she stood only a foot away, she seemed as far away as the moon.

"The letters in Josephine's dresser," Lindsay said. "They're from, like, a million years ago. When they first met."

I needed water. An ice pack wouldn't be so bad either.

Lindsay wandered around the room, moving to the far side of the sofa, and then over to the playpen. "Oh my God," she said. "Can you imagine if Larry had written those *recently*?"

Even through the pounding in my head I heard the relief in her voice.

"I don't understand," I said. "Why does it matter when he wrote them?"

"It would be the most awful thing in the world, that's why."

"But she kept them," I said, confused.

"I can't hear you," Lindsay said with irritation, walking back to where I still sat on the floor. I thought she'd kneel down, but she didn't.

I used my diaphragm to push out the words and spoke to her knees. "If their marriage is in trouble, why would she keep the letters?"

"I don't know."

I remembered the pretty satin bedspread on the king-sized bed. "Why would they share a bedroom?" I asked.

Lindsay walked away again, her voice drifting to me from across the room.

"She's probably delusional. Remember what we learned in psych class? How some people believe stuff that isn't real because it makes them happy?"

I wanted to say, *Maybe that's what* you're *doing, Lindsay*. But I did not. Between the fatigue and the headache, I was having a difficult time analyzing her crazy ideas or verbalizing my rational ones.

She said, "The first three letters were totally gross."

"First three?"

"All Larry wrote about was how much he missed his sweet Southern belle. Yada-yada-yada. Like a broken record. I guess they were apart for a while. The postmark was from New Jersey. But the dates were from a long time ago. So...whatever..."

"First *three*?" I said again. "I thought you only read *one*."

I imagined Lindsay helping me down into the family room—*dragging* me into the family room, my throbbing skull reminded me—and then leaving my crumpled body as she went back upstairs to continue reading. A surge of adrenalin helped me out as I angrily grabbed onto the sofa's arm and pulled myself up and onto the couch. I pushed a pillow behind me and leaned back.

Lindsay stared out the bay window into the darkness.

"Linds? Could you get me some water, please?"

It was the first time I'd ever had to ask her for a drink. She knew what I needed. Why was she acting like she didn't?

Lindsay paused before leaving the family room. She turned on the tap in the kitchen and brought the glass to me. I guzzled it down.

"I want to go home," I told her.

"I'll have Larry drop you off first," she said as she sat in the recliner, one leg crossed over the other, her foot shaking like she had a cramp.

Next to the coffee table on the floor, the tips of a thin stack of envelopes were sticking out of Lindsay's pocketbook.

"What's that?" I asked, pointing with my head.

"Nothing."

"You stole Josephine's letters?"

She jumped off the recliner, grabbed her pocketbook, and shoved the envelopes deeper inside. "First of all, they're *Larry's* letters, since he wrote them, and second of all, I wouldn't be stupid enough take *all* of them. What woman wouldn't notice a whole stack missing?"

"Why would you take any at all?"

Lindsay's phone chimed. She scooped it up from the coffee table like it was on fire.

"They'll be home in ten," she said, reading the text. "Thank God. I've been looking forward to this drive home all day."

***

Josephine stepped into the foyer giggling and holding onto Larry's arm. Her cheeks were flushed by the cold, her hair tousled just enough to make her a natural beauty.

"Why don't you go on upstairs, Joey?" Larry suggested. "And don't sleep with your makeup on."

Josephine pulled Larry to her and kissed him hard on the lips. "That's my lovey-hubby. Always looking out for his little Joey." She waddled up the steps, still wearing her jacket, holding onto the railing for support.

Was she going to change into one of her lacy nightgowns? Did she plan to seduce her husband later? Isn't that what married women did after being wined and dined?

Wondering about this added sorrow to my headache, and I quickly put on my coat to leave.

"Everything go okay with the twins?" Larry asked.

"Absolutely, Larry," Lindsay said. Her voice sounded breathy, like she'd just come up from under water.

"Well then," he said. "Let's get you girls home."

We walked out to the dark blue Explorer parked in the driveway. Larry opened the front passenger door for Lindsay. I tried to see if he pinched her butt, or touched her arm, or gave her a special look, but it was dark, and I was still in a bit of a fog.

"Where's your house, Erica?" Larry asked, opening the back door for me. I sat behind Lindsay.

"Over by the tennis courts."

We buckled in and Larry started the engine.

"Been living in Great Pines long?" he asked as he backed out the driveway.

"A few years," I said.

"It's a nice neighborhood."

"Yes, sir."

Larry laughed. "You don't have to call me *sir*, Erica. Call me *Larry*."

Lindsay looked back at me and grinned as Larry pulled the Explorer onto the street.

"Take Erica home first," Lindsay said. "Her mother is way stricter than mine."

We headed up the street and made a right onto Wilshire. As we drove past the recently burned house, Larry slowed the SUV. Even with the windows closed, I could smell the charred timber.

"Thank God no one was hurt in that one," he said, letting the vehicle idle in front of the rubble.

"A dog died," I said.

"We heard him barking down in the basement," Larry said. "I tried to save him. Got this for my hard work."

He turned his cheek to the right and tilted his head back. By the dim glow of the streetlamp, I could barely make out the tiny burn mark on his chin.

"Let me see," Lindsay said. She took his face in her hands and peered at the mark. "Oh, poor baby."

Larry caught my eye in the rearview mirror and gently took her hand from his face.

I looked out into the dark and pretended I hadn't noticed a thing.

"I really have to get home," I said to the window. "My mother will be wondering where I am."

"Of course," Larry said.

Lindsay turned on the radio. A new song by Adele was playing.

"Oh, I love this song, Larry. Don't you?"

Larry turned up the volume but said nothing as he pulled the car away from the curb and headed in the direction of my house.

Chapter Fourteen

"I wore Larry's boxers to bed," Lindsay said the second I got into her truck on Monday morning. "I love the little bears. Plus he gives the best bear hugs. Maybe I'll call him Lare-Bear."

I shut the door. "You can't call him that."

"Why not?" she asked.

I clicked my seatbelt in place. "Because you got that nickname from those letters."

"So?"

"So, it's weird," I said.

"Maybe you're right," she said. "He might suspect something."

"For God's sake, Lindsay. Just call him Larry. Isn't that what he asked you to call him? Shit."

Lindsay stopped at the exit to our neighborhood. "Why are you in such a bad mood?"

"Because I'm tired."

It had been an especially long weekend, keeping our snooping and Lindsay's petty theft a secret from my sometimes psychic mother. In a way, I wished my mother had suspected something.

I didn't want to carry the burden of knowledge or guilt alone. But, of course, I would never tell my mother. She'd never give me another get-out-of-jail-free card as long as I lived. And who would catch me if Lindsay was no longer there to do it?

We drove the remainder of the way to school in silence, but the second Lindsay pulled into the parking space and turned off the ignition, she turned to me.

"Erica," she said, her voice low and serious. "Something happened…Friday night…after we dropped you off."

"Something bad?"

Lindsay shook her head, shut her eyes for a moment, and opened them again. "Larry and I took a drive."

"Where'd you go?"

"To the community college."

"What for?"

"Larry has keys to the buildings up there," she explained. "He says the fire department has keys to local schools in case they have to go inside for an emergency after hours. Though we didn't go in. They have cameras in the hallways. So we hung out in the parking lot behind the auditorium."

"The parking lot?" I asked.

"You know, in his Explorer. He put the radio on that show where they play all the romantic songs, and…we made out. For like an hour."

"Oh…"

"It was so romantic. I have goose bumps just thinking about it." She held out her arm and pushed up her jacket sleeve, exposing the tiny bumps. "The whole time we were making out, he kept telling me how beautiful my eyes are, how he loves my lips, and he thinks I have a perfect body. God, Erica. He's all I can think about."

"Did you…you know…?"

"We're going to wait until the time is right."

I thought, how could there be a right time when everything Lindsay was doing was wrong?

"I always thought Adam would be the one," I told her, trying to shift the conversation.

"Huh," Lindsay said. "Me, too. Glad I held out, that's for sure."

"Does Larry know…you know…that you've never done it?"

"I made sure he knows it. Guys always want girls to be virgins."

If that was the case, then I was lucky, because I had no desire to give that part of me away so easily. But if rumors were true that scores of girls were busy losing it, then where were all the virgins coming from?

"Erica," Lindsay said. "I need a favor. Josephine's going out of town this Friday to see her mother, and Larry wants to be with me. I need you to cover for me. So he and I can have some time together. You know…alone."

"You want me to babysit so you and Larry can go on a date?"

The question was ludicrous, not only because of Lindsay's secretive plans, but because she was willing to trust me alone with the kids.

"Would you do that for me, Erica?" she asked.

"My mother will never let me babysit by myself," I reminded her, thinking it was a perfect excuse, an easy out.

"Oh, you won't be alone," she said smiling. "I've got someone to go with you."

"Who?"

"Adam."

"Wait," I said. "You talked to him?"

"Texted. But only to ask for this little favor."

"And he said yes?"

Lindsay laughed. "Well, duh. Of course he said yes. He'd do anything for me."

"Why can't he babysit by himself?"

"I thought it might be better if two people took my place," she explained. "I have that gig down to a tee. Larry said that talking Josephine into it would be easy."

My stomach rippled at the thought of hanging out with Adam, but the idea of covering for Lindsay made it turn sour.

"I don't know, Linds," I said. "That's a totally huge favor."

Lindsay's cheeks instantly turned red. Her hands gripped the steering wheel. "A huge favor? You're kidding, right? You want me to count all the huge favors I've done for you in the last two-and-a-half years? Oh, I'm sorry, we don't have time. Because it would take me another two-and-a-half years to go down the list."

My mind turned back to freshman year; back when the kids believed I was contagious. The gym teachers accused me of being lazy. The guidance counselor suggested I see a shrink. But there was Lindsay in her French braids, her long skirt and hand-knitted scarf, standing by my side in her ugly Crocs, never complaining, at the ready in case I hit the floor...

"Well?" Lindsay asked, tapping the steering wheel with a pretty polished nail.

The word "Okay" fell into the cab as a whisper, mainly because my throat had closed on the sound.

Lindsay's shoulders relaxed. A wide smile spread across her face.

"Thanks, Erica. I knew you'd say yes."

***

"Don't get busted," I told Lindsay, referring to her texting as we made our way toward the gymnasium. Cell phones were off-limits on school grounds from eight to three, except during lunch or an emergency, like a lockdown.

Lindsay's thumbs never left the keypad. "There aren't any teachers around."

"Who are you texting, anyway?" I asked.

"Who do you think?"

"Is he at his house?"

Now that I knew the layout of the Taggert home, it wasn't hard to picture Larry sitting on the edge of his Jacuzzi bathtub sneaking a phone call, while Josephine fed the babies down in the kitchen.

"No," Lindsay said, her eyes glued to the tiny screen. "He's at the station."

My viewpoint changed to Larry sitting in one of the fire trucks, tucked down low so no one would see him on the phone, the other men in the building busy watching talk shows or taking cat naps.

"Aw," Lindsay said. "Larry says he misses me. And that he's counting the minutes until Friday."

We entered the gymnasium, Lindsay's high-heeled boots clicking and my Uggs clunking against the hard floor.

"Oh my God," Lindsay whispered, stopping in the middle of

the gym and holding out her phone for me to see. "How adorable is this?"

Larry had sent a selfie, standing next to one of the red ladder trucks, wearing a fire hat with his normal street clothes. He was also wearing a creepy grin.

"I can't wait to see him," she said.

"Where is he taking you on your...you know..."

"Date? I'm not sure. But I'm going to wear this amazingly sexy dress I found for fifty percent off at Clarabelle's. I had to sneak it into the house, and I'll have to sneak it back out again or my mother will have a heart attack. The thing fits me like a very, very tight glove."

She giggled as the bell chimed on her phone. She texted something else, silenced her phone, and tucked it in her backpack.

"I don't know how you keep from stressing," I said as I walked her to the locker room doors.

"About what?"

"Getting caught."

"Those guys at the station are into their own stuff."

"I don't mean by other firemen," I explained. "I mean by his wife."

"You've seen Josephine," Lindsay said. "She keeps her head in the sand dealing with the twins twenty-four-seven. Plus her mom is really sick, so she spends a lot of time with her. Why? Are you worried for me? That's really sweet, Erica." She lightly touched my arm. "But you don't have to worry. I'm a big girl. If I can take care of you, I can definitely take care of myself."

***

My cell phone rang at ten o'clock that night.

Adam.

My stomach flittered.

"I wanted to check with you about babysitting Friday," he said. "You sure you're okay with it?"

"I wanted to ask you the same thing…you know, doing it just because Lindsay asked you to."

"Oh," Adam said. "That's not the only reason."

"It isn't?" I asked a bit too eagerly.

"No. Larry's a great guy. He's sort of been my mentor. Babysitting his kids is the least I can do."

"Oh." I heard the disappointment in my voice and wondered if Adam did, too.

"So, your mom's okay with this?" he asked.

"Lindsay worked it out."

Lindsay was always working things out, including pacifying my mother, a talent that had eluded me.

"Okay," Adam said. "So, should I bring anything?"

"Like what?"

"Like puppets, or face-painting, or something?"

I laughed. "You have puppets?" I pictured Adam with his hand stuffed inside a Kermit, entertaining the twins.

"They're not mine," he said. "The firehouse visits a lot of schools. Most of the toys are about fire prevention."

"Oh. Well, the twins have tons of their own. Plus, they go to bed at seven-thirty. So probably no time for face-painting or puppet shows. But it's cool that you asked."

There was such a long silence I thought he'd hung up. But then he said, "I'm glad Lindsay asked me to do this. It'll give you and me some time to chat."

"Chat?"

"You know, about Lindsay. I could really use some advice right now."

"Advice. Right."

"So, I'll pick you up?"

"Sounds good," I said. And then, before my brain had a chance to stop my mouth: "Why don't you come over for dinner first?"

He paused, but only for a moment. "Sure. Thanks."

"Be here at six on the dot," I told him, grinning into the phone. "My mother's a good cook, but she's also a stickler."

Chapter Fifteen

Friday came fast. At school that afternoon, Adam spotted Lindsay and me walking to class. For the first time since she'd dumped him, he made a point of waving hello from across the crowded hallway.

"Hey, Adam," Lindsay muttered, turning her head in the other direction as quickly as she said it.

"See you tonight, Erica," he called. "Six o'clock?"

I smiled and gave him a thumbs-up.

As Adam disappeared into the crowd, Lindsay asked, "Why so early?"

"My mother invited him to dinner," I fibbed. "You know how she is. Needs to make sure he's ready to jump on the Syncopian band wagon."

"Oh. Gotcha."

I gave Lindsay a sideways glance as we headed toward the classroom. I was doing a lot of that lately, inspecting her like she was a foreign exchange student fresh off the boat. She walked with her head down, cell phone in her hands, thumbs furiously tapping the keypad. She was wearing a lot of makeup. Too much for the daytime, if anybody asked my opinion. A tan stripe created a dividing line between her face and neck. Her long shiny hair was tucked behind her ears, exposing the diamond earrings she wore every day like she didn't own another pair.

"What did you tell your mom about the jewelry?" I asked.

She waved the question away like an annoying fly, the bracelet jingling against her wrist. "I told her they were gifts from Adam."

"She thinks you're still together?"

"More or less," she said.

"Why?"

"Because that's who she thinks I'm with tonight," Lindsay said. "It all works better this way. Trust me."

***

After dinner at my house, Adam and I walked out to his truck. He held the door for me and got into the driver's seat. "Your parents are pretty cool," he said.

"You think so even after the inquisition?" I asked. "I'm surprised my mother didn't burn you at the stake."

"All mothers do that."

"Yeah? Well, my mother does it for a living. It's her *thing*."

Adam started the engine and turned on the radio. Background country music that matched his fall-colored flannel shirt filled the cab. As he pulled the truck onto the street, he said, "If I had a daughter who fainted, I'd never let her out of my sight."

"She'd hate you for that," I told him.

"I'd rather have someone mad at me than see them get hurt."

"I almost never get hurt."

He gave me a narrow-eyed glance.

"What?" I asked.

"I seem to remember a certain picnic…"

"I stood in the sun too long," I said. "It could have happened to anyone."

"Whatever the reason, it totally freaked me out to see you fall like that."

"I thought you were a fireman."

"What does that have to do with seeing a pretty girl hit the ground face-first?"

I held back a grin as we pulled up in front of the Taggert house.

"You ready to play with sticky blocks?" I asked.

"That is so bizarre," Adam said, "because I've been thinking about sticky blocks all day."

I laughed as he came around to my side and opened the door. Together we walked up the sidewalk. On the front porch, I asked as subtly as possible, "Did Lindsay happen to mention where she was going tonight?"

Adam rang the doorbell. "Something about her little sister's ballet recital."

"Right," I said, knowing that Lindsay's mom could barely afford the slippers, let alone the lessons. "Ballet."

***

The top of Larry Taggert's lip was sweating like he'd been hanging out in a steam room. And he'd put on way too much cologne, like some of the men at Sunday mass who left behind a trail of Old Spice as they walked up the aisle for Communion.

"Well," Larry said as soon as our coats were off. "I should go. Don't want to keep the mother-in-law waiting."

"Mother-in-law?" I asked.

"Going to see Josephine's mother tonight," Larry said as though he'd practiced the words. "Out in Feltonville."

"That's a long drive," I said, keeping my face a stone.

"It is."

"Josephine took a separate car?"

"She left this afternoon," Larry said. "I'm...I'm going to meet her there. At her mother's."

"That's a lot of gas," I said. "Taking two cars and everything."

"It can't be helped. Her mother is ill. That's what family is all about."

"What time will you be home?" I asked.

"How late can you stay?"

Adam answered, "As long as my parents know where I am, I can stay till whenever."

"And you, Erica?"

"My mother said it doesn't matter as long as Adam is here and we don't leave the house."

"Fine," Larry said. He looked around the foyer like he was suddenly lost. "Keys..." he mumbled, patting his jacket pockets.

I picked up the jam-packed key ring from the hall table and handed it to him.

"Okay, I'm off," Larry said. "You two have fun. But not too much."

He stupidly punched Adam in the arm and I cringed.

We shut the door behind him.

"What was that about?" Adam asked.

"Old guys act weird sometimes."

"Not him," he said. "*You.* What's with all the questions?"

"I was just making conversation."

Adam and I made our way into the family room where we played with the kids for about twenty minutes. Just before seven-thirty, Adam took them upstairs one at a time. When he came back into the family room, he was smiling.

"Willie kissed me on the cheek," he said.

I smiled back. "He's a sweetie."

"They both are."

"I know, right? I feel like I'm overpaid."

We laughed as we stood in the middle of the messy family room, complete with double stroller, overused blankies, worn stuffed animals, all the typical things found in a house with toddlers. In the playpen's corner sat a couple of waterproof books and a single mini blue sock. Sadness poured over me as I stared at that tiny speck of clothing. Josephine was spending time with her sick mother while her husband was spending time with Lindsay. Here I was, acting as a human dividing line, and here Adam was, doing the same as me but not suspecting a thing.

"Want me to find a movie?" he asked.

"Sure," I said, happy for the diversion. "I'll make some popcorn."

As I headed toward the kitchen, Adam said, "You're okay by yourself?"

"Oh," I said, stopping and turning around. "I don't know. I mean, anything could happen. A piano could fall on my head.

Or a meteor might crash through the kitchen window…"

"Sorry."

In the kitchen, I microwaved the popcorn, shook it into a large bowl, and grabbed the two blue Gatorades from my bag. When I came back into the family room, Adam had paused the beginning of a Netflix movie.

"What's this?" I asked, handing Adam a bottle.

"An old Vin Diesel movie. You up for brainless?

"Always."

As I sat, Adam pulled something from his belt loop.

"Is that a pager?" I asked. "I didn't know anyone still used those."

"Our station does," he said as he turned it off. "It's mainly just for backup."

"Oh."

I placed the popcorn bowl in between us so we'd have to sit sort of close together, but not so close that our legs touched. A few times, my fingers bumped into his. He didn't seem to care, and I definitely didn't mind.

Nearly two hours later, when the movie was over, Adam clicked off the television and faced me on the sofa. His hands absently twirled the empty Gatorade bottle. My stomach flipped nervously as he pulled one leg up a little, careful to keep his work boot from touching the couch cushion. His Italian eyebrows nearly met in the middle as his face grew serious.

"Tell me what's going on," he said.

"Going on?"

"With Lindsay."

"Oh."

"You're her best friend, Erica. Does she ever say anything about me?"

"Not really…"

"Did she tell you why she broke up with me? I still can't get a straight answer."

"Adam, I'm not the one you should be talking to."

The empty bottle moved through the air as he used his hands for emphasis. "She never answers my calls. She only texts me."

When she needs something, I thought.

"What tragedy would it be if you didn't get back together?" I asked. "You'd survive. Couples break up all the time. Especially in high school."

"It probably sounds stupid, but I thought Lindsay and I would be together at least until college." He lowered his voice. "I thought I was going to be…" He tapped the empty bottle against his palm. "You know…the *one*…"

I pictured Lindsay in her dress that fit like a glove, losing her virginity to Married Larry while Adam and I babysat the man's children. We were helping Lindsay have an affair. Silently cheering her on. Aiding and abetting.

Criminals.

But Adam doesn't know, my mind reminded me. *Only you do.*

Ignorance of the law is no excuse, I told myself, if only to make to make me feel better.

"Why is your face doing that?" Adam asked.

I touched my face.

"You look worried," he said. "Like there's something you want to tell me."

"No…"

Adam shook his head. "One day she texts me, all sweet-ass, and the next day she acts like I'm invisible."

"She's moody that way."

"How come I never saw it before?" he asked.

"I don't know…forest for the trees and all of that."

"Why did she want me to do this favor for her?"

"It's hard to find someone to babysit on a Friday night," I said. "Most girls have dates or whatever."

Most girls.

Adam paused. He lowered his voice. "She's not at a ballet thing, is she?"

A click entered the air as I swallowed. "What makes you say that?"

Adam looked at the dark television screen and back to me. "I need you to be straight-up with me, Erica. Is Lindsay on a date? Is that why she asked us to babysit together? Is she doing that magician's thing? Misdirecting me, hooking us up, while she goes off with some guy—"

"Hooking us up? What? No—"

"She's out with some asshole while I sit here on my Friday night watching a bad movie in a room that smells like dirty diapers."

"Sorry I ruined your evening."

"No," he said, touching my arm. "You didn't. That's not why I'm pissed off."

"It's okay. I get it." I jerked my arm away and stood up. "I've seen enough romantic comedies to know which character I play. Lindsay gets the guys and I'm the bestie who watches from the bench. And you know what? That's totally fine with me. Because

I'd rather be alone for the rest of my life than sneak around behind people's backs."

I stormed into the kitchen and leaned my front against the sink. A handful of pacifiers sat in a soapy bowl of water, soaking. I touched one of them, causing it to bob up and down, thinking of the innocent babies sleeping upstairs in their sunshine-painted room, dreaming of ponies and rainbows. In the kitchen window, my reflection overlapped the trees outside. Tiny leaves danced around on my forehead.

Adam's reflection appeared behind my own. I didn't turn around. I noticed how soft his face looked in the glass, how his muscular body stood nearly a half-foot taller than mine.

"Erica," he said. "I didn't mean it the way you're taking it. I like spending time with you. I really do. You're easy to talk to, and we laugh a helluva lot more than Lindsay and I ever did…"

"Then why do you care what she thinks?" I asked his reflection. "Or what she's doing tonight?"

"I just don't want to look like a jackass every time I try to talk to her and she snubs me. Or every time she texts and it turns out all she wants is a babysitter. If you tell me what's going on, it will be easier to let go. Is she seeing someone from our school?"

"No," I whisper-laughed.

"A different school?"

I shook my head.

"Then who?"

I stared at a blob of baby food stuck to the stainless steel sink and pressed my lips firmly together to keep from blurting out Larry's name.

Adam said, "You should have told me she'd met someone from the start."

I turned around and faced him. "*She* should have told you, Adam. I wasn't your girlfriend. *She* was."

Tears suddenly streamed down my cheeks. I'm not sure why, exactly. Maybe because the stress of keeping Lindsay's secret was starting to consume me; because Josephine was spending time with her sick mother; because Larry was out with a girl that up until a few weeks ago still had a herd of stuffed animals covering her bed.

Adam's hand landed gently on my shoulder. "Hey. I don't want you to be upset."

"Why?" I asked. "Afraid I might faint?"

"No." He brushed a loose hair away from my forehead. "I just don't want to see you cry. Especially on account of me."

Without thinking, my arms slid around his middle. His arms made their way around my shoulders. His flannel shirt was soft against my cheek. It wasn't a passionate hug like you might see between two unbelievable actors who wouldn't be caught dead together outside a movie set. It was a desperate hug—the kind people share when they feel cast out.

"She's crushing on someone else," I told Adam, my face muffled by his shirt. "Will it change anything if you know who it is?" I pulled away from him and tore a paper towel from the holder next to the sink. "Lindsay's not the only girl in the world, you know."

Adam took the paper towel from me, folded it, and patted each of my wet cheeks. "I know."

"She's changing, Adam." I tilted my head back as he gently dried my face. "That's all you need to know. She's changing in a really big way. And there isn't a damn thing you or I can do about it."

***

119

The slam of a car door. Footsteps on the sidewalk. Footsteps on the porch.

My eyes jerked open. Adam sat next to me, his head back against the sofa cushion, tiny snores escaping his slightly open mouth. We had fallen asleep side by side, our shoes off, our feet propped up on pillows on the coffee table. In the dark, the television offered the only light. The volume was down. A late-night cartoon that only computer geeks and stoners watch flickered through the silent room.

I nudged Adam. He sat up fast, as though a fire alarm had sounded. His thick hair stood straight up like a toupee on the back of his head, and I fought the urge to flatten it down.

"It's two o'clock," I said, showing him my cell phone.

A key jiggled in the front door's lock.

After a moment, a man's voice whispered, "Adam? Erica?"

The overhead light popped on. I shielded my eyes.

Larry stood in the wide doorway of the family room. His hair was tousled. I quickly glanced at his belt buckle, half-expecting it to be undone, but it was secure. His collared shirt was neatly tucked into his pants. I squinted to see if there was lipstick on his face but noticed none in the dim television light.

"Sorry it's so late," Larry said, rubbing his hand across the top of his head. He let out a soft chuckle. "Things got a little intense tonight."

"Is she all right?" Adam asked.

"*She?*"

"Your mother-in-law."

"Oh," Larry said. "Yes. She's fine." His eyes moved from the empty playpen to the staircase. "Everything okay here?"

Adam and I nodded in unison.

Larry said, "Good…good…"

Adam worked to put on his boots. I slipped into my comfy flats and pushed my hair behind my ears.

"Well, then," Larry said. "Let me pay you."

As he pulled his wallet out of his back pocket, something square flittered to the carpet. Larry scooped it up fast and buried it in the pocket of his jacket. I barely had time to see it, but I knew what it was. My parents drove us past an abandoned movie theater parking lot on the occasional Sunday that we made it to church, the torn-open condom wrappers littering the asphalt.

I turned to Adam to see if he'd caught a glimpse, but he was lacing up his boots.

Larry opened his wallet. "I'm going to pay you double."

"Oh, that's okay," I said.

The thought of getting paid to cover up for Larry and Lindsay made it hard to take any money at all.

"No, no," Larry said, coming toward the sofa. "I came home unexpectedly late, and I feel bad, so take it."

He held out his hand. I didn't move.

"Please."

I stood up and grabbed the bills without letting his fingers touch my own.

"Thanks," I mumbled, handing half the bills to Adam and shoving the rest into my pocketbook.

Larry pulled out his cell phone. "Let me get your cell numbers, in case you both babysit again, and I'm late getting home. I should have gotten them earlier. I completely forgot…"

"You already have mine," Adam said, getting up off the couch and putting on his jacket.

"Do I?"

"You have all the volunteers' numbers."

"Of course," Larry said. "That's right. Okay, Erica, go ahead and give me yours."

I gave him my number and he tapped it into his phone.

The three of us walked to the foyer. As Adam opened the front door, a chime rang out on Larry's cell phone. Before my imagination took off regarding who might be texting Larry Taggert at two in the morning, the door shut behind us.

Chapter Sixteen

Lindsay, wearing an oversized fireman's T-shirt below her made-up face and super stylish hair, swished back and forth on the swivel chair at my bedroom desk while I sat cross-legged on my bed.

It was nearly noon on Saturday, and I was still in my pajamas, exhausted after getting home so late from babysitting the night before. My parents had gone to pick up Dad's Jeep from the mechanic, and Lindsay's visit saved me from having to go with them.

"Last night was un-freaking-believable," Lindsay said. "At one o'clock this morning, my mom called me to see why I wasn't home from babysitting yet, but my cell was off, and she called Larry's cell and hell-O! Here she is talking to him on the phone, and I'm sitting right beside him! Larry told my mom that he got stuck at his mother-in-law's. How's that for quick thinking? He never sounded nervous or anything."

"I didn't get home until after two," I said.

"I know," Lindsay said. "Me, too!"

"Did Larry go to the fire?"

"What fire?"

"The bandstand in the park. I slept through the alarm, but my parents heard it. They said it was around four this morning."

"Oh," Lindsay said. "I don't know. I'm sure if he got the call he'd find a way to go. Did you know that firemen around here hardly ever fight fires anymore? They mostly deal with car wrecks. That's what Larry told me. It totally bums him out."

"Why would that bum him out?"

"Because fighting fires is what he really loves to do."

Lindsay spun toward the closet door mirror across the room, ran her fingers through her long curls, and straightened out her posture, pushing out her boobs. Then she swiveled back toward me.

"Guess what *else* happened last night?"

"What?" I asked without enthusiasm.

"Everything!" She held onto the sides of the swivel chair like she was afraid she'd fly off. Her legs jiggled excitedly. "Oh my God, Erica. I can't even tell you what I'm feeling right now. I mean, sexually, for sure, but it's more than that. Larry showed me things and told me things...oh my God...I can't even describe it. I wouldn't do it justice."

"Did he wear a condom?" I asked.

"Are you kidding me? Of course. We're being super careful." Lindsay put her hands against her mouth for a long moment. When she released them again, she said, "I know this sounds totally corny, but I have never felt like more of a woman than I do right now. And you'll know exactly what I mean when you...well, you know...when you meet the man of your dreams."

"He's twice your age," I reminded her. Not only did my voice lack enthusiasm, it had a definite snarky undertone.

"I know…"

"You don't think someone is bound to see you together?"

She paused. "We have a secret place."

"Secret?"

"Larry has keys to some of the buildings in the warehouse district."

"You're fooling around in an abandoned warehouse?"

I pictured our downtown district, no different than a post-apocalyptic city from the movies filled with boarded up factories and threatening creatures hiding in the shadows. I'm sure the distaste showed on my face.

"It's not like it sounds, Erica," Lindsay said.

"There are drug addicts down there."

"Larry would never let anything happen to me."

"So it's a real building?" I asked. "With floors and windows and everything?"

"Of course. It's brick and has two floors. I think it used to be a store or something. There's a bunch of letters across the front, and I think the number three, but it's all sort of faded. And it was pretty dark. Anyway, who cares about the *outside*? Larry decorated the *inside*. Just for me."

"Decorated?"

"Not with wallpaper or anything fancy like that," Lindsay explained. "More like how a guy would make an ugly place prettier for a girl. Up on the second floor, there's a really cozy futon mattress with blankets and pillow shams, and he set up one of those small propane camp stoves so we can make hot chocolate. There's no electricity, something to do with city utilities, but Larry bought candles and set them up in Mason jars all over the room. He even brought a bottle of wine. It was Italian, and tasted like cherries. He said it would relax me. I only had two glasses, but it did sort of make things go smoother…"

The thought of lying on an old mattress in an abandoned building made my skin crawl. "What about a shower?" I asked. I'd at least need a toilet and a sink.

"There's a tiny bathroom," Lindsay said, "but there's no water because the pipes are old, but Larry thinks of everything. He brought bottled water and heated it on his camp stove so I would, you know, feel comfortable. I could tell he was trying hard to make me feel at home." She turned toward the window and whispered, "It's our own secret nest."

The word "nest" made me think of rats and lice. But I didn't say this to her. I didn't respond at all.

Lindsay didn't seem to notice my silence. She went on about how Larry tasted like peppermint toothpaste, his hair smelled like Axe shampoo, and even though his hands were callused, they were gentle. She talked about how awesome it was that he shaved every day, including his neck. How he was once in a garage band, and he still played guitar every once in a while.

"He's going to play for me sometime," she said. "I can't wait."

But I didn't want to hear anymore about the personal hygiene stuff or Larry Taggert's rock star fantasies. The more Lindsay spoke, the more I was disgusted by their creepy love nest and the fact that she had given herself to a married man with kids. Even working on my *Uncle Tom* essay would have been better than sitting in my bedroom on a sleepy Saturday morning listening to Lindsay gush about her affair.

"…Friday?" Lindsay was asking.

"What?"

"This Friday. Are you on?"

"For babysitting?"

"I'll sit on Saturdays if they need me and some nights during the week, so Josephine thinks everything's normal. You can sit on Fridays. Then Larry and I will have a night to call our own, and Josephine won't suspect a thing since she goes to her mother's on Fridays."

"I thought firemen had funky schedules."

Lindsay said, "Larry used his sick mother-in-law as an excuse to get a set schedule for a while."

Even though my answer should have been a quick and effortless no, that any normal high school girl would have told Lindsay to eff off, or, at the very least, that what she was doing was immoral, an appealing picture was forming in my mind, obliterating the ethical portion of my brain.

"Adam will have to come with me," I said after a moment. "You know my mother."

"I figured," Lindsay said. "I'll be sure to text him—"

"I can ask him," I said.

I was well aware of what I was doing, yet compelled to go along with the plan. After all, none of what I was agreeing to was for Lindsay's sake.

I added, "That way you don't have to worry about it."

"All right," she said.

"So, then, you're okay with it?"

"Are you kidding?" Lindsay said, again swirling the chair until it faced the full-length mirror. Staring at her reflection, she grinned and said, "I'm okay with whatever works for Larry and me to be together."

Chapter Seventeen

Biannual check-up day.

As my mother made a right into the hospital parking lot, I announced, "I think it might be over."

"What's over, honey?"

I held up the log book that I'd grabbed from the kitchen drawer. "My spells."

"Why do you think that?"

"Read the log," I told her. "I haven't fainted in two weeks. *Two weeks.* Don't you think that's a good sign?"

"I like to think that every day without a spell is a good sign."

"So," I said, "I was thinking, if this keeps up, I'd like to get my learner's permit."

"To drive?"

"Lots of Syncopians go into remission or stop fainting forever. Maybe I'm one of the lucky ones."

"Stop calling yourself a Syncopian," my mother said. "It makes you sound like an alien. Even if you were suddenly spell-free, getting your permit is nothing to jump into."

"Who's jumping?" I asked. "My whole class has been driving for two years."

"Let's take it one step at a time."

My mother parked the car and turned off the ignition.

"You don't want me to get better," I said.

She jerked her head toward me. "Excuse me?"

"Sometimes I think you want me to stay this way." I handed her an exaggerated pout.

"Did you really just say that to me? I've spent nearly three years driving you to appointments, losing sleep, keeping your diet in check. You're not the only one with a log, you know."

"I just want it to be over—"

"You think I don't want the same thing?" she asked, redness filling her cheeks. "I'd like to have a life outside of this disease, too. What the hell do you think I do all day, eat bonbons?"

"That's not what I—"

"Sometimes you make me out to be a monster, Erica, and it really kills me. You don't think I want my daughter to live like a normal teenager? Go tubing on the river? Try snowboarding? Hit a concert with her friends? Shit."

"I'm getting better, Mom. I know it."

"Because you haven't fainted in two weeks."

"Yes."

"In case you've forgotten, you made it through three weeks last spring without a spell. And then, bam! It got you while you were trying on shoes at the mall."

She looked at me as though expecting an answer, but when I didn't respond she unbuckled her seatbelt and grabbed her pocketbook from the console.

My voice was no longer convincing, but still I said the words: "I'll talk to Doctor Seymour. He trusts me."

"Erica, this has nothing to do with trust."

"He'll take one look at my log and know that I'm ready."

Before my mother got out of the car, she placed a warm hand against my cheek. "I hope that's true, honey. All I've ever wanted is for you to get better; for you to have a wonderful life. I pray for it every day, even if you don't believe I do."

***

I sat in the waiting area while my mother stood in line at the check-in window. Four girls and two boys sat scattered around the room. Most parents were mothers. One boy brought his dad along. The grownups watched *Good Morning America* playing on the television with the volume turned down. Most kids were glued to their cell phones.

An elfish girl of twelve or thirteen came through the door. While her mother spoke to the receptionist, the girl sat in the chair next to mine. Her skin was bluish and pale and her eyes were sunken. She played nervously with a gold pinky ring on her left hand.

"Are you getting the tilt-table test?" she whispered.

The tilt-table test is known by seasoned Syncopians as the *TTT*, as though calling it by its initials makes it less of a monster.

"No," I said. "I had it done two years ago. Is that why you're here?"

The girl nodded. Even though she was very pale, she was slender and pretty, like a miniature cheerleader, or a gymnast. But she would probably never become either of those things.

"Don't worry," I told her. "It's a piece of cake."

"Do you faint a lot?" she asked.

"Actually, I'm on a two-week break."

"I fainted three times yesterday alone. And I have to wear *this* stupid thing."

She lowered her dress at the collar bone to show me the tip of the tiny machine, the same type I had worn back in the beginning when they were trying to figure out why I fainted. Some kids at school asked if they could use it for video games, while others ran away from me like I was half-robot.

The girl whispered, "I might have POTS."

I nodded, letting her know I was familiar with POTS, also known by its longer name, *Postural Orthostatic Tachycardia Syndrome*. I knew all the types on the syncope spectrum. Fainting itself isn't uncommon, even though no one really talks about it. It's the amount of fainting and the reason why a person faints that differentiates one type from another. The doctors categorized my fainting as a cross between *vasovagal* syncope and *othorstatic hypotension*. But the words sort of blur together and really mean nothing other than "You're a chronic fainter and we don't have a freaking clue why."

POTS is one of the worst types. I used to follow a girl with POTS on the Internet, where she kept an online journal. During her entire fifteenth year, she only made it out of bed a handful of times, and that was for doctors' appointments. Her skin was gray, her voice barely audible. She wore a pacemaker, and her friends eventually abandoned her when they got tired of hanging out on her bed watching television. She became very depressed. Her story was so hard to watch that eventually I stopped following her, but it was that POTS girl that often kept me from falling into my own state of depression. I'd had my share of dark days, but none as bad as hers.

Now, while I sat and waited for the receptionist to call my name, I remembered back to the day my life changed. Ninth grade. The day before Valentine's Day. I thought it was silly to think I could faint by lying on a tilt table. That it would take a lot more than that to make me black out. Bring on a roller coaster, or the monkey bars.

But I was wrong.

Doctor Seymour and two nurses had helped me onto the table on my back. With my feet planted against a footboard, they fastened me in with wide straps and dimmed the lights. The machine next to the table monitored my heart rate and blood pressure. No one spoke. I was slowly tilted halfway up and left in that position for five minutes. Then they pushed me all the way up.

When I came to, Doctor Seymour was staring down into my face. I could see my reflection in his glasses. He and a nurse unstrapped me, whispered to each other near the EKG machine, and left the room. I wiggled my fingers and toes. The overhead lights killed my retinas, the monitor boasted my heartbeat, and that constant hospital odor of alcohol burned my sinuses.

My mother was holding my hand.

"How long did it take?" I had whispered.

She shook her head sadly. "It was instantaneous."

Instantaneous rang through my head for the next year as Doctor Seymour tried to find the correct medicine and dosage that would help me stop hitting the ground when I least expected it.

Now, years after that tilt-table test had become my judge and jury, a nurse called my name.

I smiled at the girl sitting next to me with her pale skin and nervous fingers. "Don't worry," I told her. "You'll be fine."

The assistant brought me to the back. While waiting in one of the chilly rooms for Doctor Seymour, a poster on the wall caught my eye. The photo showed a group of young people in preppie shirts and shorts, sailing a boat over an enormous wave, the sun setting in the distance. The caption read: *What would you do if you weren't afraid?*

Before my mind had time to answer the question, a different nurse came in and took my weight and blood pressure, and asked me the usual questions about diet, caffeine, alcohol, drugs. She drew some blood and had me pee in a tiny cup. A few minutes later, Doctor Seymour came into the room. He placed a clipboard on the counter.

"Well, little lady," he said, sitting in his rolling chair and facing me. He pushed his thick black glasses up his nose. "How are you feeling these days?"

"I haven't fainted in two weeks," I said. "See?"

I proudly opened my book and moved my finger along the empty row.

"That's wonderful," Doctor Seymour said. "How are you feeling right now?"

"Good enough to drive."

"I'm sorry?"

"I think my spells have stopped," I said.

"Driving isn't the best way to test your theory."

"It's not a theory."

"Erica, I want you spell-free for three months before you get behind a wheel."

"It's not like that's a magic number."

"It is to me," he said.

"What if I go to another doctor?" I asked.

"They may tell you something different, and that's certainly their choice. But this office chooses to follow the same guidelines for syncope as we do for seizures."

"I don't have seizures."

Doctor Seymour paused. "Erica, your mother told me about your teeth. Imagine what could happen if you suddenly fainted behind the wheel of a vehicle moving at sixty-five miles an hour."

"I'm telling you, I feel better than ever."

"Feeling well is important," he said. "But *being* well is a different thing altogether. So until you are spell-free for three months—"

He held up three fingers as though I didn't understand the number.

"Okay," I said. "I get it. But please. You have to tell her I'm getting better."

"Your mother?"

"She's like a Homeland Security drone."

"Your mother is your caregiver. It's my job to make you healthy, but it's her job to keep you safe."

I said nothing.

Doctor Seymour grabbed his clipboard from the counter. "I have some good news," he said, smiling like we were getting our picture taken for a Christmas card. "I'm putting you on two new drugs."

"New drugs?"

"Many of my patients are finding that the combination helps. I'm excited about the prospect." He jotted something on his clipboard. "Any questions?"

I thought a moment, then said, "Even if these drugs are the latest and greatest, I'm never going to get better, am I? I used to think so, but I don't anymore. Two weeks means nothing, does it? It keeps tricking me."

"It tricks all of us," he said.

"I eat right. I sleep well every night. I try not to get overheated. I stay away from caffeine. Don't do drugs. Don't drink alcohol. I don't...do...anything..."

I pressed the heels against my eyes to stop the tears.

"Erica," Doctor Seymour said. "You need to trust that somewhere out there is a cure. That's what I'm here for. That's what doctors do. We look for the miracles in the midst of hopelessness."

I took my hands from my eyes. "I'm not asking for miracles. I just want a normal life. Even a normal month would be nice."

"Will you do me a favor?" he asked.

I waited.

"Focus on all the great things in your life. Because one day, when there is a treatment and all of this is behind you, or one day should you outgrow it, and you probably will, I want you to be able to look back and remember the moments that happened in between the spells. Not the spells themselves. Promise me you'll do that."

"I'll try."

"Good." He stood up. "We'll call your prescription in for you. You can pick it up later today."

Chapter Eighteen

Adam and I sat on the couch watching the movie credits scroll up the screen. It was nine-thirty on Friday night. The kids were sound asleep in their beds, Larry and Lindsay were hiding out in their secret nest, and Josephine was at her mother's in Feltonville. Lindsay's mom believed her daughter was babysitting with me, my mother believed Lindsay was at another ballet recital, and Adam believed Larry was working. Even if I hadn't been a seasoned fainter, all the twists and turns would have made me dizzy.

"How did your doctor's appointment go yesterday?" Adam asked me.

"Sucked. But thanks for asking."

"Isn't there something they can give you? Like medication?"

"I've been on everything from blood pressure pills to salt tablets. My doctor put me on a couple of new drugs, so fingers crossed. It would be nice to do some fun stuff my last year before college."

"What kind of stuff?" he asked.

"I don't know. Everything, I guess. Drink a couple of beers. Maybe ride a horse. Though not necessarily in that order. And I'd really love to spend some time at the beach."

"I don't want a beer gut," Adam said. "And horses are way too much work. But I love the beach. Did you know that I surf?"

"Really?"

"I try to get in the ocean as much as I can, especially when the water's warm. I offered to teach Lindsay to surf, but she never wanted to get her hair wet. Maybe I could teach you."

"I can't go in the waves."

"Oh."

"But not because I'm afraid of getting my hair wet," I quickly added.

Adam said, "I asked Lindsay to a festival on Ocracoke Island a few weeks back, but she said she didn't like riding the ferry. One Saturday, I surprised her with tickets to a killer motocross event, and she told me she wanted to go to the mall instead. So I gave the tickets away."

There were so many things I craved to do, yet could not, and all these things Lindsay was invited to do, but she declined.

I thought about the blue gown Ms. Bennett had saved money for so her daughter could go to Winter Formal. I wondered if Lindsay would give Larry Taggert a private fashion show instead, spinning in a wide circle in the candlelit warehouse with a glass of wine in her hand, showing off her ball dress like she was accepting an Oscar.

The burden of knowledge nearly strangled me.

Adam ran his fingers through his thick curls. "You know what?"

"What?"

"This is nice, just hanging out. I like it."

"Me, too," I said, smiling. "Weekends for me are all about decompressing."

"That's because you take those crazy AP's. I don't know how you do it."

"It isn't easy," I said, "but it's something I need to do. Back when the spells first started, my parents tried to get me to home school. Had to do a lot of begging to stay at Grayson. I need to prove they made the right decision."

Adam said, "I'm counting down the seconds until college."

"Me, too."

"Where did you apply?"

"Duke, Chapel Hill, and Wake Forest. You?"

"I went for those three, too," he said. "My mother made me, even though they're probably out of my ballpark. I also played it safe with Wilmington and ECU. And the community college is always there as a default."

Upstairs, one of the babies cried out. Adam and I both cocked our heads and listened, but the crying stopped and all was silent again.

"You know," Adam said, "Lindsay and I could never talk about ordinary stuff. It's like she has all these walls up. Like when she was with me, she wished she was somewhere else." After a moment, he asked, "Want me to get your Gatorade out of the fridge?"

"Sure. Thanks."

While he was gone, I took off my headband and readjusted my hair. When Adam came back, he unscrewed the lid from the drink and handed me the bottle. Then he sat back down and hit the remote, and we watched a few reality shows.

Halfway through *Hoarders*, we heard an engine cut and the slam of a car door.

"Larry's home early," Adam said, hitting the button on the remote. "It's only ten-thirty."

The front door opened.

"Hello?" a woman's voice called.

It was Josephine. Panic sank into my gut.

"We're in the family room," Adam called.

Josephine appeared in the doorway. She wore a pretty plaid jacket, high-heeled black boots, and a beret. She looked like a Parisian artist. She clutched a small suitcase in her hand.

"What are you two doing here?" she asked.

"Babysitting," Adam told her.

"Where's Larry? I drove by the firehouse, but I didn't see his Explorer. I've texted him twice, and called him twice, and he hasn't responded. Do you know if there was an emergency?"

Adam looked at his pager, then at his cell phone. "I never got a message."

"Never mind," Josephine said. "He didn't expect me home anyway. My mama's part-time caretaker offered to stay the weekend to give me a break. Larry's phone is probably on silent by mistake. I do that all the time."

"So do I," I said.

Just then, my cell phone chimed.

"Oh," I said, reading the words. "Larry will be home in twenty minutes."

"He texted you?" Josephine asked.

"To let me know he's on his way."

"Well," she said after a moment, "I don't have any cash on me...I didn't know y'all were coming over. Larry said he'd be watching the kids tonight. At least, that's what I thought he said..." She shook her head slightly and slid off her hat. "Anyway, do you mind if I go on upstairs? I'm wiped out after the long drive. Y'all can stay here and wait for Larry to pay you, or Adam can meet up with him later."

"No worries," Adam said. "I'll see him at the station Monday night."

Josephine walked us to the door. As Adam and I stepped onto the porch, she asked, "How come Lindsay didn't sit tonight?"

I held my breath.

"She went somewhere with her mother," Adam said.

"Oh," Josephine said. "Well. Y'all drive safely."

We said goodnight as she closed the door behind us.

In the truck, as Adam started the engine, I looked toward the house. The room at the end of the hall, which had been sitting in darkness, now came alive with light. Josephine was in Larry's shrine. She hadn't gone up to bed right away like she said she would.

Adam said, "You've never taken student driving, have you?"

I turned my eyes away from the house. "What?"

"Lindsay said you don't drive. That you don't have your license."

"That's true."

"I could teach you," he said.

"That's not the best idea," I told him. "My mother would freak."

"Your mother isn't here."

"You mean, *now*? You be brave, but crazy, *Seniore* Carchelli."

"I may be *mucho loco*," he said, "but that has nothing to do with what I asked you."

"Why do you want to do this?" I asked.

"Why not?"

"I don't know..." The gauges behind the steering wheel were lit up like green specks of jade. My mother's apprehension coursed through my veins. "What if I black out?"

"What if you don't?"

I looked toward the Taggert house. The light in the shrine was still on.

"We'll only go a couple of blocks," Adam said. "Just up to your street. One right and one left."

I moved my eyes from the house to the dark road ahead. My heart skipped at least one beat.

Adam said, "I'll put my lights on so you don't run into any trees."

"Ha-ha," I said. "I drove my dad's rider mower when I was little, and I never hit a tree that didn't deserve it."

"I didn't think the yards in Great Pines were big enough for a rider mower."

I explained, "We didn't move here until after my freshman year, but I actually grew up on the river. We used to have a huge yard. My mother thought it was safer to live in a house away from the water. Less mold. Less chance of stepping on a water moccasin..."

"You do know that a rider mower is different than a Dodge Ram?"

"You do know that a nice guy is different than a sarcastic butt-head?"

Adam laughed. The streetlight made his brown eyes sparkle. "Put your money where your mouth is." He got out of the truck and jogged around to my side. He opened my door. "Move over, Rover."

I slid into the driver's seat.

He got in and closed the door.

"Seatbelt," he ordered.

"Yes, sir, right away, sir!" I saluted him and clicked in the belt.

My palms were sweaty. It was nearly eleven o'clock but I was suddenly wide awake. Adrenaline pumped through my veins. For the average person, that's a good thing—for a person with syncope, not so much.

"I'm not allowed to get overly excited," I whispered.

"Well, lace up, girl, because I happen to be one helluvan exciting guy."

He leaned over me to adjust my seat and mirrors. His hair smelled lemony. I took a whiff and planned to take that smell to bed with me. If I didn't kill both of us in this death trap first.

"My truck is totally safe," Adam said, reading my mind. "Just had my brakes checked. And I gave her a bath."

"Well, that's a relief. Shiny hubcaps should protect us."

"Okay," he said. "Put your right foot on the brake. Take the shift and slide it into *DRIVE*. It's marked by a green letter *D*. Right there." He pointed to the gauge.

I slid the shift into *Drive*. "What do I do with my left foot?"

"Pretend you don't have one. Everything is done with your right. Both the gas and the brake. Right now your foot is on the brake. The gas pedal is to the right of the brake."

Adam spoke slowly, quietly. He seemed so patient; so happy to be giving driving lessons on a late Friday night.

"Put your hands where they feel comfortable on the steering wheel," he instructed. "Some driver's ed classes tell you to put them at ten and two o'clock."

I shifted my hands around the wheel until they sat at ten and two.

"Good. Now. Slowly…very slowly…let your foot off the brake and place it on the accelerator."

"The accelerator?"

"The gas."

"Oh. Right."

I felt like an idiot. Like I was learning how to drink from a sippy cup, or tinkle in a potty seat. Slowly, I took my foot off the brake and placed it against the gas.

"Watch your wheels," Adam said. "The curb is a little close to my right tire, so be sure that when you hit the gas, you move the wheel to the—"

The truck jerked forward. In a matter of seconds, the front right tire had hopped onto the curb.

"At least you hit the brake," he said, laughing. "Now, keep your foot where it is…that's it…and put the shift into *REVERSE*…and slowly…super slowly, take your foot off the brake, give it a little gas, and get off the curb."

I did as he asked, and the truck's tire fell back onto the street.

"I did it!"

"You did."

"That's the farthest I've ever driven," I said, laughing.

"Okay," Adam said. "Right foot back on the brake. Now turn the wheel a little to the left...that's it...now take your foot off the brake and put it back on the gas. Good. Good. Keep it up. You're doing it, Erica! You're driving!"

We inched our way up the street.

"How fast am I going?" I asked.

"Look at your speedometer. No. Don't. Keep your eyes on the road." He leaned over so he could see the gauge. "You're going about ten miles an hour."

"Is that all?"

"If you want to go faster, give it more gas," he said. "But only a little at a time. The speed limit is twenty-five."

"I only plan to go half that fast."

My foot pressed more firmly against the accelerator. The truck moved faster and in the right direction.

"This is awesome!" I shouted. "Take a picture of me!"

Adam pulled out his cell phone and snapped a shot of my profile, since I wouldn't dare take my eyes off the road.

"Do you see that stop sign?" he asked.

"Yes."

"Take your foot off the gas and gently apply it to the brake."

My brain heard the word "gently," but my foot obeyed the word "brake." We both lurched forward as the truck stopped a yard before the stop sign. I realized I was holding my breath. My ears started buzzing.

As Adam waited for me to continue toward the stop sign, Josephine's face came to me. Then Larry's. Then Lindsay's. Then the twins'. My head began to swim, like someone had stuck a fish bowl on top of my shoulders.

145

"I think I'm done for the night," I said, finally taking in a breath, keeping my foot glued to the brake.

"Aw, no way."

"Yes way."

"Sure," he said. "Okay."

He stepped out of the truck. It seemed like he was moving in slow motion. And then, the all-too-familiar fog was seeping through the truck.

No! my mind screamed. *Not now!*

My hands grew clammier. My face flushed with heat. The tunnel vision that for some reason was worse at night than in the daytime pulled me into its center. I could no longer see Adam as he disappeared from my sight in front of the headlights. I could only feel the fog as it streamed into my ears and wrapped its intrusive hands around my brain.

Then the cab of the truck went black.

Chapter Nineteen

I took in the smell of damp earth and chimney smoke. My eyes fluttered open. The cold ground was my bed. Stars dotted the ceiling.

"You'll be fine, Erica," a deep voice said. "Just breathe."

Adam's smiling face was close to mine.

"You caught me," I whispered.

"You mean I caught the truck. Before it rammed into that mailbox over there. I should have had you put it in *PARK*."

The truck. I'd been in Adam's truck.

"I drove," I croaked, smiling.

"You did."

"How far?"

"Almost a whole block."

I frowned.

"Even NASCAR drivers have to start somewhere," Adam said.

I wanted desperately to laugh at his joke, but I could barely make my throat muscles move.

"I grabbed the wheel and hit the brake," he said. "You were as limp as a jelly fish."

"I am a jelly fish."

He touched my cheek. My stomach flipped, but not with panic. It was a good flip. A soothing flip.

"You're sort of pale," he said.

"I was born this way."

"You feel clammy."

"Totally normal."

"Oh."

"Help me sit up," I told him. "Go super slow."

With his chest against my back and his legs straddled on either side of me, Adam placed his strong arms under me and pushed me into a seated position. For a few minutes we sat there on a stranger's lawn, neither one of us speaking as I concentrated on getting steady air into my lungs. With his arms protectively around me, his warm breaths matched my own.

I whispered, "She was right."

"Who?"

My mother had known I wasn't ready. Just one big fat I-told-you-so waiting to happen.

"No one," I said.

He helped me stand and nearly lifted me into the truck.

A few minutes later, with the engine idling in front of my house, I mumbled, "I'm sorry, Adam."

"For what?"

"What do you think?"

"Erica, it doesn't bother me."

"You're just saying that to be nice."

"I am nice, but that's not why I'm saying it. Really. It doesn't bother me. Why would you assume it did?" When I didn't answer, he placed a hand on my arm. "You gotta get over it."

"Over what?"

"Defining yourself by this fainting thing. It really doesn't make you attractive."

My eyes grew wide.

"That's not what I mean," he said. "I mean that carrying your disease around like oversized luggage isn't attractive. Everyone has stuff going on. I've seen scary shit you don't want to mess up your head with. Believe me. I know life is short. Don't let the fainting thing become who you are."

"But it is who I am."

"Fainting is something you *do*. It isn't something you *are*." He nodded toward my house and whispered, "Your mom's peeking through the curtains."

There she was, a black silhouette with the light glowing behind her, like the little old witch waiting to cook Hansel and Gretel.

Adam jumped out and came around to my side. He opened the door and gingerly helped me to the ground. "Thanks for tonight, Erica. I had fun."

"You did?"

"Didn't you?"

"Yes," I said.

"See? You fainted, and you still had fun. A helluvua lot better than fainting and *not* having fun."

Adam walked me to the door, gave me a super tight hug, and said goodnight. I watched as he got into his truck and drove away.

Then the porch light came on over my head. The front door opened wide. As soon as I stepped into the foyer, my mother started the inquisition.

But I cut her off at the pass.

"Super tired, Mother," I said, ignoring her questions and walking up the hallway toward my bedroom. "Babysitting twins takes a lot of energy."

I shut the bedroom door behind me, changed into my jammies, and crawled into bed, the idiotic grin never leaving my face.

Chapter Twenty

Lindsay stopped at the BP station on our way to school Monday morning.

"I'm falling in love, Erica," she said as we sat waiting for the tank to fill. "Big-time."

"He's married, Lindsay."

I wondered how often our conversation would go around and around in this inane circle.

"It's not my fault my heart is telling me what to do," she said.

If Lindsay had shared that sentiment a few weeks before, I would have argued the point, but now, with Adam never leaving my thoughts, I had little room to judge what the heart does or doesn't do without our permission.

"Does Larry feel the same way?" I asked.

"Neither one of us has said the words yet, but I know how he feels. I can tell."

"How?"

"By the way he looks into my eyes," Lindsay said. "I feel like I could drown. And the way he touches my face, like I'm a valuable statue or something. Like if he touches me too hard I'll crack. Sometimes I think I will."

"What if he does say the words?"

"I guess we'll have to tell his wife."

"Tell her—"

"Not right away," Lindsay said. "Maybe wait until the kids are old enough to understand."

I suddenly missed the old Lindsay, the one who would've hung out in the sci-fi section of Books-a-Million on a Saturday night rather than sneak into a high school party like the other kids; who used to think that wearing her hair in two pigtails high up on her head like a Hello Kitty character was sexy.

But that sweet and innocent Lindsay had been replaced by an imposter. This Lindsay had stopped talking to the cheerleaders in the cafeteria and the football players in the hallways. This Lindsay had decided that lying through her teeth to her family, my family, Larry's family, and Adam was perfectly normal, all in the name of love. This Lindsay seemed completely unaffected by the fact that if her secret got out, she could be branded a joy-girl, a ho-bag, or worse.

By Wednesday, we had run into Adam six times. I know the exact number because I was counting.

Once a day on the way to gym, he and some of his weight-lifting buddies passed us. Adam walked on the outside of the group, closest to Lindsay and me. He smiled at both of us, and even though Lindsay assumed the smiles were for her, I was secretly hoping they were meant for me.

We saw Adam again after school as Lindsay and I got into her truck. There he was, taking his time as he came through the school's front doors, giving a quick nod as he shuffled by, finally disappearing into the vast parking lot.

Lindsay complained, "Two thousand students and he *still* manages to stalk me."

Then, on Thursday, I was in the cafeteria buying real milk to go with my packed lunch, because I'd accidentally left my thermos in Lindsay's truck. It seemed like every student and their brother stood in line that afternoon. The heating system in the school had gone into overdrive, and we were being baked alive inside a human incubator. November sweaters were slung over the backs of chairs. Most of the girls had put their hair up in buns or ponytails. Some of the boys remained in their gym shorts.

While Lindsay went to grab a table near the windows, Adam approached me in line.

"Hey, Erica. We on for tomorrow night?"

"Sure."

He paused. "You okay?"

"Why?"

"You look flushed."

"Guess it's just hot in here."

He nodded in agreement. "Feels like a greenhouse."

I grabbed the container of milk and reached for a straw. The straw fell to the ground, and I did the worst possible thing an overheated Syncopian can do: I bent over to pick it up. Bending over wasn't the worst part. Standing back up was.

Which I did.

Way too quickly.

A mixture of Pine Sol and tater tots rolled into my sinuses. I opened my eyes. High above me, paper turkeys and pumpkins and cornucopias dangled from the ceiling. Fifty or more students had gathered around me as I lay on the cafeteria tiles. Most of them by now knew about the weird girl who fainted all the time, no matter how much I hugged the woodwork. But there were always a few who didn't.

One boy shouted, "This is so going on Youtube!" He hovered over me with his cell phone a foot from my face. A hand came out of nowhere so fast I thought it was a separate entity, flying through the air. It grabbed the phone out of the kid's hand. I heard the crash as it slammed against a wall.

"That's my phone!" the boy screamed.

"Not anymore," Adam said.

Some students backed up when Adam's buddies collected around me like a pod of dolphin. Then Adam was behind me, his strong thighs offering support beneath my head. Gentle fingers lay against my neck.

"Where's Lindsay?" my mind said, but I wasn't sure if my lips moved.

Adam didn't answer. He whispered into my ear, "Breathe, Erica. That's it."

Miss Toni, the school nurse, pushed her way through the crowd. Someone blew a whistle. A man's authoritative voice shouted, "Break it up! Give her room!"

A finger pointed over my head as a boy whined, "He threw my phone across the room. He needs to pay for that!"

Our vice-principal, Mr. Kershaw, loomed over me. His eyes traveled to a place beyond my forehead.

"Adam Carchelli, did you break this young man's phone?"

"Who cares about that right now?" Adam responded.

The nurse knelt down and held my wrist. "Your heartbeat is erratic, Erica," Miss Toni said. "Let's keep you here for a minute or two until it evens out." She turned to Mr. Kershaw. "Stan, please break up the crowd."

The vice-principal ordered, "Everyone back to your tables. Finish eating your lunches. Do not give me a reason to call security. You have five seconds before I start taking down names! Five…four…three…"

The crowd thinned. Adam's thighs remained under my head, and the nurse lingered by my side.

"Where's Lindsay?" I asked again, this time sure I'd said the words out loud.

I looked toward the windows. With most of the kids at their tables or back in the lunch line, I got a better view. There she was, sitting at a table, her back to me.

"Linds?" I said, my voice so quiet there was no way she could have heard me.

"She's on her cell," Adam said.

"What?"

"She's texting someone."

Heat rose to my cheeks. "Pig."

The whining boy said, "He broke my cell phone, Mr. Kershaw. Tell him he has to pay for it."

Adam said, "I'm not paying for a fucking thing."

A suited arm reached down and snatched Adam from beneath me as the nurse helped me into a seated position.

"Come with me, Carchelli," Mr. Kershaw said. "Perhaps you need to take a breather. Using foul language is offensive enough. But throwing things that belong to others…damaging school property…do you see that dent in the wall? I wish you boys would get your act together. You're seniors, for God's sake. You're supposed to set an example…"

The rambling vice-principal led Adam out of the cafeteria. As the nurse helped me stand, I turned in Lindsay's direction. She didn't seem to notice anything unusual was happening. She was too busy texting.

***

Home early from school, I was relaxing in the sunroom hammock when my cell phone rang.

"What happened today?" Lindsay asked.

"*Now* you want to know?"

"I heard you fainted."

"I heard *you* were busy texting—"

"There were too many kids in the way—"

"—while I was on the floor."

"Sorry."

I wanted to say, "Did you know your ex-boyfriend might be suspended for protecting me?" But a tiny ring sounded through my cell, saving me from starting an argument. I looked down at my screen: a text from Adam. I read his message while Lindsay went on with her lame excuses.

You ok? Adam wrote.

Better now. You suspended?

Sweet talked the VP. Detention for a week.

Awesome.

"Hell-*O*," Lindsay said. "Did you hear what I said?"

"No."

"I had to cancel my date with Larry tomorrow night. My mom is taking my sister and me to Myrtle Beach to see our stupid cousins. That's why I was texting Larry during lunch. Anyway, you don't have to worry about babysitting with Adam tomorrow, since I'll be out of town, and Larry and I can't be together—"

"But we are babysitting," I said.

"You are?"

"Larry called Adam and asked him directly. I guess he made other plans for the night, since you'll be out of town."

Lindsay paused. "Huh. Maybe he decided to work or something. To take his mind off the fact that we won't be together..."

I waited for her to say something else.

"Oh, well," she finally said. "I'll text Larry later. Have fun babysitting."

I responded, "Have fun in Myrtle Beach."

***

On Friday afternoon, Adam texted me to be ready early, that he was taking me out to dinner before babysitting. Invisible worry beams from my mother's eyes bore into the side of my head as Adam helped me into the truck. I wondered if she knew I was burying my support hose under my pillow on Friday nights.

I clicked on my seatbelt.

"What's that smell?" I asked, scrunching up my nose and thinking of roasted marshmallows.

"I started the fireplace for my mom," Adam said. "She doesn't trust herself to do it, and she's got friends coming over for book club. Or, should I say, red wine club." He started the engine. "You like pizza?"

"My number one favorite food group."

We drove across town to a strip mall which housed Sartini's Pizza. In the restaurant, Adam headed to the restroom to wash his hands while the hostess led me to a booth. After a few moments, he scooted onto the bench across from me.

Once the waitress had taken our order and brought our drinks, Adam said, "You called Lindsay a pig."

"What?"

"In the cafeteria," he said. "When you came to."

"Sometimes crazy junk rolls off my tongue when I come out of a spell. Like when you come out of anesthesia."

"So, you didn't mean it?"

I shrugged.

"I thought you were besties," he said.

It occurred to me that Lindsay and I had become more like cats than friends, learning to adapt to one another because we were forced to occupy the same territory.

"Bestie is a loose term these days," I told him. "Anyway, I wasn't calling *her* a pig."

Adam paused. "The person she was texting?"

I sipped my un-sweetened tea.

"Her new boyfriend, right?" Adam said. "Is he a total loser or something?"

"It doesn't matter what I think," I told him. Then I added, "She says she's in love with him."

Adam took a swig from his mug of root beer.

"Want to hear something crazy?" he asked. "Lindsay doesn't like pizza. Who the hell doesn't like pizza?"

"There are a lot of things she doesn't like, Adam."

Like swimming and boogie-boarding and dating hotties her own age...

We watched as customers came and went, as pizzas dripping with cheese were set on racks in the center of tables. My mouth began to water.

"You and Linds don't have much in common," I said after a moment. "It surprises me you two ended up together."

"Surprises me, too," he said.

"And it might be my bitchy alter-ego saying this, but I think you're too good for her."

Adam smiled. "So are you." He took the jar of hot peppers and grated cheese and nervously tapped them together. Then he said, "You know what? Let's not bring her up again. I want to have a good time. Just you and me."

"Sounds like a plan."

He held up his mug. I picked up my glass.

"To letting go," he said as our glasses clanked against one another.

Since Adam wasn't the only one feeling liberated, I added, "And to having some freaking fun for a change."

"Hashtag, true dat, *mama sita*," he said, laughing at his deliberate use of poorly mixed slang.

The giggles came on hard then, causing customers in the restaurant to shoot us curious looks. Maybe we both felt a sense of relief. Or maybe we just liked laughing together. Whatever the reason, it felt amazing, and we didn't stop until tears streamed down our cheeks and our pizza finally arrived.

Chapter Twenty-one

After Larry kissed his babies, Adam and I stood with him in the foyer.

"Josephine's at her mother's," Larry said as he put on his jacket.

"Where are you off to?" I asked casually.

"A movie."

"Which one?" Adam asked.

"What?" Larry said. "Oh. I forget the name. Some bang 'em up film. Anyway, I might stop for a bite to eat afterward. And a buddy of mine is having a late poker game, so I might stop by there for a little while, too. Probably gonna be a late night."

He fiddled with his mass of keys a moment, then said goodbye.

As soon as he left, Adam and I went into the family room. Samantha and Willie sat in the large playpen, staring out at us through the slats.

"Do you think he's good looking?" Adam asked.

"Willie? He's a little young for me."

"No," Adam said, laughing. "Larry."

"Gross. No. Why would you ask me that?"

Adam pulled Willie over the edge of the playpen, placed him on the family room rug, and did the same with Samantha. Samantha shouted, "House!" and ran to a giant dollhouse in the corner. She began moving furniture around. Willie shot his arms under the couch and retrieved two toy fire trucks. He banged them together in the air.

Adam said, "Did you know that girls are always coming by the station to see him? Larry, I mean. Not to see the other guys, just *him*. Sometimes they bring cookies or brownies. One girl brought him a CD of her college choir. He gets texts all day long, and I'm pretty sure they're not all from Josephine. It's like he has this James Bond thing going on. No one at the station gets it."

"To be honest with you, Adam, he gives me the creeps."

"He does?"

"You won't tell him I said that, will you?"

"I don't share anything you tell me," he said. "I like our private conversations."

"Me, too."

"Why does he give you the creeps? He hasn't hit on you or anything, has he?"

"No," I said. "Thank God."

Adam knelt down next to Willie. They played with the fire trucks, pretending to heroically douse a burning sofa leg. I squatted next to Samantha as she placed a miniature bed in the dollhouse kitchen. She pointed, laughing at her intentional mistake.

A half-hour later, after the kids were put down, Adam and I

watched some television. Two shows in, he stood up and stretched and reached out his hand to help me off the couch.

He looked around the room. "I'm sort of tired of TV."

"I hear ya."

"What do you feel like doing?"

"We could play with some of the kids' toys, or a board game," I suggested. "Let me kick your butt at Candy Land."

"Nah," he said. "The pieces are all snotty."

"We could—" I stopped myself.

"What?"

"Have you ever, you know, looked around the place?"

"Looked around?"

"Yeah."

"No." Adam narrowed his eyes. "Have you?"

"Not by myself."

"You and Lindsay?"

"Sort of…"

"That's not cool, Erica."

"Oh. No. It wasn't any big deal. Lindsay was bored, so we checked out the back office. It's a shrine."

"A shrine?"

"Wanna see it?" Before he had a chance to answer, I said, "It's not locked," as if an unlocked door was the same as a personal invitation. I walked up the hallway. Adam followed a few feet behind. I opened the door. "Larry has the whole room dedicated to himself."

We stood together in the doorway.

"What are those?" Adam asked, pointing to the framed clippings.

"Newspaper articles about firefighting. More specifically, station thirty-two. Don't you think it's weird?"

"He risks his life for a living," Adam said. "If he wants to pat himself on the back, who cares?"

I didn't answer as I walked to the other side of the desk and opened the center drawer. The secret latch was just underneath the lip. I placed a finger on it.

Adam remained in the doorway. "Football stars have trophies on their shelves, and rock stars hang gold albums on their walls. Besides, I wouldn't want someone making assumptions based on my personal stuff. Would you?"

I thought about all the goofy boy-band posters I'd taped to my own walls over the years; piles of embarrassing diaries hidden in my closet; the support hose buried under my pillow.

"No," I said, taking my finger off the latch.

He turned and went back up the hall.

"It was Lindsay's idea," I called after him as I shut the drawer, and then the office door. I followed him back to the family room where he leaned against the arm of the sofa, his arms crossed. Was that disappointment on his face? I wasn't sure, so I added, "*Lindsay* was the one who wanted to snoop, not *me*. I swear."

Even as I said the words, I cringed. Where was this nasty side of me coming from? I didn't want to be like Lindsay. I didn't want to be sneaking around behind anyone's back for *any* reason. I didn't roll that way.

"I might be over Lindsay," Adam said, "but I don't want to hate her."

I felt like an idiot. "You're right," I told him. "I'm sorry. I don't know what—"

A beeping sound cut me off.

Adam stared at his pager.

"What is it?" I asked.

"I don't know." He tapped a number into his cell phone and placed it against an ear. "Yes, I will," he said into the phone. "Ten minutes. Yes, sir."

Just then the fire department alarm sounded, echoing through the neighborhood. Adam's jaw twitched. "I have to go."

"What is it?"

"Two fires," he said, grabbing his jacket from the back of the recliner.

"*Two?*"

"They need every volunteer they can get."

"What about the twins?" I asked, a tiny seed of panic sprouting in my gut.

"They're sound asleep, Erica," Adam said calmly. "Just stay put on the couch. I'll grab your extra Gatorade."

As Adam disappeared into the kitchen, I sat on the sofa and concentrated on my breathing. When he came back, he put the drink and a power bar on the coffee table. He watched me, my knees tucked up to my chest like I was adrift on a raft.

"Too bad Lindsay's out of town," he said.

"Yeah."

"What about your mom?"

"Sure," I said. "I'll call her."

But I was lying. I had no intention of calling my mother.

Adam let himself out and his tires squealed as he sped away. Within minutes, I could feel the large empty house surrounding me. I clicked on the television and turned up the volume to block out the overwhelming silence, settled into a rerun of *Family Guy*, and eventually fell into a restless doze.

***

The theme song to *Halloween* interrupted my dreams.

"Have you seen the news?" my mother asked.

"What time is it?" I asked, trying to make out the time on my cell phone.

"Almost ten." She paused. "Erica, is Adam still there?"

I whispered, "No."

"The second I heard the alarm, I knew it," she said. "I should have called you sooner."

I could see my mother, standing on our front porch, her nose in the air like a wolf.

"They needed him," I said, defending Adam. "He did the right thing."

"When did he leave?" she asked.

"About an hour ago."

"Is everything okay?"

"Everything's fine. No fires to put out over here. Ha-ha."

"*Two* fires," my mother said, ignoring my weak joke. "One at the community college. Culinary arts building, I think they said. The other one is an abandoned building down in the warehouse district."

I barely heard my own voice: "The warehouse district?"

"Let's talk when I see you," she said. I could hear the jingle of keys through the phone. "I'll be there in five."

"No. Don't come over. I'm fine. Really—"

"Erica," my mother said, her stern voice pounding in my ear, "you are responsible for someone else's children."

"You didn't even know I was by myself," I reminded her. "All I did was sleep. The babies are fine."

"If those were my children, I wouldn't want...I wouldn't have...you'll understand when you have children one day. Trust me. I am already dressed and the keys are in my hand. Your father agrees with me; he's standing here nodding his head. I'm coming over. End of story."

***

At twelve-fifteen, my mother and I sat on the couch, our feet up on the coffee table, a large afghan covering the two of us. As we both semi-dozed, I held the remote, switching back and forth between local news stations.

A car door slammed outside.

"Someone's here," she said, pushing off the afghan.

I muted the television as she went to the door.

"Adam," my mother said through a yawn.

I quickly rubbed the crusties out of my eyes and pinched my cheeks as they came into the family room.

My mother looked from Adam to me. "I'll put on some water for tea," she said, heading to the kitchen.

Adam sat next to me on the couch.

"I've been watching the news," I told him.

"It's totally insane," he said. "As of now, seven fires since mid-summer. More than half are red-flagged."

"Red-flagged?"

"Arson."

It looked like he might cry with exhaustion. Dark circles

cupped his eyes, and dirt was caked under his nails.

"Sorry I'm so gross," he said. "My shower at the station was quick. I wanted to get back to make sure you were all right."

"I'm fine," I said, happy he was safe, happy he'd come back to check on me. "I told my mother not to come, but you know how that goes."

"Let's go somewhere, Erica," Adam said. "I'm tired, but I have all this energy."

"What about the twins?"

"Maybe your mom would be willing to stay."

"You're joking, right?"

My mother spoke from the kitchen doorway. A pot holder dangled from her hand. "Erica...it's after midnight..."

"Told you," I said to Adam. "I'd have to get my name on Schindler's list to get out of here."

My mother frowned. "Schindler's list? That's the metaphor you came up with?"

I shrugged. "It's late."

"Exactly my point," she said.

Adam stood up. "Mrs. O'Donnell, Erica is probably safer in my hands than anyone else's. I'd never let anything happen to her. You have my word."

"I thought you were seeing Lindsay."

"We broke up," Adam told her.

Mom chewed on a hangnail and considered Adam for a long, hard moment as he stood next to the couch, composed, confident.

"Where will you go at this hour?" she asked.

"For a bite. You like eggs, Erica?"

I nodded as I mentally crossed my fingers.

"Eggs where?" my mother asked.

Adam said, "The Waffle House over by the mall."

During the next pause, my mother's eyes drifted from Adam to me, and back to Adam again. Finally, she said, "Fine."

"Really?" I asked, unbelieving.

"I'm way too tired to argue," she said. "Besides, I like you, Adam. I trust you, too. Anyway, it's been a long time since I've babysat. Maybe dirty diapers will bring back some fond memories."

I slipped on my flats, grabbed my pocketbook and jacket, and nearly ran out the door, worried she'd change her mind.

As Adam and I headed to the truck, my mother called from the doorway, "Erica, leave your cell phone on. And no later than two."

Two o'clock? The number itself felt like a miracle.

As soon as he pulled onto the street, Adam let out a heavy breath, like he'd been holding it for a while. "Someone died in the fire."

"At the college?"

"No," he said. "Downtown. A homeless man."

A thin layer of smoke drifted over the moon, reminding me of a vampire movie.

"I want to take you somewhere before we eat," Adam said.

He left the neighborhood and merged onto the highway. His jaw was firmly set, his eyes alive with excitement.

Already I could smell the fiery remains as we took the downtown ramp toward Division Street. A half-dozen blocks of warehouses lined both sides of the potholed street. I wondered which building was Larry's nest; just as quickly, I wondered if it was Larry's nest that had burned. Lighting candles or making hot chocolate on a camp stove could be hazardous in any of these old buildings.

"Do they know what started it?" I asked.

"They have their suspicions," he said, "but no one's saying anything for sure. They have to look at everything: combustibility of the materials, oxygen levels, available water supply, evidence of any chemicals used…"

We approached the yellow tape and orange cones preventing vehicles from driving past the destroyed structure. Down either side of the street stood dilapidated brick or cement buildings, most with broken windows behind rusty bars, and chunks of plywood nailed across front doors. In the quiet darkness of the night, it felt more like a Hollywood set than a real city.

Adam pulled up to the curb and let the truck idle. A block away, policemen, a handful of firemen, and about a dozen suits moved around the scene. News camera crews scanned the ruins.

"The building used to belong to the old paper mill," Adam said. "The main part was torn down years ago, but some of the smaller buildings are still standing. Well, minus one now. There must be dozens of buildings in the district, just sitting here, empty."

"I've never been down here," I said. "My parents think it's too dangerous."

"I know this place like the back of my hand," Adam said. "When I was little, my buddies and I used to ride down here on our bikes and look for treasure."

"Treasure?"

"Old bottles and cans and junk like that. The city keeps talking about turning this section into a theater district, or some kind of restaurant row."

"Where did the fire start?" I asked.

"In the back of the building." He turned toward me. "You should have seen it, Erica. Flames shooting up ten feet higher than the roofline. They had to bring out the bucket."

"Bucket?"

"The truck with a tall ladder and a bucket attached for one of the veteran firefighters to stand in."

"Adam, don't you ever get scared?"

"I'm always a little nervous when a page comes through," he said. "But by the time I'm in my uniform, adrenaline takes over. I feel pumped up. I think all firemen do. They say that once you get the firefighter bug…"

A homeless man in a tattered coat and a frayed ski hat stood watching the scene from a nearby doorway.

"Maybe the man who died was trying to keep warm," I said, thinking how awful it must be to have nowhere to go with so many cold nights ahead.

We sat in silence until I noticed the clock on Adam's dash.

"I turn into a pumpkin at two."

"You still hungry?" he asked.

"Yes," I said, surprised that my appetite was stronger than my exhaustion.

Adam made a U-turn and went back up Division Street toward the other side of the district, crossing beneath the highway overpass.

"Aren't we going toward the mall?" I asked.

"There's a Waffle House down here that's closer," he said. "It'll save us some time."

I spotted the restaurant's black and yellow sign up ahead.

As we entered the parking lot, my mouth fell open, but I slammed it shut before Adam could see. Backing out of a spot on my right was a dark blue Explorer, just like Larry's, with a fireman's license plate bracket, just like Larry's. Adam was busy talking and didn't notice.

"I like downtown, at least some parts," he said as he pulled into a parking spot two spaces to the left of the Explorer. One car sat between us. "I think it could be a cool place if they ever rebuild it."

The Explorer backed out and went to the right. I spotted the driver's profile under the glow of the restaurant lights. Then I noticed a second person, sitting in the passenger seat, and even though I couldn't see a distinct face, it was clear that his passenger was female. A *blond* female.

"Did Larry show up to help with the fire?" I asked as the SUV left the parking lot.

"Not down here," Adam said. "Probably went out to the college fire."

"But he had plans tonight."

"I don't know any fireman who'd choose poker over fighting a fire."

Had Larry been hanging out in his nest when his pager went off? Maybe he'd dragged the blond girl along with him. I pictured her, hanging out in front of the community college sign, wearing her Friday night heels and mini skirt, shivering in the cold while watching her hero in action.

Adam turned off his headlights, cut the engine, and came around to open my door. A little bell tinkled over our heads as we stepped into the Waffle House.

The room was filled with mostly male patrons, either sitting alone at the counter or looking miniature while reading the paper in an oversized booth. A tired-looking waitress stood chatting with a customer. I glanced at the truckers and other late-nighters as the hostess led us to a table, wondering how many of them were lonely, how many were married, how many would have an affair if they thought they could get away with it.

Chapter Twenty-two

Late Sunday night, after saying goodnight to my parents, I was putting my freshly-printed *Uncle Tom* essay into my binder when my cell rang.

"What a wasted weekend," Lindsay whined. "Myrtle Beach this time of year is a ghost town. And my cousins are so boring. All they wanted to do was play video games. How did things go here?"

"Things?"

"Babysitting," she said. "Did you see Larry?"

"Yup."

"Did he go to work? Or did he have a Fake Date Night with Josephine? God, it makes my stomach sick to think about it."

"Josephine was at her mother's."

"Oh, well," she said, "that's a relief."

"How come you didn't know what Larry's plans were?" I asked. "I thought you guys kept tabs on each other."

"Our number one rule is that I don't text him unless he texts me first. Way too risky."

"Oh."

"Hey," Lindsay said. "I heard about the excitement."

"You mean the fires?"

"I saw the downtown one on the news. It was huge."

"I know," I told her, then, after a beat, "I was there."

"At the fire?"

"After they put it out."

"What were you doing downtown?" she asked.

"Adam took me."

Silence filled the other end.

"Linds? You there?"

"You went downtown with Adam?"

"To see the fire. It's no big deal—"

Lindsay's voice grew snippy. "Maybe your mother should babysit with you from now on."

"My mother?"

"She told me she came to sit with you after Adam left. But she failed to mention—"

"When did you talk to her?"

"We talk all the time," she said.

"About me?"

"I am in charge of you, Erica, remember?"

"You are not *in charge* of me."

"If you say so…"

"And I don't think talking to my mother behind my back is cool."

"Well," Lindsay said, "I don't think sneaking around with Adam is cool."

"You're the one who hooked us up to babysit together," I

reminded her. "And obviously, I wasn't sneaking, or I wouldn't have told you. But while we're on the subject, you totally blew a good thing. Adam is one of the sweetest guys around."

"Oh my God," she said. "He's only being nice to you to keep a paw on me. I'm sure there are other things he'd rather be doing on a Friday night."

"Didn't seem like he was having too bad a time," I said. "We talked and laughed. He likes to have conversations, in case you didn't know. Intelligent conversations. It just so happens we like a lot of the same stuff. We had a great time until he got paged. Then, after the fire was out, he picked me up and took me to the Waffle House."

"So, what are you telling me, Erica? That you're honing in on my boyfriend the second we break up?"

I laughed. "If you're so broken up, then stop calling him your boyfriend."

"Okay, my *ex*-boyfriend."

"Lindsay, you can't keep Adam on a back burner in case things with Married Larry don't work out."

"Is that what you're hoping for?" she asked. "That Larry and I break up? Then you can work on him, too?"

"You're crazy—"

"It's not my fault Adam still likes me," she said.

"No, Lindsay, he doesn't. He's over you."

"Right."

"He told me so."

"Really?" she said. "And what exactly did he say?"

"That he's *over you*."

"He's lying."

"Okay, Linds. He's lying."

"He is."

"Well," I said, "if that's the case, then he's not the only one who lies."

"What does *that* mean?"

"Forget it."

"No," Lindsay said. "You started this. Who's lying?"

"Larry."

"What are you talking about?"

"As it turns out, there's a whole line of girls just waiting to get a piece of him."

"What girls?" she asked.

"The ones who show up at the fire station bearing gifts."

"Who told you that?"

"Adam."

Lindsay paused. "Did you tell Adam about Larry and me?"

"No."

"That's why Adam's saying these things, because he knows it'll get back to me. He wants to get even with me for—"

"No, Lindsay, I swear Adam doesn't know. I've never said a word to him or anyone about you and Larry. I never would. For a lot of reasons."

"Even if what Adam said is true," Lindsay said, "that girls are going to the station, Larry doesn't care about any of them." She snorted into the phone. "He's crazy about me."

"When you talked to my mother, did she mention that Larry didn't get home on Saturday until seven in the morning?"

"So?"

"He told her it took all night to put out the college fire."

"What's your freaking point, Erica?"

"It took less than an hour to put it out."

"How do you know?"

"Newspaper," I said.

"Maybe they made a mistake."

"I don't think so…"

"Why are you acting like this?"

I paused. "Because I saw him. I saw Larry."

"Where?" Lindsay asked.

"Downtown. When Adam took me out to eat. Larry was there in the Waffle House parking lot. And he wasn't alone."

"Stop it, Erica."

"He had another girl in his car."

"You're lying."

"No, Lindsay, I'm not."

"First you go and hit on my ex, and then you tell me lies about the man I'm in love with. You suck."

"I'm not hitting on anyone," I told her. "If anything, I've deliberately held back because I didn't want to hurt you. But you know what? As of now, I don't give a shit. What Adam and I do is our business. Just like what you and Larry do is your business. I don't want to know your business anymore anyway. Because it's wrong, Lindsay. You're hooking up with a married man. You know his wife. You know his kids. It's disgusting. And you won't admit to yourself that he's probably playing the same game with a bunch of other girls."

A deathly silence filled the phone. I was hoping Lindsay had hung up. But she hadn't.

Her voice was low, her words spoken slowly like she was

reading them from cue cards. "I had to twist Adam's arm to babysit with you that first night," she said. "Did he happen to mention that? Twist his arm. I almost offered to pay him like your mom does with me."

"What are you talking about?"

"The money she pays me."

"To do what?" I asked.

"Be your bodyguard."

"That's a bold-faced lie."

"You think I do this gig five days a week for brownie badges?"

"You're just trying to hurt me."

"Hurt *you*?" Lindsay said. "What about *me*? Do you realize how much I've missed? All the stuff I've turned down for you? Like being a cheerleader? You have no idea how much I wanted to do that. But you don't exactly see me walking around shaking my pompoms, do you?"

"I never stopped you from being a cheerleader or anything else."

"Yes, Erica, you did. Half the practices are during last period and go until after five. I've been busy driving you home every day, in case you forgot. Not to mention the homework load. All the hard-ass classes you signed up for? You think I wanted to take them? If I'd known how tough this was going to be, I never would have done it. I wanted to have a little fun in high school, especially during my senior year."

"Then you should have gone and had your fun, Lindsay. I never asked for a bodyguard. I never asked for your help, or anyone else's, for that matter."

"Well, your mom did," Lindsay said. "She begged me. And the contract kept my hands tied."

"*Contract?*"

She paused, reloaded her gun, and sprayed the bullets in my face.

"Between your parents and my mom and me. So you could have a halfway normal life. So if you crashed to the floor during school, at least there was someone you could trust to help you. And now you're stabbing me in the back, after all I've done for you."

"How much have they been paying you?"

"Ten dollars for each school day, plus my first year of college."

"College?"

"They expect me to go with you. They said they couldn't afford to send us to Harvard or Princeton." She laughed sarcastically and I wanted to punch her.

"You could have said no," I said, ignoring the throbbing behind my eyes. "You could have walked away."

"With my dad bailing…and my mom working two jobs…I did what I had to do."

"Why didn't you tell me?" I asked.

"Because I promised your parents I wouldn't."

"You're telling me now."

"Yeah…well…things have changed," Lindsay said. "As soon as I graduate, Larry will probably get a divorce. He said something about moving to Hawaii or the Caribbean. And I plan to go with him. Which sounds way better than hanging out with a bunch of college freshmen. As it turns out, I took care of you for nothing."

The temperature in my bedroom felt like it had climbed twenty degrees. But my mouth was frozen. I didn't know what to think or say. So many questions jammed together in my brain like tiny car wrecks, crashing into one another, shrapnel slicing through my skull.

"Adam knows," Lindsay said.

My stomach knotted. I could barely form the words or hear them once they entered the air. "Knows what?"

"About the contract, Erica. As close as you say you two are, I'm surprised he didn't let that cat out of the—"

I hung up.

My earlier dinner of chicken pot pie threatened to rise into my throat, and even though putting my head between my knees is on the no-no list, it was the only thing stopping me from throwing up on my pink shag rug. Soon, the sweat pouring down the back of my neck gave me the shakes, my only warning before hitting the floor.

Chapter Twenty-three

The smell of toast.

My eyes fluttered. Pale morning light made its way through the crack in the curtains, spilling onto the ruffled edge of my bedspread. I had spent the whole night on the floor and in my sleep had managed to pull my Grayson Falcons blanket on top of me.

In the kitchen, the tea kettle's whistle screamed and died.

I sat up slowly, pushed the hair from my eyes, and scanned my body.

Bruises: none.

Teeth: all accounted for, including caps.

I held onto the bed post to pull myself up and accidentally stepped on my cell phone.

Who had I spoken to the night before? Had I fainted in the middle of a conversation?

My cell showed two texts from Lindsay. The first one was sent at 10:20 P.M.: *Bring my blue wool hat to school tomorrow.* The second was sent ten minutes later: *And my chunky pearl necklace.*

And my sweater. And anything else of mine you still have.

I plucked the necklace from where it hung over my jewelry stand, and the moment the pearls settled in my hand, it all came back: Lindsay's angry words; her hurtful remarks; the secret contract that everyone knew about but me, including Adam.

I got dressed, brushed out my matted hair, slid a fabric headband in place, and grabbed my backpack.

I texted Adam: *Pick me up for school. ASAP.*

He wrote back in an instant: *10-4.*

I wrapped the fake pearl necklace in Lindsay's sweater and shoved them both into my backpack, then grabbed her wool hat from my desk and deliberately squashed it against the bottom.

I tossed my bag on the chair by the front door and lingered in the arched doorway of the kitchen. My mother stood at the counter dishing scrambled eggs onto three plates. Steam spiraled up from a cup of herbal tea next to the stove. Dad sat at the table reading the morning paper. To any outsider looking in, we were the center of a Norman Rockwell painting. Minus the tats and multiple earrings and Syncopian daughter staring from the doorway.

And minus the shit that was about to hit the fan.

"Morning, honey," Dad said. He sipped from his orange juice glass.

"Just in time for breakfast," my mother said. "I added cheddar for extra—"

"Traitor," I said from the doorway. I didn't want to step all the way in. I was afraid if I did, those scrambled eggs might find their way to the wall.

"Excuse me?" she asked. Her hands were in the air like a

conductor, the wooden spoon in one and the dirty egg pan in the other. I did not answer as her hands slowly settled to the counter.

Dad folded the paper. "Erica?"

"I *know*," I said, glancing at my dad, but saving the cold, intense glare for my mother.

She turned her back to me and put the pan in the sink. She squeezed out some dish liquid and ran the water. "What exactly do you know?"

"Everything."

I felt the way an adopted child must feel when she discovers her parents aren't her own; that she was found in a basket in the woods or conceived by rape or some other tragedy.

"Did you hear what I said?" I asked, raising my voice. "I know *everything*."

Dad said, "You're talking about Lindsay?"

I nodded.

"Ruthie," he said, "I told you this would happen…"

My mother turned off the water and spun around. Her eyes bulged out like she had a sudden attack of hyperthyroidism. I wanted to press my thumbs into her sockets to push them back in place.

"Don't tell me you told me so, Marcus," she said. "I can't take it. That, along with having a child who expects me to save her and then gets mad when I do." She turned her angry bulging eyes toward me. "And you! Maybe it's about time my daughter, the only one I have, offered me a thank you. Need some help? Try this on for size: Thank you, Mom, for protecting me."

"I never asked you to protect—"

"Or how about this one: Thank you, Mom, for trusting me

to make my own choices in school. Or maybe this will work for you: Thank you, Mom, for moving our family close to the only friend willing to stand by me!"

"You moved us from our old house so I'd be closer to Lindsay?"

Silence filled the room. My mother's face was red and her eyes blinked fast, like a high-power fan was blowing air into them.

Dad's voice stayed calm. "It was the best plan at the time, honey. Lindsay's family was struggling financially…and you were fainting so often. Your mother did what she thought was best—"

"We *both* did what we thought was best. Christ, Marcus, you make it sound like you were never there. How many times did you save Erica from bashing in her nose or drowning in the river?"

The doorbell rang.

"I'm out of here," I said, storming into the foyer and grabbing my backpack from the hallway chair. "And FYI, Mother," I shouted, even though she could hear me without raising my voice, "your Princess Lindsay doesn't plan to go to college. As a matter of fact, if I told you what her real plans were, you'd know what it feels like to hit the kitchen floor."

I opened the front door and slammed it behind me.

Adam said, jogging in his boots to keep up with me, "You okay?"

"Nope."

"What's going on?"

"A helluva lot."

We got into the truck.

The front door of my house opened. My mother stood in the doorway and Dad appeared behind her. She stepped onto the porch like she planned to run after me. Dad grabbed her by the elbow.

For the first time that morning, I was grateful.

***

We drove past Larry Taggert's house on our way out of the neighborhood. I turned away.

"What's going on between you and Lindsay?" Adam asked. "She flipped out this morning."

"You talked to her?"

"No," he said. "She texted me like a dozen times."

"What did she say?"

"Read them for yourself."

He pulled his cell phone from his jacket pocket and handed it to me.

The first message said, *Don't believe anything Erica tells you.* The second said, *She's jealous.* The rest were variations of the first two. One-liners, like a stand-up comedian. Only these texts weren't the least bit funny.

"Is there something going on that you haven't told me?" Adam asked. "Something I need to know?"

I put the phone on the seat between us. "Yes."

After a few moments, he said, "Maybe I don't want to know."

"You just might."

"No, I don't," he said, stopping at a stop sign. He turned to look at me. "What you two have going on is a mean-girl thing. And I'm not getting in the middle of it."

"This is not a *mean-girl thing.*"

"Come on, Erica. First you're like twins, doing everything for one another, and then you have a falling out and do everything you can to destroy each other."

"No," I said. "I'm not like that…"

What was I like? Was I spiteful enough to tell Adam about Lindsay's affair to get even with the two of them for knowing about the contract? Or was I simply afraid, needing a guarantee that if Larry dumped Lindsay, she wouldn't go running back to Adam?

The second reason was the clincher.

"I can tell you who she's seeing," I said.

"Why now?"

"Because you need to know that Lindsay didn't dump you for just some other guy. She broke up with you for an *older* man."

A car behind us lightly tooted their horn. Adam got the truck moving and drove out of the neighborhood. He remained silent as we passed the cotton field. White tufts spread out over the hundred or so acres like fuzzy ghosts floating among the leaves. Soon, that cotton would be tilled under, the leftover stalks that the combine missed sticking up like explosive shards from an artillery shell.

"*Way* older," I added.

Adam's hands gripped the wheel harder. "I don't care."

"You should."

"Well, I don't. She and I are through, in case you've forgotten."

"Drive to school the long way," I told him. "Make a right up here."

"Too many lights."

"Just do it, Adam. Make a right."

Adam did as I asked. In less than a minute, the fire station was in view.

"Slow down," I said.

We moved past the station at twenty miles an hour. One of the garage doors was open. A handful of men stood inside polishing the red engine. In the shadows, they all looked the same. Even though I wasn't sure if Larry was one of them, wasn't sure if he was even working that morning, I said, "He's in there."

Adam glanced into the garage as he drove past. Then he increased his speed, zooming up to the red light on the corner. He barely stopped before making a hard right and heading toward the school.

"Why are you going so fast?" I asked.

"Getting to homeroom on time."

"Did you see—"

"I don't need this right now, Erica. I just got out of one bullshit relationship; I don't need to get into another."

We pulled into the school parking lot. In front of the school, Adam stopped the truck next to the curb. He didn't make an effort to open my door. I didn't take off my seatbelt.

"When did Lindsay tell you about the contract?" I asked.

"What contract?"

"The contract about her taking care of me."

"When she and I first started dating."

"Huh," I said. "Good for you. I just found out about it last night."

"You didn't know?" he asked.

"No, I didn't know," I said. "What the hell kind of question is that?"

"Why are you getting mad at me? I didn't do anything."

"Lindsay didn't tell you that the contract was written behind my back? Between her and my mother?"

Adam shook his head. "No. She just told me not to mention it because it was a sensitive issue for you."

"Well, she's pretty good at telling half-truths, isn't she, Adam?"

"If you're blaming me for something, you'd better just spit it out."

"No…"

"You know what?" Adam said. "You're acting just like Lindsay."

"No, I'm not."

"You snoop like her…you talk junk—"

"I am *nothing* like her."

"Then tell me how you're different," he said.

"I don't keep secrets from the people I care about."

"I'm sure the only reason she kept the contract a secret was to protect you."

"I don't need protecting," I said.

Adam didn't respond.

I went on. "You think you know so much about the girl you used to date. But you don't know jack. She lied to you, Adam. She's lying to her mom. She's lying to herself. That contract with my parents isn't Lindsay's only secret. Not by a long shot."

I jumped out of the truck, grabbed my backpack from behind the seat, and slung it over my shoulder. I could feel Adam staring after me as I melded with the crowd rushing into the building.

Chapter Twenty-four

Lindsay didn't waste time dropping out of our AP classes. On Monday, I spotted her in the cafeteria, but she turned her head the other way when I went past.

Thanksgiving was Thursday, so the school week was cut short. In the cafeteria, Adam nodded his head when he saw me. Three days, three nods. I could handle letting go of Lindsay. After all, that contract had obviously defined our relationship. But I couldn't stand the thought of losing Adam's friendship, especially if I was the reason. I had misdirected my anger, unconsciously shoving him between Lindsay and me like a hefty chunk of insulation.

So, if all Adam offered me at the moment was a polite nod of the head, I would humbly take it.

***

I overheard my mother on the phone Wednesday night as I got out of the shower. With Dad away at a conference in Mexico, my mother didn't use a filter.

"Please, Lindsay," she was saying, like an addict begging for one more hit. "We need you."

In my towel and wet hair, I shouted from my bedroom doorway: "Why don't you offer her more money, Mother, since that seems to be a motivator!"

That outburst, followed by hours of grueling silence, prompted my mother's obsessive quest to make me her friend again.

"Your dad's enjoying the conference in Cancun," she told me during supper.

"Cool."

"He says he wishes we were there."

"Uh-huh."

"He's going to celebrate the holiday with turkey tacos. Isn't that cute?"

"Guess so."

"So…how's school?"

"Fine."

"Anything new?"

"Nope."

"Gearing up for midterms?"

"Yup."

"If you like, Erica, you can spend your second semester at home," she said, slipping in the offer like arsenic into my herbal tea. "I can help you with everything except science and math. But we could hire a private tutor."

"No, thank you."

"You sure? Because—"

"I'm sure."

And then, on Thanksgiving morning: "How about we go Christmas shopping tomorrow? Black Friday."

"I haven't made a list yet."

"That's all right. We could get an early start."

"Too much homework."

"Over Thanksgiving break?"

"Sorry."

And I was sorry; or, at least I *felt* sorry for her. I found myself hiding in my bedroom so I wouldn't have to see the lonely desperation on her face.

On Thanksgiving afternoon, a different voice came through my door; a softer, calmer one; a voice of negotiation: "I'll give you all the space you need, Erica. If that's what you want. And I won't talk to Lindsay anymore." And then, when I didn't answer, "Is that what you want?"

Pause.

"Yes," I said.

"Will that make us friends again?"

A second, longer pause.

"I guess so."

"Okay," she said, her voice drifting away. "Okay…"

***

While Dad discussed sales charts at a conference table in Cancun, and I was busy trying not to overanalyze Ruth O'Donnell's outlook on our mother-daughter bond while making homemade turkey stuffing, all humidity got sucked from the North Carolina air.

And fire loves dry air, or so I've heard.

On Thanksgiving night, another blaze hit our county: An abandoned horse stable out at Pleasant Ridge burned to the ground. The fires seemed so frequent, we barely paid attention when the anchor person spoke to us from the television.

For my mother, it was business as usual.

"You sure you don't want to go to the mall tomorrow?" she asked after her second slice of sugar-free pumpkin pie.

"I don't think so."

"We don't have to buy anything," she said. "We can just tool around."

"Going to the library with Adam," I lied.

"The library's open this weekend?"

The question was left hanging between us. My mother had kept her end of the bargain by taking a dozen steps back, and I had pushed her another ten. The space around me felt infinite. I was a new star in the middle of a black hole.

And I liked it.

A band geek who worked at Magic Wok over by the movie theater lived on my block. I asked him to pick me up the next afternoon at the entrance to Great Pines. After he dropped me off, I threw him a couple of bucks for gas and headed into the theater. I couldn't think of a better way to exercise my newfound independence than by disappearing into the darkness and soaking up a B-movie.

The previews were blaring when I got a text.

Larry Taggert: *Can you babysit tonight?*

My wheels turned slowly. If I told him yes, I would indirectly be doing it for Lindsay, or some other unsuspecting jailbait.

On the flipside, it was none of my business what Larry's plans were. I was done caring about what grownups did with their personal lives, no matter how psychotic.

Me: *What time?*

Larry: *Seven.*

Me: *What about Adam?*

Larry: *Couldn't reach him.*

I hesitated, then tapped the letters: *You sure you're okay with just me?*

I waited through an entire movie preview before I received his final text: *Yes.*

"Please turn off your cell," someone whispered from the seat behind me.

"Sorry," I whispered back.

I texted one last time: *See you at seven.*

To prevent my mother from being a buzz kill, I'd tell her that Adam was with me. But I'd be babysitting alone. No one knew the truth but Larry and me.

As the movie began, I thought how strange it was that of all the people in my life, Larry was the one who seemed to trust me the most.

Chapter Twenty-five

The wind nearly pushed me into the foyer as Larry opened the door.

"It's blustery out there," he said as I followed him into the family room. The house smelled homey, like gravy and cinnamon. "Josephine's with her mother. She plans to be home by midnight, but I'll be back before her. If she knew I had you sitting alone, she might get worried."

"She doesn't know?" I asked, staring down into the playpen at the twins, already dressed in their pajamas.

"I have something important tonight," Larry explained. "Something that can't be helped. Emergency, you might say..."

I took off my beanie and shook out my hair. Leaves fell to the carpet.

"Sorry," I said, fighting the urge to stoop down to collect them. Always the chance I wouldn't come back up.

"Your hair looks good like that," he said.

My stomach twisted. I tried to throw away the compliment with a joke. "The windblown look is *tres chic* these days."

Larry laughed. I pretended to join him.

Samantha reached up to Larry, her tiny hands opening and closing into miniature fists. He picked her up and placed her on his hip.

"Sure you're ready to handle this by yourself?" he asked.

I nodded.

"Lindsay told me you'd jump at the chance," he added. He rubbed his nose against Samantha's baby cheek.

"You saw Lindsay?" I asked.

"What?" Larry said as he placed Samantha back in the playpen. "Oh. I happened to run into her. At the Food Lion. She was…buying milk…and I was…buying a newspaper."

I said nothing.

"So," he said, "you're ready then?"

"Yes, sir."

"What's with the 'sir' stuff?" Larry asked. "You make me feel old."

My skin was naturally pale, and heat suddenly rose to my cheeks. I wondered if Larry could see the rosiness in the dimly lit room.

The babies were watching Larry and me. I could have sworn Samantha shot me a doubtful look, and I agreed with her. How could their daddy leave me alone with them? Why did he trust me more than I trusted myself?

I wanted to shout, *How dare you leave your children with someone like me just so you can cheat on your wife!*

The wind gusted, pushing branches against the roof.

"Wind is the enemy," Larry said quietly. "Keeps us firemen on our toes. Especially when there's an arsonist on the loose."

"Adam mentioned that."

"What did he say exactly?"

"That some of the fires were deliberate," I told him.

"And?"

"That's all."

"Arsonists are meteorologists and geologists put together," Larry said. "Incredibly astute. They see the signs. They follow the arrows."

"You think they'll catch him?" I asked.

Larry smiled. "You automatically assume it's a man."

"Oh. I didn't mean to—"

"No, you're probably right. Most arsonists throughout history have been men. Mostly *young* men." He smiled then, a creepy leer that made the saliva in my mouth dry up. "Anyway, our fire department is well overdue for a new leader. I don't think we'll catch the person until we have one. So, hopefully…sooner than later…"

The branches scraped against the roof again.

"All girls dig firemen," Larry told me. "Looks like you're no different."

"I'm sorry?"

"Adam."

"Adam?"

"Reminds me of myself when I was his age. Strong. Confident bordering on cocky. Ready to prove himself to the world."

I didn't respond.

"Did you know I was in a calendar a while back?" he suddenly asked. "You want to see it?"

I wanted to shake my head no, but the word popped out of my mouth instead: "Okay."

I stared at the babies as he went down the hall and into his personal shrine. A moment later, he was back in the family room holding out a calendar. He turned it to the month of April.

"That's you?" I asked, trying not to laugh.

In the glossy but faded photo, Larry sat on a beach cross-legged with waves crashing behind him. He wore a pair of disturbingly short shorts, a fireman's hat, and a pair of large sunglasses. His body was tan and fit. He barely had any hair on his chest.

"We did it voluntarily," he said, grinning. "You know, to make money for the Fireman's Fund. I had just joined the department up in Jersey. Barely older than you are now."

I wondered, did Larry still think he looked like the young guy in that goofy photo?

He closed the calendar and set it on the coffee table. "Those were the good old days. When people looked up to firemen the same way they look up to doctors and pilots." He shook his head. "What good would it be to be a surgeon without patients? Or to fly an airplane without passengers? Last year, we had twenty-four car wrecks but only one structural fire."

"Aren't you glad when there aren't any fires? I mean, aren't you relieved?"

I had seen photos of wildfires in California and Colorado. Even if I was a firefighter, I'd be happy knowing that people and wildlife were safe.

"Not much of a livelihood when a fireman doesn't have fires to fight," he said. "That's why I became one. To fight fires. Got a slew of them now though, that's for sure. The universe is making up for lost time."

I gave him a weak smile to show I understood what he was

saying, when in reality I thought he was bonkers.

"You know something, Erica?" he said. "For a high-schooler, you're easy to talk to. I can see why Adam likes you so much."

My eyes grew wide.

"As if you didn't know," Larry said. "And why wouldn't he? You're pretty and sexy and a great listener. You seem way older than other girls your age. Adam's a lucky guy. Make sure you let him know that." He glanced at his cell phone. "It's getting late. I'd better scram."

The two words that got stuck in my head as I shut the front door behind him were "sexy" and "scram." "Sexy" because it disgusted me that Larry was the first guy to call me that, and "scram" because it's a word my dad would have used.

In the family room, I leaned against the arm of the couch and picked up the calendar.

"Daddy?" Samantha asked, pointing.

I held up the photo for her to see. "Yup. That's your daddy."

Willie jumped and said, "Daddy, daddy, daddy," then fell back onto his bottom, laughing.

Outside, the wind blew harder, causing the fake shutters to rattle against the siding. The chime on the front porch made a tinkling sound.

In the calendar, I sifted through the pictures of men who looked like actors from vintage re-runs of *Miami Vice* or some other disco cop show. When I turned back to the month of April, something profound occurred to me as Larry's grinning face peered from the photo. He wasn't only infatuated with himself. Larry Taggert was madly in love with fire.

***

To stay on the safe side, I walked the kids upstairs one at a time instead of carrying both on my hips like Adam and Lindsay did. Willie went first.

As soon as I put him down in his bed, he screamed, "Sammy! Sammy!"

"I'm going to get her now, Silly Willie. Calm down."

He cried for his sister as I made my way down the stairs, and by the time I reached into the playpen and picked up Samantha, the wooziness covered me like an invisible cloak, and I knew what was coming.

"CLIFF," I said out loud.

"Cliff?" asked Samantha as she slid out of my arms to the floor.

"Cross legs, lie down, feet up," I said, chanting by rote the never-ending mantra that would one day be chiseled into my headstone.

I crossed my legs. When the dizziness didn't subside, I lay down on the family room carpet with the backs of my legs up against the side of the sofa, perpendicular to the floor. Willie was whaling upstairs, and now Samantha cried, too. I told Samantha to lie down next to me, that I was playing a game. But with her brother screaming upstairs, it was impossible to get her to listen. She ran over to the bottom of the steps.

"Willie!" she screamed. Then, "I want Mama!"

I heard the slap-slap-slap of tiny bare feet on the tiled floor, and the sound of the front door opening. I felt the swish of cold air as it streamed across my body. Barely time to count my breaths, I forced myself to stand, holding onto the couch arm for support. The tunnel vision was sniffing me out, trying to grab me. Again I crossed my legs. After a moment, the wooziness subsided just enough for me to walk by leaning against walls and doorway frames.

"Mama!" Samantha yelled from outside.

I stumbled out the front door. The dry wind wrapped around me, whipping my hair across my face.

Samantha stood in the middle of the driveway in her pink pajamas and bare feet. She called into the dark for her mama. A light in the house next door came on and a face appeared in the window.

I grabbed Samantha's shivering body and pulled it to my own, praying to God I didn't faint on the driveway with the child in my arms; praying that the neighbor didn't call the police to report an insane babysitter who allows toddlers to run amok in their jammies.

"Don't cry, baby doll," I whispered.

Samantha's head lay against my shoulder as I carried her back into the house. I closed and double locked the door behind me. She wiggled out of my arms and scurried up the steps on her hands and feet like a dog. When I believed I'd avoided the crash and burn, I followed behind.

In his bed behind the safety railing, Willie sat with his worn stuffed rabbit in his lap and a thumb in his mouth. His face was wet but he had stopped crying.

"How's my Silly Willie?" I said, smoothing out his soft baby hair.

"Sammy crying," he said with his thumb still stuck between his tiny teeth.

"She's just a tired camper," I told him.

Samantha had already climbed up the side of the bed and scurried over the railing onto her Lion King comforter. I wiped her damp cheeks as she stood there. "You gonna be okay, Sammy Wammy?"

She nodded.

"That's my girl. Give Erica a big hug before you go night-night."

Sammy put her arms around my neck and hugged me tightly. Her wet cheek touched my own. I grabbed one of her dolls from the corner of the bed and handed it to her. As she lay down and I pulled the blanket over her, the dizziness that had tried to destroy me a few minutes earlier came back with a vengeance. My neck grew hot, then my ears, then my cheeks.

"No, no, no," I whispered.

Willie repeated, "No, no, no" and giggled.

Samantha held the doll in her arms and stared at me through the wooden slats.

Repeating my earlier routine, I lay on the floor, this time with my legs pressed up against the end of Willie's bed. The smell of scented baby wipes engulfed me. The room spun me around like I was on the Tilt-a-Whirl. My eyes throbbed. Blood rushed to my ears and throat.

Willie's giggling stopped, and Samantha cried for her mama again. I could barely see her blurry face, her miniature arms reaching down between the wooden slats like she was trying to save me from drowning. And I was drowning. Spinning into that whirlpool where I didn't hear, see, or feel. The tunnel vision was headed right for me, its goal to suck my head into its center.

And it succeeded.

Chapter Twenty-six

I smelled lemons. Strong thighs supported the back of my head. A warm hand stroked my cheek. My eyes fluttered. I lay stretched out on a couch.

"You'll be fine," Adam whispered.

I tried to say, "The kids," but it came out "da kiz" like the fainting spell had turned me into a German woman.

Adam's breathing remained steady as he checked the pulse in my neck.

"How?" I asked.

"I finally listened to Larry's voicemail," Adam said, "but I didn't call him back."

When my tongue came back to me, I whispered, "How did you get in?"

"Key. Under the yard gnome."

"How did I get on the couch?"

Adam smiled down at me. "I carried you," he said.

Like a real fireman, I thought. I tried to swallow, but my throat refused to let me. "The twins…"

"They're fine."

His calloused fingers ran circles against my cheek.

"Thirsty," I said.

He tucked a bolster pillow under my head in place of his legs as my eyelids shut. When I opened them again, a bottle of blue Gatorade sat on a coaster on the coffee table. Adam helped me sit up. He unscrewed the cap, handed me the bottle, and sat beside me on the sofa.

"I can't believe your mom let you babysit alone," he said.

"I told her you'd be with me." I downed a quarter of the blue liquid. "And now you are."

"Why didn't you ask me for real?"

"You were mad at me."

"I just needed a couple of days to chill," Adam said. "I knew you were taking your anger toward Lindsay out on me. But it still hurt."

"I'm sorry."

"Erica, I had no idea that contract would upset you. If I had, I would have told you about it sooner. I swear."

"I believe you." My tongue moved against my teeth in a familiar stretching exercise. "So you would have come tonight if I'd asked?"

"You could have twisted my arm," he said, pulling his arm behind his back and grimacing. Then he placed a hand on my thigh and left it there. "Did you walk over here?"

I nodded.

"Larry's a douche," Adam said. "What was so important that he'd have you babysit alone?"

"A date."

"I can't believe Josephine would have agreed—"

"Not with Josephine."

Adam hesitated. "You mean he had *plans* with someone…"

"No, Adam. A *date*."

"Lindsay has to be lying to you," he said. "To make you jealous, or make me jealous, or something crazy—"

"She's not lying, Adam. I've seen his texts…and that's not all…"

Everything spilled out of me in snippets as my throat muscles came back to life and the fog drifted away: the snooping in the bedroom drawers; the stolen boxer shorts and love letters; Larry's jewelry gifts; the secret dates; the real reason I was asked to babysit each week; the jokes behind Josephine's back, including the phrase "Fake Date Night."

When I mentioned the nest, Adam said, "That's disgusting."

"I think Larry has a God complex," I said. "Like he needs to have people glorify him. I learned about it in my psych class." I pointed to the calendar where it sat closed on the coffee table. "Take a look at April. Larry showed it to me himself."

Adam opened the calendar, glanced at the photo, and folded it closed again.

"He called me *sexy*," I said.

"What did you do?"

"Pretended like I didn't hear him."

"Loser…"

"And there's one more thing."

Adam waited, his face as still as a windless night.

"I suspect him," I said.

"Of what?"

"Of starting the fires."

Adam let out a laugh that sounded forced. "You must have hit your head…"

"Think about those newspaper articles in his office. He's doing more than patting himself on the back. Let me show you something. Then you can judge for yourself."

Adam removed his hand from my leg. "No."

"What if he's the one, Adam, and we don't say anything? What if the next fire kills another person? Someone we know? What if it turns out that Lindsay isn't safe with him? I know she's done some awful things, but she doesn't deserve—"

"You think Larry is capable of physically hurting someone? That because he's hooking up with a girl half his age—"

"Not *girl. Girls.*"

"Erica…"

"I have proof, Adam. I'll show you."

I slid off the couch and made baby steps up the hallway, leaning against the wall for support. I looked back to see Adam still sitting on the couch. At the end of the hall, I opened the office door, flicked on the light, and stepped into the room. By the time I got to the other side of the desk, Adam was standing in the doorway. He crossed his arms.

"Erica, you can't accuse someone of arson just because you don't like him. You have to have *real* proof. Not a room filled with newspaper articles."

"You need to come all the way in," I told him.

After a moment, he walked over to the desk and stood on the opposite side. I opened the drawer, pulled out the leather book, placed it on the desk, and turned it around so he could read it.

"It's a record of all the fires he's fought since last summer," I said. "Dates, names…do you see now?"

In silence, Adam moved his finger across and down each column of names and dates.

I said, "Forest fires, a chimney fire, the one out at the stables…"

"Erica," Adam said, "some of these were caused by lightning, and at least one by campers too stupid to read signs."

"I didn't mean all of them…"

"And if Larry is what you say, then why isn't this book hidden any better?"

"The drawer was locked," I said.

"You managed to open it," he said. "And the office door isn't locked at all. I think you're grasping at straws."

Adam closed the book and slid it back across the desk toward me, but his push was too forceful. The book slipped over the edge, crashing into the open drawer below. He walked around to my side, squatted, picked up the ledger, and rubbed his hand along the spine.

"Is it damaged?" I asked.

Adam shook his head, placed it back on the desk, and squatted down again. He held up a flat piece of wood about a quarter-inch thick and nearly the same size as the drawer's bottom. It was a cheaper wood than the rest of the desk, but it had been stained to match.

"Where did that come from?" I asked, confused.

"It's a fake bottom." He handed me the piece of wood as he stood up. We inspected it, and then our eyes made their way back to the drawer. There, in the bottom, sat another book.

Adam pulled it out and placed it on the desk beside the first book. A photo of Larry's twenty-something face decorated the front.

"I'm afraid to open it," I said.

"It's too late for that, don't you think?"

Adam flipped opened the book. Inside was a yellow Steno notebook with horizontal and vertical lines typically used for everything from grocery lists to doctors' appointments. It wasn't all that different from *Erica's Book of Spells* in my own kitchen drawer, minus the glitter.

Adam and I silently read the headings along the top of each page: *Temperature, Humidity, Barometric Pressure, Wind Speed, On-duty, Off-duty…*

Beneath the headings were tally marks and percentages, and symbols that looked like they belonged on an ancient cave wall, not in a modern-day ledger.

"What is this?" I asked.

But Adam didn't have time to answer. The muffled sound of tires coming up the driveway came through the closed window.

"It's Larry!" I said.

Adam pulled the drawer all the way out and placed the second book back in the bottom. He tried to get the piece of wood to slide along its track, but it kept missing.

"Hurry," I whispered.

"I'm trying. It won't go back in…"

A car door slammed.

Adam fiddled with the piece of wood, rotating it this way and that.

"Turn it over," I suggested.

Adam turned it over, and it slid up the track.

I handed him the first book. He placed it on top and shut the drawer. As we ran out of the room, I pulled the door closed behind me. It wasn't until we had high-tailed it back to the family room that I realized I'd forgotten to turn off the light.

By the time we heard the click of the key in the front door, we were falling onto the couch.

"We left the light on," I whispered in a panic.

"Shit," Adam said.

I counted to ten as I breathed in and out, two fingers against my wrist, checking my heart rate.

Adam grabbed the remote from the coffee table, but it fell to the floor. He left it there. Footsteps clacked against the tiled floor in the foyer. Adam's eyes shifted to a place behind me. I followed his gaze.

Josephine stood in the doorway. She took off her hat, but left her coat and scarf and gloves on.

Adam stood up. I moved to my feet slowly, like an old turtle.

"Josephine," Adam said.

"I was all the way out at my mama's," she said. "But when Larry called and said he'd be out until eleven or so, I thought it best to come on home. He told me not to, that things here were taken care of. But then I asked who was watching the babies." Josephine moved her eyes to me alone. "He told me it was the two of you, but I got the feeling he was fibbing. For some reason, I thought I'd only find Erica here." She rubbed the back of her neck. "Guess my exhaustion is taking over my senses."

"Yes, ma'am," I answered, as though she'd asked a question.

And now we are all part of the lie, I thought as the sick feeling crawled into my core and festered.

"Erica," Josephine said, "I have to be honest with you. I told Larry when you first started sitting for us that you being alone with the twins worried me, so I'm relieved Adam's here. No offense. It's just that, well, I'm sure you understand."

"Yes, ma'am."

Adam said, "How's your mother?"

"Running me to an early grave," Josephine said. "I'm sure I'll do the same to my own children when I get old."

Josephine looked back and forth between us. She had to have seen the light on in the back room as she pulled into the driveway. How could she not? Maybe she believed Larry had left it on. After all, it was his shrine. Maybe *not* turning off the office light was the best thing possible. If Josephine had been pulling into the driveway just as the light clicked off, she'd have caught us for sure.

"And how were the twins?" she asked.

"A little fussy, but good," I told her, convinced she could hear my rapid heartbeat.

"Did y'all have some apple pie?" she asked, glancing toward the kitchen. "I make a mean pie, you know. It's in the fridge."

"No, ma'am," I said. "Still stuffed from yesterday."

"Of course." She pressed her hands against her lower back. "Well, then. I'm dog tired. All this driving back and forth is draining the blood out of me. And my mama's restaurant that she refuses to let go of, like it's an appendage. Trying to sell a business that hasn't seen a profit in a decade, well, that story could take all night."

The three of us stood in the thick silence until Josephine said,

"I should pay you." Still wearing her pretty leather gloves, she fiddled with the bills in her wallet and handed some to me. "Y'all can split it?"

"Sure," Adam and I said at the same time.

"Of course you can," she said, smiling. "You two are—what do the kids call it today—hooking up?"

Adam blushed and looked at his boots.

"Oh, I'm sorry," she said. "I just thought…I mean…y'all would make a cute couple, being the same age and all, and going to the same school…sort of convenient…I should just learn to keep my mouth shut…"

Her voice drifted off as her eyes traveled to the fireman's calendar sitting on the coffee table. "Why on earth is that out here?"

"Larry showed it to me," I said. "To *us*, I mean."

"I haven't seen that old thing in years." She peeled off her gloves and let out a small yawn. "Alrighty then," she said. "It's time to shuffle off to Buffalo, as the old folks say. I'm going up to see my babies. Kiss their sweet faces before I hit the hay."

She moved back into the foyer and waited for us to put on our coats and hats with the door open and chilly air streaming into the house.

"Goodnight, y'all," she said, ushering us onto the porch.

As we started up the sidewalk, Josephine called to me. "Erica, could you come back here for a quick sec?"

Adam's boots clacked against the cold cement as he walked to the truck and I headed back to the porch.

"Yes, ma'am?" I said.

"He's got the hots for you," Josephine whispered.

My stomach moved into a knot. "Who?"

"Who do you think? That gorgeous boy over there."

I looked over my shoulder to see Adam leaning against the passenger door, waiting.

"You ought to hook up with him," Josephine said. "That way, there's nothing to worry about."

"Worry?"

"It's always good to have someone to watch over you," she said. "To be there through thick and thin. To help you in a time of crisis." She waved her hands in the chilly air. "So go on now and have a good time. Ya'll look adorable together. The perfect couple. Like Larry and me."

She stepped back inside the house and closed the door. The porch light went out over my head. Through the dark I made my way to the truck. Adam helped me in and shut the door behind me.

When he got into the driver's seat, he said, "What was that about?"

"I think she knows."

"That we were snooping? Damn it, Erica, I told you—"

"Not just snooping," I said.

"What else?"

"I'm not sure…"

The heater was turned on high. Warm air blew against my face. I put on my seatbelt and turned toward the Taggert house. The downstairs sat in complete darkness now, including the shrine. Upstairs in the master bedroom, a thin trickle of light seeped through a sliver separating the curtains.

"Take me downtown," I told Adam as he pulled away from the curb.

"What?"

"I want to see it. Larry's nest."

"Are you insane?" he asked. "Why would you want to do that?"

"Just take me there."

"Do you even know where it is?"

"I might be able to find it…"

"It's already eleven, Erica." Adam stopped at the stop sign on the corner and turned to me. "We could be looking all night."

"Larry is setting those fires, Adam. You saw the book. How can you even question it?" When he didn't respond, I said, "If you don't take me, I'll sneak out in my mother's car. She's playing BUNCO at a neighbor's. She won't be home till after midnight. Her Prius is sitting alone in the garage, just waiting for me to take it for a spin."

"You'll never do it."

"Is that a dare?"

"You *can't* do it," he said. "And not just the driving part. Who knows what maniacs are creeping around the warehouse district on a Friday night? It's way too dangerous to go down there alone."

I smiled to myself in the dark. I knew I had him.

"I'm only doing this to pacify you," Adam said, turning up his favorite country station to show me he was finished talking.

I sucked on my bottom lip for the next ten minutes, and by the time the silhouettes of buildings appeared on the horizon, Keith Urban was singing about desperately loving someone, and I could taste the tang of blood in my mouth.

Chapter Twenty-seven

We crawled at a snail's pace along Division Street. I squinted to see through the shadows, convinced there were drug addicts or rapists in every sinister doorway, rodents in every dark alley. As if on cue, a mangy rat scurried along the gutter and disappeared down a storm drain.

We drove another block. I stared into the dark. "Larry has keys to some of the buildings down here," I told Adam.

"Fire departments have keys to a lot of places."

"Why would Larry choose to have an affair at this end of town?" I asked. "Why wouldn't he rent an apartment somewhere nice? Or get a hotel room?"

Adam shrugged. "This is free. Besides, who'd have the balls to follow him down here?"

I nearly answered, "We do," but he shot me a look, and I held my tongue.

We drove a few more blocks. The shadows grew darker. Each time we crossed an intersection, I caught a glimpse of the river beyond the buildings on our left. Some of the streetlights in the district weren't lit; some lights were missing altogether, their holes left behind in the sidewalk. As we approached the burned-out paper mill, I remembered something.

"Lindsay said the building is brick."

"Well, that narrows it down," Adam said sarcastically.

"That's not all. She said there's a number on the front of the building."

"What number?"

I squinted up at the occasional number that hadn't eroded in a century's time. Twenty-four…eighteen…

"I can't remember," I said.

"You can't remember the number. And the building is brick like all the others."

"Please, Adam," I said. "Just a little longer."

"I'm giving us thirty minutes, and then we bail. Got it?"

I nodded.

We weaved up and down old, chipped cobblestone streets, half of them dead-ending into the river which seemed to be waiting for us in the dark. Up on the main drag, I peered through the darkness at the building fronts, trying to decipher fragments of letters and numbers. Business signs that used to be lighted were either burned out or smashed. Painted advertisements on the brick walls—tobacco goods, household products, company names—had nearly faded away over time.

As Adam turned left onto South Bend Street, I glanced at the brick building on the corner on my right. The streetlight flickered as it tried to cast a dim yellow haze across the building's façade where two empty flagpole holders stuck out from the top.

As we made the turn, I shouted, "Three!"

"What?" Adam slowed the truck, but it was too late to see the number clearly since most of the front was in shadow, and we'd already passed the building.

"That's what Lindsay told me," I said, excited. "The number three."

Adam wound his way around the large square block again. Back in the front of the building, he let the truck idle at the curb. Together we peered up into the shadows. I read the letters *E* and *N*, but my eyes could not make out the rest. A large circled "3" was sculpted in the cement near the roofline, with a scrolled cement ribbon underneath.

"Do you know what this is?" Adam asked.

My eyes worked in the dark as they connected the carved letters above the two garage doors. "It says *ENGINE*."

"That's another name for a fire department," Adam said. "And that "3" up there is the station's number. These were built near mills because fires were pretty common back in the day. Probably hasn't been used in fifty years, maybe longer. As long as the mill's been shut down, anyway."

The building was small compared to the others on the block, but it seemed to have withstood the test of time. Only a few bricks were missing, and the glass window panes at the top were in tact. Out front, an old shoe lay in the gutter, and pieces of trash covered a nearby storm drain.

"What do we do now?" I asked.

"We go home."

"We can't."

"Yes, we can."

"Adam, we didn't come all the way down here not to see the inside."

"No way."

"We'll be careful," I told him. "We'll stay hidden."

"It's too dangerous," he said. "There are crazies down here."

"I haven't seen a single person tonight."

"They're probably staying warm inside the empty buildings. Like that homeless man who died."

"Please," I begged. "Just a looky-loo. What if it turns out that Larry keeps a bunch of evidence down here? What if this is where he stashes the kerosene or whatever he uses to start the fires?"

"Grease," Adam said.

"What?"

"The fires were started with grease."

"Oh," I said. "Well, I'll bet Larry's got gallons inside this place."

"Erica…"

"We might be saving lives, Adam."

He put the truck in *DRIVE*, made a second turn onto South Bend, and parked by what I assumed used to be a picturesque river walkway.

"This is a block away," I said.

"What if what you say is true, and Larry's in that building? You don't want him to see me, do you?"

"*Us.*"

"*Me,*" he said. "You're going to wait here. You're going to sit in the driver's seat with the doors locked and the engine running and your cell phone on your lap."

"That wasn't part of the plan," I said.

"We never made a plan."

"Yes, we did."

"What if you faint?" Adam asked.

"I won't."

"Cross your heart."

We both knew I could not make that promise.

"You see?" Adam said. "I'll run up there by myself, take a quick look around, and get my ass back to the truck." He reached over and grabbed a heavy-duty flashlight from inside the glove compartment.

Invasive thoughts entered my mind that if something did happen, it would be my fault. "What if something happens to you?" I whispered.

"I have my cell and my Swiss Army knife," he said. "Satisfied?"

"No."

"Then we can leave." He put his hand on the lever.

"No way," I told him as I pushed him out the driver's door and slid into his seat. I put my hands on the steering wheel at ten and two. "Be careful, Adam. Don't let anyone see you."

"Yes, ma'am."

He hesitated, leaned into the cab, and gave me a quick peck on the lips. Then he became nothing more than a shadow in the mirror.

Chapter Twenty-eight

When Adam's soft warm lips connected with mine, it took all I had not to grab him by the collar and pull him back into the truck. Instead, I sat in the cab alone, stalking a grown man who split his time between coddling his babies and cheating on his wife.

The river glistened under a moonlit sky. A slight breeze turned the sparkles into wide ribbons, seemingly endless as they rippled their way to the opposite bank nearly half a mile away. The river disappeared from view as I slid down a little in the driver's seat and set my cell phone timer.

One minute drifted by.

Two minutes...

Three minutes....

It was like waiting for a meteor to fall inevitably to earth; no control, just the waiting. I kept checking the mirrors, thinking I saw movement, sighing with a mixture of relief and anxiety that there was nothing, only the same thin streams of light in between the wide masses of shadows.

The numbers on my cell seemed extra bright as they glowed through the dark. Adam had been gone nearly eight minutes.

Eight minutes is a long time. *Too* long, I reasoned.

I did what I'd promised *not* to do. I cut the engine and got out of the truck. After locking the doors and putting the keys in my coat pocket, I headed up the sidewalk. Acrid smells of urine and mold and ancient brick mortar rose up to my sinuses. I hopped over narrow strips of light to keep my cover. The nighttime wrapped itself around me like a tight-fitting coat, making me claustrophobic. I glanced back at Adam's truck, realizing how much safer I'd felt with the walls of the vehicle protecting me. Still, I made my way along the brick wall to a cul-de-sac behind the firehouse.

As I snuck into the alcove, I prayed to God that my footsteps couldn't be heard by anyone, including whatever rodents lurked in the shadows or storm drains. Cockroaches scattered outward like the balls on a pool table. The cul-de-sac was a large empty square with a metal ramp that led up to a large roll-top door. I walked up the ramp and shook the door handle, but a rusty deadbolt held it in place. I left the cul-de-sac and made my way to the building's front. The two large garage doors were also locked, these from the inside, the rectangular windows too high to see through.

The temperature had dropped to the mid-thirties. I shivered uncontrollably. Adam had been MIA for nearly fifteen minutes. My cell showed 11:25. My mother would be getting home from BUNCO a little after midnight.

As I rounded the opposite side of the building, I spotted a narrow open door, a seemingly endless black abyss looming behind it.

219

"Adam?" I whispered loudly at the edge of the opening.

No answer.

"Adam?" I called again as I stepped through the doorway. The sound of tiny feet pattered in front of me, and I screamed.

"Erica?" Adam's voice fell from somewhere above me.

"There's something crawling around down here!"

"Stay put." His feet clomped down a set of metal stairs, and he appeared before me, flashlight in hand. "Why aren't you in the truck?"

"I was worried about you."

"I'm fine."

"Did you find anything?"

"Larry's not here," Adam said. Then, after a pause: "I'm pretty sure you were right about this place."

He guided me through the dark, the flashlight beam leading the way. We walked toward the metal steps which were against a wall to the right. He held my hand as he led me up the staircase. At the top, he shone the beam slowly around a large open room. Each time the light landed on something Adam wanted me to see, he let it linger a moment.

"Futon," he said. "Blankets, pillows, candles, camp stove...but that's not all."

I followed him across the room. A bachelor's version of a bookshelf unit stood against the wall, three long boards and lines of bricks holding one plank above the other. On the shelves sat stacks of books and magazines and a single Dalmatian bookend.

"What am I supposed to be seeing?" I asked.

"This," Adam said, shining the flashlight to a spot on top of the dog's head.

I could barely make out a small glass circle peering out like an evil eye.

"What is it?" I asked.

"A camera."

"We're being watched?"

He shook his head. "I don't think so. The light's not flashing."

I peered more closely. "It's so small."

"I think it's supposed to be so no one will see it. Like a nanny cam."

"How did you find it?" I asked.

"My flashlight just happened to land on it. Look where it's aimed."

I followed Adam's gaze back to the twin futon mattress on the floor. "Why would Larry—?" I cut myself off. "Oh," I said. "Do you think Lindsay knows?"

"It's not like it's out in the open." He let the flashlight dangle from his hand. For a moment he didn't say anything. Until recently, Lindsay had been Adam's girlfriend. I could only imagine what was going through his mind.

"You okay?" I asked.

He nodded. "I just find it hard to believe this is Larry's place."

"*Nest*," I corrected. "It's exactly as Lindsay described. Except for the camera. Did you find anything downstairs?"

"Couple of old chairs, leftover pieces of fire hose, some trash."

"No proof?"

"Not that Larry's an arsonist," Adam said.

"Oh."

"You sound disappointed."

"No. Just tired."

I thought discovering the nest would thrill me, but it did the opposite, and a heavy weariness draped over me.

"We should call the police," I told him.

"And report *what*?"

Adam was right. There was no evidence of arson. But what about the camera? Or the affair? Was any of this illegal if both were willing participants?

"I'll talk to Lindsay," I said. "If I explain what we found, and that we're worried about her, maybe she'll listen."

Adam turned away from the shelf. "Let's get out of here."

"Should we take the camera?" I asked.

"I'm not touching that thing or anything else."

I followed him back down the stairs. We made our way through the side door, and Adam pulled it closed behind us. The door knob made a clicking sound.

"It just locked," Adam said, jiggling the handle. "But it was open when I got here."

"Maybe Larry was here earlier and forgot to close it," I suggested.

Adam said, "Larry Taggert isn't the kind of guy who forgets anything."

Well, I thought to myself as we headed down the sidewalk toward the truck, *if it turns out he's busy juggling affairs and starting fires, maybe this won't be his only slip-up.*

Chapter Twenty-nine

The same night we found Larry's nest, I dreamed that my bedroom was engulfed in flames. My desk, the curtains, the rug, all burning, the flames reaching toward the ceiling, smoke filling the room. On my bed, I stood in my SpongeBob pajamas and bare feet with a fire extinguisher in my hands. I pulled the lever, but it broke off. Then my door opened and Larry, dressed in firefighter gear, stepped into the room. He set up an old-fashioned camera on a tripod in the corner and threw a large jarful of grease onto the fire, all the while grinning like he was auditioning for a Colgate commercial. The flames jumped higher—

My mother's voice broke through the nightmare: "Erica! Get up! Quick!"

By the time I made my way to the kitchen, the awful dream began to slip away.

My mother was standing with her arms crossed, facing the small flat screen on the kitchen counter. The early sky beyond the window was orange and blue.

"It's Saturday, Mom. Barely seven o'clock—"

"Shush. It's your school."

She turned up the volume as I stood next to her. On the television, the sound of helicopter blades whirred behind a female reporter's voice.

"…with a live report from Grayson High School. As you can see below, emergency vehicles are lined up along the sidewalk in front of the entrance doors. Sources tell us the third-floor cafeteria is engulfed in flames, but that is only hearsay at this point, although black smoke can be seen behind the windows. It's suspected that the fire started hours ago, before the weekend janitors were due to arrive…"

Our ninth through twelfth grade high school was a massive building housing kids bused in from two counties, a student body of over two thousand. The second-floor cafeteria, where most of the jazz-band kids and Goths and other sub-groups ate lunch, didn't have any windows because it sat in the center of the building. The third-floor cafeteria was much brighter, with a wall of windows looking out over the main parking lot. I had eaten in that room nearly every school day since freshman year.

The helicopter news camera zoomed in on an extension ladder as it made its climb upward. I tried to see if the man on the ladder was Larry, but his back was toward the camera. By the time the faceless fireman reached the top, other firefighters appeared on the inside of the cafeteria windows. Within seconds, two of the large windows were shattered.

A handful of early-morning spectators stood at the edge of the parking lot, held back by a long piece of yellow tape, taking pictures or videotaping the scene. Internet videos would be streaming by midmorning, if not already.

My mother shook her head. "What the hell is going on in this town?" Her cell phone chimed. "It's the ABS," she said, staring at the tiny screen. ABS stood for *Automated Buddy System*, used by the public schools in case of a lockdown or other crisis.

"What's it say?" I asked.

"They advise all students, parents, and faculty to stay away from the school grounds until further notice. They'll notify us as to whether or not you'll have school on Monday."

On television, the thick smoke streaming through the wide window frames was slowly turning from black to gray.

I texted Adam, curious if he was part of the fire crew. When he dropped me off the night before, he'd mentioned sleeping in.

I tapped the letters: *You awake?*

About five minutes later, Adam wrote back: *Barely.*

Did you hear the news?

What news?

I typed: *Grayson cafeteria on fire.*

What????

Channel 11.

I waited for what felt like forever.

Finally, another message: *Holy crapoli.*

I texted back a frowny face.

My mother and I ate breakfast and watched the news for the next hour until it looked as though the fire department had everything under control, and the last little bit of smoke sliding through the broken windows had turned thin and milky white.

***

Adam didn't text again that Saturday. I texted him twice and called him once, but he didn't respond. Maybe he'd had enough of fires and speculation.

Maybe he's had enough of me…

The ABS notified us again: School was cancelled until Thursday. I didn't know what I was going to do with myself with so much free time.

Sunday morning rolled around. Dad was due home that evening, and my mother seemed more excited than usual when I crawled out of my cave for breakfast.

"Check this out," she said, tossing the Sunday paper next to my placemat.

I read the headline out loud. "'Pig farmer arrested in connection with fires.'" I looked up from the paper. "Pig farmer?"

"Read the whole thing." My mother scooped scrambled eggs into a gluten-free pita pocket and put it on the table for me.

I scanned the article. "It says he could have fed evidence to his livestock."

"Pigs have a reputation for eating most anything," she said. "Even bones."

"That's disgusting."

My mother nodded as she bit into her bagel at the counter.

"He lives out in the county, over by Juniperville," I said. "Why would someone come all the way out here to start fires?"

"People who are mentally unstable do all kinds of strange things."

"How did he get into our school? We have security."

"Maybe he had help from the inside," my mother said. "Who

knows? I'm sure they'll figure it all out."

After breakfast, my mother's cell phone rang. I left her in the kitchen going over flight information with my dad. I took a shower and got dressed. Getting ahead in my studies was an option, but I couldn't imagine sitting at my desk all day knowing that a fire had nearly burned down my school, and now a suspect was in custody.

I tapped Adam's number into my phone, and this time he answered. "I was getting worried," I told him.

"Sorry I didn't call you back. My mom lost her cell yesterday and borrowed mine. It was under the seat in her car."

"Oh. Did you make it over to the school?"

"I started to go," Adam said. "I grabbed all my gear, but then, about a mile away, I changed my mind."

"Why?"

"I knew Larry would be there. As much as I love volunteering for the fire department, I can't work beside him without saying something."

"You're quitting?" I asked.

"Taking a break. I've known Larry for a long time, Erica. After seeing his nest...and that camera...I don't think I can look him in the eye."

"I get it."

"Did you hear they caught the arsonist?" he asked.

"I read it in the paper," I said. "Guess we were wrong."

"*You* were wrong."

"That's what I meant. Anyway, we don't have school until Thursday."

"Want to get together tomorrow?" Adam asked. "Maybe get

out of Dodge for the day? I sort of need a breather."

"Sure. Where do you want to go?"

"It's supposed to be in the seventies. How about heading down to the beach?"

"The beach?"

"Don't worry," he said. "I'll do the surfing. You can do the admiring from the shoreline."

"Okay," I said. "I mean, I'd love to."

"Think your mom will let you go?"

"My dad will be on my side."

"So…it's a date?"

"It's a date," I said, rolling the phrase around on my tongue and loving the sweet taste of it.

Chapter Thirty

As thrilled as I was to see Adam again, the idea of that camera hidden in Larry's nest wouldn't stop nudging me. Even though the suspected arsonist had been arrested, Lindsay had the right to know what kind of loser Larry was. And even though she'd betrayed me, I felt the need to protect her. But I wasn't only defending Lindsay. I was heartbroken over Larry's unsuspecting wife and kids; worried about all the naïve girls Larry might be manipulating.

On Monday morning, before Adam picked me up, I texted Lindsay: *We need to talk. Important.*

Ten minutes later, her cold reply: *I have nothing to say to you.*

I typed: *You need to know something about Larry.*

Again, I waited. I pictured Lindsay cozied up next to Larry himself, maybe on the futon in his nest, sharing my texts, laughing behind my back. Then the thought changed to him and the blond I'd seen at the Waffle House. Larry convincing her she's the only one, making up disgusting lies about his wife, leaning in for a kiss…

When Lindsay didn't respond, I wrote, *Adam and I are worried about you.*

Her text came back within seconds: *MIND YOUR OWN BUSINESS!!!*

I stared at the caps and sighed.

***

Tiny seabirds zigzagged in front of the surf, digging into the sand for miniature crabs before the waves had a chance to chase them back again. A row of gulls sitting on an empty lifeguard stand kept me company as I watched Adam, a lone surfer, sitting on top of his yellow surfboard, waiting. The sun felt divine against my face. The salt air licked my cheeks. The wind was cool, and I zipped my sweat jacket up to my chin and pulled the hood down over my head. I sipped my Gatorade and watched from the large picnic blanket as an old man waved a metal detector over the dunes, a large pair of headphones covering his ears. The man bent down, dug into the sand, picked something up, and tossed it into a canvas bag attached to his belt. Nearby, a mother and a small boy collected seashells. Every once in a while, the child shouted, "Look, Mommy! It's the best one in the world!" Then he handed the treasure to his mother, who admired it and dropped it into a plastic bucket.

"Erica!"

I turned toward the call. Adam waved to me from across the water fifty yards away. I waved back. For an hour, I watched as he patiently waited for the wave he felt was his. Finally, a rising swell grew into a barely two-foot wave, and he stood up on the board. Without losing his balance, he glided across the top all the way to the break.

He picked up his board and jogged over to where I sat on the blanket.

"Waves are blown out," he said. "Perfect for skim boarding; not so much for surfing."

"It didn't seem like you were having too bad a time," I told him.

Adam stuck his surfboard upright in the sand. "I never have a bad time on the water," he said, drying himself with a beach towel. He shook his wet hair and pulled down the top of his wet suit until it fell around his waist. I saw the rugged contours of his bare chest, the shapely deltoids and biceps, and wondered how Lindsay could have let such a sexy boy slip through her fingers.

He plunked down beside me.

"I really miss coming down here," I told him. "I don't think there's a better smell than the ocean."

"Me too."

As if it was the most ordinary thing in the world, Adam put his arm around my shoulders.

"You look cold," he said, squeezing me.

"Not anymore."

Adam gazed out over the turquoise water. I stared at his profile. His nose was straight and strong. His lips were full, his cheek bones high. With his mop of black hair, and those thick lashes and brow, he could have passed for a Roman leader, just add a toga and an ivy wreath.

It came to me in a sudden rush that Lindsay had *accidentally* let the right guy get away; that eventually she would want him back. If Lindsay's relationship with Adam was an accident, maybe their breakup was an accident. That meant our being together could be an accident as well.

Adam pulled me to him, thankfully forcing out the fearful thoughts. He pushed back my hoodie and pressed a hand against the back of my head. First his lips touched mine, and then his tongue. I tasted salt and air and sunshine in that kiss, and I drank it up like an expensive glass of champagne.

He leaned back again. "Surfing makes me hungry."

I smiled. "Watching you surf makes me hungry."

He changed back into his clothes in the public restroom, and we drove to a small café on the boardwalk. Because it was a Monday, there were few customers seated on the restaurant's deck.

After we ordered a couple of burgers, I said, "I know we weren't going to talk about Lindsay..."

"But?"

"I tried to get in touch with her. You know, to tell her about Larry. She's flat-out ignoring me."

"Then that's that," Adam said.

"What about the camera?"

"If Lindsay gets hurt it's because she set herself up."

"She's in love with him, Adam. Girls do crazy things when they're in love."

"So do guys. But that doesn't mean they should be saved every time they do something stupid."

I shifted the conversation a bit. "Did you know that Larry had plans to leave Josephine for Lindsay?"

"What?" Adam laughed. "That'll *never* happen, Erica."

"How do you know?"

"First of all, there are a lot of girls out there. Who knows who else he's hooking up with? And secondly, Larry Taggert would never mess up his opportunity to advance. If you think he's high on himself now, wait until he makes chief. He'll toss Lindsay to the curb so fast, it'll skin her knees. If he hasn't done it already."

Our burgers came, and we devoured them in near silence. When we were through and the waitress had taken away our plates, I told Adam, "I want to help her."

"Help Lindsay? Why?"

"Because she helped me."

"She got *paid* to help you," Adam reminded me.

"She was still there for me."

"So you feel like you owe her?"

I nodded.

"You know, Erica, I crawl inside burning buildings. I pull people out of mangled cars. But I never expect anyone to pay me back."

"I want to keep trying."

"You'll be wasting your time."

"How do you know?" I asked.

"Trust me," he said. "You can't help someone who doesn't want to be helped."

What Adam said was true, but I couldn't stand the idea of Larry buying flowers for his wife when he'd just finished videotaping God-knew-who doing God-knew-what. The more I thought about it, the more I wanted Larry to get caught. Wanted to *help him* get caught. Even if it meant helping Lindsay in the process.

As Adam drove me back to Great Pines, I silently decided that with or without his blessing, I would make a plan. I would prove to Lindsay, myself, maybe even Adam, that everyone—not just me—needed saving every once in a while.

***

On Monday night, I sent Lindsay another message: *Please. Call me so I can tell you what I know.*

Lindsay: *The only thing that counts is what I know.*

Me: *There's a camera hidden in Larry's nest.*

Short pause.

Lindsay: *That's a lie.*

Me: *It's the truth.*

Lindsay: *How do you know?*

Me: *Adam and I both know.*

Lindsay: *How?*

Me: *We were there.*

Longer Pause.

Lindsay: *When?*

Me: *Friday night.*

Lindsay: *Bullshit. I would have seen you.*

So, Larry hadn't dumped her yet…

Me: *You must have left before we got there.*

Lindsay: *If you know so much, then tell me where the nest is.*

Me: *The old fire department.*

The next pause lasted a few minutes.

Lindsay: *Good for you. Now you can see I wasn't lying about our love for each other.*

Me: *He's videotaping you.*

Lindsay: *Liar.*

Me: *He doesn't love you.*

234

The last text Lindsay sent ended our conversation: *Fuck off.*

***

Adam decided to talk to Chief Miller in person, and I offered to tag along for support. After all, the main reason he'd made the decision to quit was because of what I'd shared with him.

In front of the firehouse, Adam pulled into a parking spot.

"Have you ever been inside?" he asked.

"No."

We stepped through the glass door to the right of the garage doors. A row of tall boots lined the hallway floor as far as I could see. Above the boots, orange and yellow jackets hung from wall pegs, along with helmets. An older man with blond-white hair sat behind a metal desk.

"Adam," he said, standing up.

"Morning, Chief Miller."

The man had a sweet grandfather's smile and an old-timer's accent like he belonged in the Appalachians. "Who is this?"

"This is my friend, Erica O'Donnell."

Chief Miller leaned over the desk and shook my hand. "Nice to meet you."

"You, too."

"Something on your mind?" he asked Adam.

"Yes, sir."

"Private matter?"

"No, sir," Adam said. "I just wanted to tell you that I'm planning on leaving the squad."

"May I ask why, son?"

"I have a ton of stuff on my plate with college right around the corner," Adam said. "That's sort of where my head is right now. So maybe you can take my name off the roster."

"Why don't we keep your name in that book just in case?"

"But you don't need to."

"Adam, for thirty years I've seen boys and men alike think they need some time off or want to leave altogether. They disappear for a while, but most of 'em slowly creep back in, coming to visit on an occasional Saturday, then putting on a helmet for old time's sake. Before you know it, a car accident or a fire goes over the wire, and lo and behold, those men are sitting right up there in the cab of that engine. So let's keep your name on the active list." Chief Miller winked. "Just in case."

A man's voice broke into the conversation. "Thought I heard a familiar voice."

Larry stood in the doorway. He was dressed in a pair of navy blue sweats and a long-sleeved T-shirt. On his feet he wore corduroy slippers. His eyes moved between Adam and me.

"Everything okay, Carchelli?" Larry asked.

Chief Miller said, "Adam has decided to go on a bit of a respite."

"That right?" Larry said. "Sort of an odd time to bail, considering all the fires we've had lately."

"We'll keep him in the book," Chief Miller said.

Larry again let his eyes travel between the two of us. Then he said to Adam, "That fire out at your school was a rough one. Could have used your help."

"Yes, I know," Adam said. "I wish...I mean...I couldn't come. Had other stuff to do."

"Other stuff?"

I shuffle from one foot to the other and stopped when Larry looked at my feet.

"Funny seeing the two of you here together," Larry said, suddenly smiling like a used car salesman. "I wanted to ask if you both can babysit this Friday."

Adam said, "Sorry. Busy."

Larry looked at me. He still wore that oversized grin. "You sure? It'll be extra money for Christmas."

I spoke to Larry's clean-shaven neck instead of his face so I wouldn't have to meet his eyes. "We're going to a…party…"

"A party," Adam repeated.

"No worries," Larry said. "I'm sure I can round up somebody else."

"What about Lindsay?" I suggested.

"She has other plans."

Neither Adam nor I responded.

Chief Miller said, "Keep in touch, Adam. You're one of the best volunteers we've had."

After a quick and uncomfortable goodbye to Larry and Chief Miller, Adam and I made our way across the parking lot.

In the truck, Adam's jaw was clenched tight. "I don't want you around him anymore."

I didn't reply. As I reached for my seatbelt, I noticed the yellow volunteer fireman's jacket still laid out on the cab's back seat. Black gloves and a yellow helmet sat on top.

Heading back onto the road, the chief's words, *Just in case*, entered my brain, and I had a strong feeling they'd stuck with Adam, too.

Chapter Thirty-one

Grayson High reeked like a Southern plantation smokehouse.

At lunchtime on Thursday, Adam and I ate together with a few of his buddies. Since the third-floor cafeteria would be off-limits for another week or so, the second-floor cafeteria was overrun, so we got there early. Some students who brought their own lunches ate at tables set up in the lobby. Pods of other kids chose to eat in the second-floor hallway instead, sitting on the floor against the wall like backstage groupies after a concert.

Lindsay hid from me so well I would have sworn she'd moved. Not seeing her actually offered some relief. But on Friday after school, as I sat at the kitchen table dipping apple slices into the peanut butter jar, a text from Lindsay popped up on my cell: *Have a problem.*

I didn't respond.

Immediately, another text came through: *Can you babysit tonight?*

I almost wrote: *Are you on crack?* Instead, I typed: *Are you kidding?*

Lindsay: *It's my birthday weekend.*

Me: *I will never sit for Larry Taggert again.*

Lindsay: *Then do it for me. You owe me one.*

I had tried to be honest with her. Had tried to warn her.

Me: *No.*

Lindsay: *Please.*

Me: *No.*

Lindsay: *I need you to.*

Me: *Too bad.*

Lindsay: *Larry has something he wants to ask me. I think he might be proposing.*

I almost fell off the kitchen chair. There was no way in any universe that Larry would propose to Lindsay. Even if he wasn't an arsonist, and even if he wasn't seeing other girls, that hidden camera made him a disgusting creep.

Me: *In case you forgot, you told me to fuck off.*

Lindsay: *I'm sorry.*

Me: *You're not sorry. You want to use me, the same way you used Adam.*

Pause.

Lindsay: *Just this once. Please, Erica.*

Me: *You need someone to look after his kids? Do it yourself. Sounds like you're signing up to be their stepmom anyway.*

Lindsay did not respond.

***

That night, I begged my parents to go out on a date together, especially since Dad had been away so much.

"You're the only parents I know who never go anywhere."

After I assured them that Adam would hang out with me, they made last-minute reservations at a restaurant down by the beach. Dad whistled as my mother came down the stairs, her bluish black hair swishing against her shoulders, her tats covered by a knitted, long-sleeved dress, a pair of high heels showing off her runner's calves.

I had traded my support hose for compression socks and wore my jeans, a comfy black turtleneck, and my Uggs. My long hair was curled and rouge brightened my cheeks.

"You look especially pretty tonight," my mother said.

"So do you."

We smiled at one another's reflection in the hall mirror.

The doorbell rang. My dad greeted Adam as he stepped into the foyer, the cool evening air sneaking in behind him.

"Be safe," my mother told me, pushing a strand of hair from my forehead.

"Behave," Dad told Adam, putting on his extra-deep voice usually saved for teleconferences.

Adam and I shut the door quickly behind them. Together we cooked a store-bought pizza and chose a Netflix comedy. We snuggled on the couch holding hands, my head against his shoulder for a long while.

An hour into the movie, which was way more stupid than funny, my cell chimed.

I stared at my phone. "It's Lindsay again."

Adam paused the movie. "*Again?*"

"She had the nerve to ask me to babysit so she could spend her birthday with Larry. I blew her off." I glanced at the text. "How's this for drama? She says she's stranded."

"Where's Larry?"

I shrugged and ignored the text, but as soon as we restarted the movie, my phone rang. I pressed the button and waved for Adam to pause the movie again.

"What?" I asked with deliberate meanness.

Lindsay panted into the phone. "I need someone to come and get me."

"Why?"

She sniffled into the phone. "Larry cancelled our date tonight."

"And why should I care about that?"

"No, Erica," she said. "You don't understand—"

"I do understand. That's why I'm hanging up now." Which I did. "She is really starting to annoy me," I told Adam.

My phone dinged. I read the text: *Please!!! I'm in trouble!!!*

I sighed and called her back. "You are totally selfish to think you're the only one—"

Lindsay cried into the phone. I put it on speaker so Adam could listen. In between sobs she meandered her way through the evening's events.

"When I asked Larry why he was cancelling, he said that Josephine was at her mother's. And since you wouldn't babysit for us, he wouldn't be able to see me."

I ignored Lindsay's finger-pointing.

"So," she went on, "I told Larry I'd come over, you know, and help *him* babysit, and we could be together that way, but he said no, it was way too risky. So then I said, 'Bring the kids with you. We can take them out for ice cream and cake.' He said that was a stupid idea. He called me *stupid*…" She sobbed into the phone. "He cancelled, Erica, for the first time ever. And it's my birthday weekend. So I did something…something crazy…"

I waited.

"I drove to his house, and all the lights were on, and his SUV was in the driveway. So then I thought I'd knock on the door, and Larry would realize how much he wanted to see me, and he'd let me in, and we could hang out in his family room, and not have to go to the warehouse where it smells like pee…"

"Where are you now?" I asked.

"Downtown."

"What are you doing down there?"

"I wanted to see him."

"Rewind," I told her, confused. "I thought you went to Larry's *house*."

"I did," she explained. "I drove back and forth a few times, but I worried that a neighbor might see me, so I parked my truck around the corner, and then I snuck into his backyard and peeked through the curtains."

"Oh, Lindsay…"

Adam rolled his eyes.

Lindsay said, "I saw a blond girl playing with the kids in the family room, but I didn't see Larry."

"Obviously, he found another babysitter," I told her.

"Duh, I know that!" she shouted. "But he *told me he couldn't find one*. He *lied* to me. On my birthday! I called his cell after I saw that scumbag in his house, and he wouldn't answer his phone. I texted him like twenty times and still no answer."

"Maybe he went to the movies…"

"No! He would never cancel our date to go to the movies. *Never*. I know him. Anyway, when I got back to my truck and drove past the front of his house again, I saw that his SUV was gone. He must have left while I was in his backyard. I figured that maybe he went to our secret place alone. You know how guys are, needing space and all. Or maybe he planned to set something up for later, you know, like a surprise for me or something…" She bawled into the phone.

Adam and I waited as Lindsay got herself under control.

"But that's not what happened," she finally said. "I drove past the alley where he usually parks. I was sure I'd find his Explorer there, but it was empty. I wracked my brain trying to think of where he might have gone, believing that everything was okay, you know, that if he suddenly showed up and saw me, he'd be surprised and happy. So, I decided to look for him. I had my fingers crossed that maybe he'd parked his SUV in a different place. I dressed in my super high heels and my awesome skinny jeans, but I could barely walk without my heels clacking, so I tippy-toed all the way to the other side, thinking if he was inside, the door would be unlocked, because sometimes he leaves it open when he first gets there to air the place out, you know, cuz it's so stuffy. The door was open, and I started to go in, but then I heard a shuffling inside, and I suddenly had this crazy feeling that it wasn't Larry, so I said, 'Screw this,' and I ran back to my truck. While I was running, I tripped on some old cobblestones and tore my jeans and skinned my cheek. I took off my shoes and ran in my bare feet, but I'd left the headlights on by mistake, and when I tried to get the truck started, it wouldn't turn over. It's dead."

"Where are you now?" I asked.

"In my truck. Behind the building. Erica, I'm really scared."

"Lindsay, call the police."

"No. They'll call my mother."

"Then call Larry."

"I did," she said. "He won't answer his phone. What if it was him up there in our nest? What if it turns out he's with someone else? Oh my God, I don't want to know…" She whimpered into the phone. "Please. I need you two to come and help me. Adam will know what to do."

"How do you know I'm with Adam?" I asked.

"I saw his truck when I drove past your house."

Adam mouthed the word "stalker" and I smacked his arm.

Lindsay said, "I know you told him about Larry and me. And why wouldn't you?" She paused, and her next words came out in a whisper: "Hurry, Erica. It's totally dark…what if someone sees me, just sitting here…"

I looked at Adam. He frowned and put up his hands in surrender.

"Stay put, Linds," I told her. "We'll get there as soon as we can."

Chapter Thirty-two

The radio's country music drowned out the somber thoughts invading my brain. I had never been so worried about another person before, even if that person was standing on my last nerve. I suddenly had an inkling of what my parents went through dealing with a kid like me.

The song ended and a reporter came on with the news. I barely listened as the woman churned out the headlines: a lumber truck accident on Interstate 95; the Farmer's Market this Saturday overflowing with homemade Christmas gifts; a man held for arson released earlier today…

Adam turned up the volume.

"…Raymond Parker, Junior, who owns RP Farms in Harkins Township, said he was filled with relief he'd been released. He told reporters he was never near the locations where suspicious fires had occurred recently, including Grayson High School; that he's been spending most of his time at a hospice center in Fairfield, where his wife suffers from cancer. Mr. Parker says he thanks God they released him; that being falsely accused was a grueling experience. Authorities are now convinced the arsonist is still on the loose, but they aren't offering any additional information at this time. In other news today, a fisherman off the coast of Hatteras—"

Adam clicked off the radio.

In dark silence, the two of us made our way toward the off-ramp. I texted Lindsay to let her know we were only minutes away, but she didn't reply. When I called her, it went straight to her voicemail.

"Something's wrong," I said.

"Try calling Larry," Adam suggested.

"Are you kidding?"

"It's because of him that we're down here at all."

My nervous fingers pulled up Larry's number, but after five rings, the call went to his voicemail. I hung up.

Downtown, we reached the ancient firehouse and headed down the side street. Adam slowed the truck. The cul-de-sac behind the building was dark and empty of vehicles. Stray pieces of paper trash swirled around, trapped in tiny whirlpools of air.

"She said her truck was behind the building," I said, trying to keep my voice steady so I wouldn't slip into straight-jacket mode. "Where is she?" Blood rushed from my neck to my face to my skull. I wrapped my scarf more tightly around my neck and pulled my beanie down over my ears so Adam wouldn't see how flushed I'd become.

He drove to the end of the block and parked in the same spot as a week earlier. He pulled his heavy-duty flashlight out of the glove box and put his pocketknife in his jacket pocket. He said nothing as he came around and opened my door.

"You're letting me come with you?" I asked, surprised.

"I think it might be safer."

Our hands clung to one another's as we hiked away from the river and up the shadowy sidewalk. Cockroaches scurried. A rat moved slowly along the gutter across the street. Pieces of gravel and chunks of dry earth crunched under our feet as we peered into empty cul-de-sac.

I called Lindsay's cell again. "Still not answering," I whispered. "We should call the police."

"No," Adam said. "No police."

"But—"

"Maybe she already found Larry. Or maybe she brought us down here for some other reason altogether."

"Like what?" I asked.

"If she's willing to have an affair with a married man, I wouldn't put anything past her. You really want to get the authorities involved in her stupid games? And the police will probably call our parents, too. I can see your mother now. She'd never let me near you again."

I thought about his reasoning. "Okay," I agreed. "No police. But we can't leave, Adam. Lindsay's counting on us."

He fanned out his arms. "Then tell me where her truck is."

I didn't answer.

We stepped out of the cul-de-sac and walked around the front, past the two garage doors, to the other side of the building. The narrow door stood open a crack like it was offering a private invitation.

"Let me go in first," Adam whispered, pushing the door wide. He stepped inside, shone the flashlight around, and motioned for me to follow. "I don't think anyone's here."

"But the door was open—"

As soon as my words entered the darkness, loud footsteps thumped outside, along the front of the building.

My heart pounded in my ears. I grabbed Adam's arm. "Somebody's out there."

"Stay here," Adam whispered.

"Maybe it's Lindsay."

"Or someone else."

I pointed a stern finger. "You've got three minutes before I call the police."

He pushed me behind the door, put a finger to his lips, and headed outside. I heard his boots as they made their way down the sidewalk and into the night. Then all was silent.

Adam had taken the flashlight with him. Until he got back, I would remain alone in the old dark building, the perfect setting for a *Ghost Hunters* episode.

I poked my head through the doorway but could only see dirt bordering the side of the building. Tiny hairs rose on the nape of my neck. Cold air streaming in through the cracked door attacked my cheeks. Tremors moved through my body, but it was easy to tell the difference between chills from winter weather and chills from fear. I quickly pulled myself back inside, afraid of being abandoned, but more afraid of being exposed.

A sliver of light from a distant streetlamp trickled through the rectangular windows at the top of the garage doors, lending me a bit of help as I awkwardly moved toward the staircase. I sat on the bottom step and silently counted to thirty, my shaking arms wrapped around my bent knees. I took slow deep breaths...in and out...in and out...

Why the hell wasn't Adam back yet?

"Shit shit shit…"

As the profanity slipped through my lips, a shuffling sound against the upstairs floor tumbled down the steps. My head jerked upward. I stood up fast, instinctively crossed my legs, and called out without thinking, "Hello?"

The shuffling stopped. I froze. No one answered, but I was convinced I heard breathing. I opened my mouth to speak and shut it again, placing a hand against my lips.

Maybe it was a rat.

Then again, maybe it was Lindsay.

Adam! my mind screamed. *If Lindsay is upstairs, then who did you run after?*

I peeked into the shadows along the staircase above me, my eyes trying to adjust to the dark.

What if the person upstairs wasn't Lindsay, but someone looking for something to entertain them on a Friday night? What if that person turned out to be a desperate homeless man? A drug addict? A maniac?

Or Larry?

My cell phone nearly fell to the floor as my gloved hand cautiously pulled it from my pocket. With my teeth, I pulled off both gloves. I scrolled to the word "Adam." It rang six times before going to his voicemail.

While weighing my limited options—whether to call the police or make a run for Adam's truck—a girl's whisper floated down from upstairs: "Hello?"

I nearly wet my pants with relief as I grabbed the railing that led up the metal steps.

"Lindsay?" I whispered, peering into the shadowed abyss at the top of the stairs. "It's me, Erica."

Apparently, neither one of us had the courage to use our normal daytime voice. Hers was so soft, I could barely hear her. "Come up here. Please."

"You come down here."

She paused, then said, "I can't."

I placed a foot on the second step. "Are you hurt?"

"Of course I'm hurt," she said. "Everyone gets hurt. Even the men we love."

Darkness like a heavy tent pressed down on my head. Gripping the railing, I took another step up.

"Please, Erica." Her words carried an odd combination of patience and desperation.

"Is Larry with you?" I asked.

She let out a small laugh. "No."

This fact should have offered some relief, but it did not. I ascended slowly, counting steps. The light from outside disappeared. When the railing was no longer beneath my hand, I knew I was standing on the upstairs landing. I peered into the dark, trying to make out the layout from when Adam and I had discovered the nest. But without Adam's bright flashlight I was blind, and without his hand in mine, I was terrified.

I tried to say the word "Linds," but it entered the room as a squeak. With a shaking hand, I lit my cell phone. The glow moved like an alien's headlight around the room. Everything appeared the same as before: the futon on the floor, the shelves over on the side, the Dalmatian statue—

Her voice startled me from somewhere across the cave, but

my phone's light didn't reach that far.

"I need you, Erica," she whispered.

"Need me for what?" I asked, fear again rolling through my bones.

"I'll show you."

But I did not want her to show me. Not without Adam by my side. I would call the police, something I should have done to begin with. Holding my cell phone out in front of me, I tried to focus on the glowing keypad.

I let my finger hit the first number, and then the second, and as I was about to press the last digit, the lighted 9-1 became a psychedelic trail as my cell phone slipped from my hands, tumbling through the shadows to the floor, falling on its face, taking the light with it. I bent over, felt around, and clutched the phone in my fist.

Then I stood.

The familiar buzz of white noise entered my ear drums. Heat rose to my cheeks and my feet grew numb inside my furry Uggs. My heart climbed into my throat. My stomach rolled beneath a twenty-foot wave. *CLIFF!* I crossed my legs fast. My body was designed to cave under the weight of the spell, but I refused to give in. Slow breaths moved in and out of my lungs by rote but with precision. The white spots in front of my eyes dissolved. The spell ebbed, leaving me with clammy hands and shaking legs.

I held the phone out in front of me again, brightening before my eyes. The 9-1 still showed on the screen. I managed to press the third number. Just as my thumb went to tap the call button, the pounding of heavy boots rose up behind me, and before I had a chance to turn, a piece of material slammed against my mouth and nose. I grappled but failed. My flailing hand lost control of my cell phone and again it hurtled toward the floor. I gasped for air but found none. Only the smell of something sweet, strong, and suffocating as it entered my sinuses.

In less time than it took to give in to one of my spells, I fell into the arms of the shadows; banished to a place darker than an abandoned firehouse; a place emptier than the life of a girl with syncope; a place where the world disappeared, and I became nothing.

Chapter Thirty-three

Was I at a barbeque? Was there a juicy Christmas ham nearby? Maybe I was lying on the linoleum floor at the Waffle House surrounded by plates of freshly cooked bacon and hash browns.

I was flat on my back. Beneath me there was softness, and under my throbbing head what felt like a pillow. My fingers and toes wiggled, but when I tried to move my arms and legs, they wouldn't work. My eyelids fluttered open, eyes darting around, expecting to find objects that would help me remember.

The universe was black.

"Hello?" I croaked through my burning throat. "Is someone there? Am in a hospital?"

No one answered, but I was not alone. Soft breathing other than my own filled the pitch-dark room. The scent of fragrant shampoo or perfume lay just beneath the smell of fried meat.

A piece of furniture scraped against the floor. Heavy footsteps followed.

The darkness suddenly came alive with a stripe of purple-yellow light which bounced around the room. Shadows jumped across the cracked ceiling over my head.

At that moment, everything that had happened before hitting the floor tumbled into me: Lindsay's frantic phone call...driving downtown...Adam running down the sidewalk...Adam not returning...

A lit candle sat on the top shelf of the bookcase. Through blurry eyes, I spotted someone in an orange coat sitting on a chair in the corner. Legs up. Arms wrapped around bent knees. Fingernails coated in bright polish. I could barely make out the outline of the navy blue hat, the one Lindsay had loaned me when the weather turned cool; the one she had demanded back after our fallout.

I wanted to see more clearly in the dim light, worked to raise my head above the pillow. But each time I tried, I fell back, exhausted.

Why couldn't I sit up? What was wrong with me?

"Please help me," I begged as the light on the ceiling flickered.

"Help *you?*" she whispered. "No, Erica. *You're* going to help *me.*"

The wool hat rose into the air as she stood. Heavy shoes thumped against the floor as she moved beyond my sightline.

"Water," I said.

"No water. Sorry."

The smell of grizzle or rotting meat was all around me now. I wiggled my fingers and toes, aching for the rest of me to follow, but when I commanded my arms and legs to move, they refused.

My eyes traveled down my body. My coat and gloves and boots had been removed. A draft swished around my head and neck, and I knew that my beanie and scarf were gone, too. I lay in my jeans and turtleneck and socks on the same mattress Lindsay had bragged about.

I was in the middle of their nest.

My long sleeves had been rolled up to the elbows. Each arm was stretched out straight, my fingertips dangling over the edge of the narrow mattress.

And then I saw why I couldn't move: A thin white rope was tightly wound around each of my wrists. The tips of my fingers brushed against the floor. I raised my head as far as it could manage, straining my neck. My legs were straight and tied together at the ankles by the same type of rope. I yanked hard, but the ropes didn't budge.

She appeared at the foot of the futon with the blue wool hat pulled down past her eyebrows. The bottom half of her face looked blurry and far away, like a photo taken in bad light by a photographer with a shaking hand.

"Untie me," I said, forcing my weak voice to carry as much weight as possible.

She mumbled something unintelligible as she turned away, humming as she headed toward the bookcase against the wall. With my eyes barely adjusted to the muted light, I recognized the orange coat she wore: a fireman's jacket, identical to the one all the certified firefighters wore.

Including Larry.

Moving like a ghost, she grabbed the candle and brought it to the end of the bed, holding it near her cheek. For a moment, I was afraid she would set the wool hat on fire. But that fear was replaced by a more overpowering one, as the flickering light showed the soft angle of her jaw, the roundness of her face. As she stood there, she pushed the hat back until it sat high on her head like it belonged on a Doctor Seuss character.

She grinned like the Grinch.

Insanity flickered in her eyes.

Anger reddened her cheeks.

And my frozen mind suddenly comprehended that the person standing at the foot of the bed, although Lindsay's relative size and shape, was not Lindsay at all.

It was Josephine.

Her incessant grin terrified me more than the fact that she was wearing Lindsay's hat.

"Where is she?" I asked.

"Who?"

"Lindsay."

"Oh," Josephine said. "Was tonight Lindsay's night?"

"Untie me," I commanded, ignoring the cruel rope burns as I moved my wrists in wild circles. Fear oozed from every pore. Anxiety dripped down the back of my throat. Even though it was nearly freezing outside, and not much warmer inside the old firehouse, sweat trickled from my forehead to my temples and into my hair.

"Funny," Josephine said. "The moment I heard someone downstairs, I knew it was you. Something about the way y'all...shuffle your feet. Like you're afraid if you pick them up when you walk, you might trip over them."

"You were waiting for me?"

Her shoulders moved up and down in a deliberately slow shrug. "You or whoever else happened to drop in."

She walked away from the bed again, taking the dim light

with her. She slid one of the blackout curtains along the track and looked through the small window.

"Temperature in the low thirties," she said like a bored Southern weatherman. "Winds from the northwest. Cold front moving across the Southeast. Super. Duper. Dry." She opened the window and took a deep breath. "Seems all the humidity went out the window…"

"Please, Josephine, if I've done something—"

She spun around and the wool hat fell to the floor. Her unbrushed brown curls fell across her face and stood out in a cockeyed mess all over her head. "*Done something?*"

I glanced around the brutal environment, my eyes as alert as a tiger's, darting back and forth from Josephine to the shadows on the cracked ceiling to the tiny open window, too small to crawl through, and too high to jump from. My analytical brain worked to find a way out. The binding ropes were attached to something in the shadows beyond the mattress that held them in place.

There was no way out.

"Bookshelves are a nice touch," Josephine said, walking toward the futon. "And the blackout curtains. Just like the Hilton. Did y'all help him decorate?"

On the end of the mattress, she sat near my feet, the candle still in her hand.

"I suspected for a long time," she said. "It just took me a little while to plan it out. But we true-blue Southern gals are born with patience, aren't we?" Her voice was calm and smooth, like she was speaking to a confidant over a cappuccino. "I used to be madly in love with him, too, you know. He was my hero."

Josephine frowned. "My sweet Larry. Firefighting was what drew me to him. His dedication to helping mankind. He seemed so happy each time he was called to action, each time he fought a blaze. A happy husband is an attentive husband. So, I thought, why not make him even happier? Why not help Larry become a small-town hero?"

She looked at her nails as though she were inspecting the color.

"It was easy setting them," she said after a moment. "Especially in the heat of the summer. At first they were only small fires, a little one that popped up in a trash can or near the campground late at night. But by autumn, just as I was growing fearless, well, my plan backfired. Pardon the pun."

She snickered at her own lifeless joke.

"Larry started moving *away* from me. The more fires he fought, the less I was the center of his world. I could have been any one of his groupies, for all he cared. I had to buy myself flowers. Had to twist his arm to go out to dinner or see a movie. So we'd have some time together. Alone. But we barely spoke to each other. I could tell he had something on his mind other than me. Even the kids could sense it. He wasn't in love with their mama anymore. He was in love with her."

"*Her*?" I squeaked.

"*Fire*. She stole him away from me. But Fire didn't come alone; she brought Fame with her. Once upon a time, Larry Taggert shared the glory with me, his wife, the one who put him through the Academy, then quit her nursing job to manage his home and push out a couple of babies; the one who gave up her life's work so hubby could move up the ranks in his own career.

But the bastard grew selfish. All my hard work up in smoke. All those months of planning, just to keep him happy…"

"It was you…"

"It was me who put him up on that pedestal to begin with, so I guess I'm partially to blame. But he kept the glory all to himself. His little wifey wasn't needed anymore; I was just another peon expected to bow down to him. For a while, I believed I could make it work. I shared him with Fire. But that turned out to be a combustible combination…"

"You killed a homeless person," I said. "An innocent man."

"Larry should have been more careful," she said. "Everyone should be more careful not to sneak around in someone else's world. Don't you agree?"

Josephine looked toward the window and cocked her head as if someone had called her name. When she faced me again, her eyes were wide with excitement.

"Stealing lard from my mama's restaurant was the easy part. God knows she had enough in storage to choke an elephant. And when I found Larry's little hidden camera, it was like winning the lottery. Then, when they released that poor pig farmer, their temporary scapegoat, I thought, how lucky can one woman get?"

She looked at a thin watch on her wrist.

"I must ask you, Erica, since it is getting late, and I still have a few things on my honey-do list, how does it feel to be caught sleeping with another woman's man?"

"No…it wasn't me…"

"Oh, I know it wasn't *only* you. I know about his entourage of girls. Ya'll are on the tapes he made, surprise surprise."

"What? No—"

"I know how upset you must be, thinking you were his one and only."

"I never did anything with your husband, Josephine. I swear."

Josephine pulled her cell phone out of the pocket of the orange jacket. She pressed a button and held it up for me to see, even though I couldn't make out the numbers. "What do we have here?" she asked. "Looks like you called Larry just a little while ago."

"That's because...I..."

"You wanted to meet him here? Well, Larry certainly is a popular man." She scrolled through the phone. "Let's see...Lindsay called him tonight as well. Though she has much less restraint than you. Sixteen times, if you can believe that. And why didn't he take your calls, you might be wondering? Couples often buy two of the same thing, you know, like his and her bathrobes. Heck, switching cell phones was simple. All I had to do was swap covers. I almost answered your call, by the way, just for fun. But speaking with you in person is way more entertaining."

"How did you know I'd be here? I didn't even know until tonight."

"I didn't know it would be you for sure," she said. "But after following the idiot around for a few weeks, it would take a deer in the headlights not to see the pattern. The wifey goes to see her dying mama, the hubby goes and gets some tail. Who did he get to babysit tonight? Obviously it isn't you. Some other girl? I'm sure he never runs out of prospective pubescent whores to choose from. So...how did this work, exactly? Did he have y'all on rotation? Sweet Jesus, I had no idea my husband could be so cliché. Bible Study on Wednesdays, barbeque on Thursdays, a little strange for dessert on the weekends…"

"We were never together, I swear," I told her. "I think your husband is a loser."

"You say that now, after you get your panties caught in a trap. I've seen the look in your eyes, the same look all the girls give the firemen, like they're a gang of modern-day saints. But they're nothing more than narcissistic Neanderthals."

"You're wrong," I told her. "Most firemen want to help people. That's why they put their lives on the line."

"You are so naïve. But I have to forgive you for that. I was the same way once. Back before I knew that being married to a hero would cost me. So tell me, what did you think of the Larry Taggert Memorial? Find anything interesting? And how about our bedroom? Did you happen to snoop through his drawers? Or mine, perhaps?"

I said nothing as the flash of guilt moved across my face.

"Gutsy," Josephine said. "And where are my letters now, because, let's say for old-time's sake, I'd like to have them back."

"I don't have your—"

"And my charm bracelet. And my earrings. Did you steal those, or did one of the other girls? Did Larry take them himself? That's the question of the century. But, I suppose it doesn't matter now. I bought the bracelet at a Belk sale. And those earrings aren't real, in case y'all wondered. Cubic Zirconium."

"I didn't know—"

"I was a teenager once, Erica. I know how boring it can be to watch someone's babies on a Friday or Saturday night. You stole some letters, woop-de-do. And some cheap-o earrings that I don't give a pig's snout about."

"I never stole anything!"

"Maybe you did, maybe you didn't. But y'all looked, didn't you? I'm sure you read Larry's I'm-so-fucking-awesome ledger. Lord knows hanging photos on the wall wasn't enough for his ego. But I'll bet you didn't dig deep enough through my granddaddy's old desk. Bet y'all didn't find the surprise I left for the police."

"Surprise?"

"A second and much more interesting book. At least it will be to the police when they find it. I've become quite the handwriting expert as of late. Plenty of time to practice when your husband's never home."

I said nothing.

"Well," Josephine said, "it doesn't matter what you do or don't know. Just like all the other trailer trash in this town, you're expendable." The yellow jacket let out the sound of crinkled rubber as she bent down and picked up the wool hat. She twirled it on her finger as she spoke. "I found this in the back of Larry's Explorer."

"It's not mine," I told her.

"Oh. Maybe it belongs to Lindsay…"

I didn't respond as Josephine twirled the hat.

"What's the matter, Erica, you really didn't know your bestie was cheating on you with the man who was cheating on me?"

"I was never with your husband!"

"And I really hate to be a washwoman," she went on, "but I think he's been with half the girls in this town. At least that's what I gather by the videos. So many girls…so little time." She laughed as she tossed the blue hat onto the bed next to me. "You bitches are spoiled. Lindsay, wearing those short skirts and ridiculous high heels. You, using your pitiful disease. Did you want Larry to feel sorry for you? Like that day at the picnic? Feel sorry for poor little Erica, save her from the evils of fainting spells."

"I don't faint on purpose," I said flatly.

"Maybe not. But y'all sure know how to use what you've got to your advantage." A ring of keys appeared in Josephine's hand. She dangled the bunch in the air. "I wonder when King Larry will realize he's missing his precious keys to Teenager Town?"

"You incriminated him," I said.

"He incriminated himself," Josephine said, smiling again. "I could have ratted him out regarding his underage indiscretions, but that's not half as fun as framing him for arson. I like the ironic twist in the whole thing, don't you?"

"He's probably on his way over here right now."

"Afraid not," she said. "I told him to meet me at my mama's out in Feltonville tonight…that she was taking a turn for the worse." She put her hand against her chest in feigned Southern surprise. "Won't Larry be beside himself when he finds out she had a stroke a month ago. She's been in a care facility ever since. Can't even feed herself."

She laughed like a madwoman.

When she was through, she said, "In a little while, I'll make two anonymous calls from that ancient phone booth across the street. One to the police—there just happens to be a container of grease hidden in Larry's spare tire compartment—the other call to our trusted fire department to put out a blaze that suddenly popped up in old firehouse number three. Oh," she added, patting my foot, "I almost forgot to mention…that second call will go out a bit too late."

"Please, Josephine," I said, crying. "You have to believe me. I was never with Larry. Take another look at the tapes."

"You think I get my kicks watching my husband with other women? Five-minute's worth was all I could stomach. Anyway, I've already mailed a copy to the police and a copy to the news station. They'll get them first thing tomorrow."

She looked somewhere beyond me and whispered, "In case you didn't know, Erica, fire doesn't discriminate. It won't feel sorry for you like Larry did. Oxygen, fuel, skin…to fire, it all tastes yummy."

I cried harder, tears dripping past my ears and soaking the flat pillow beneath my head. "You'll be caught. No one will believe that any of this was Larry's doing."

"Of course they will. They'll think Larry and one of his pieces of jailbait had a spat, and she threatened to spread the affair on social media, so Larry was forced to get rid of the evidence. It's a perfect crime of love-gone-wrong."

"They'll put the pieces together."

"I don't think so," Josephine said. "I've crossed my tiny *t*'s. Dotted my itty-bitty *i*'s. I haven't missed a single thing."

"You missed one thing," I told her.

"And what is that?"

"Adam."

"What does Adam have to do with anything?"

"How do you think I got here?" I said. "You think I drove myself? I don't even have a driver's license!"

"Adam drove you here? He knows about you and Larry?"

"There is nothing between me and Larry! Adam and I came down here together. He's here." I screamed then, hoping that the open window would help carry my voice. "Adam, help me! I'm upstairs!"

Josephine looked around the room. "Well, where is he, honey, playing olly-olly-oxen-free?"

"He heard something. Outside. But he'll be back. I know it."

"Y'all willing to bet your life on it?" she asked. When I didn't answer, she said, "Let's wait a bit. Let's see if Adam magically appears."

"He will."

Josephine walked over to the window and stared down at the sidewalk below.

"He will," I said again. "I know it."

Chapter Thirty-four

It felt like eternity before Josephine said, "Looks like your imagination isn't strong enough to make someone appear out of thin air."

"I'm telling you, Josephine, we came here together."

"The only thing that matters is he's not here now."

Josephine was right. That was all that mattered.

"Adam!" I screamed again.

Josephine yanked the window shut and slid the curtain back in place, blocking out the pale streetlight. She pulled something out of a black bag by the chair and placed it on her head: a fireman's helmet with the number thirty-two on the front. The oversized helmet wobbled as she clomped toward me in the boots.

She knelt down next to the futon, gently pushed some wispy hairs from my forehead, and whispered, "You weren't the first girl, but by the grace of God, you will be the last."

Moving away from the mattress, she went to the corner off my right shoulder, a place I could not see.

Sulfur filled my sinuses. The room suddenly grew bright, making me flinch. Furniture shadows danced along the walls. I smelled cured meat. Fried chicken. Hush puppies. It was as though all the deep-fried items from a Southern restaurant menu had been left to rot.

What will it feel like to burn to death?

I had once stumbled onto a horrific video of Tibetan monks committing suicide by fire, sitting passively as the flames ate them alive. I pictured my parents, identifying their only child's charred body at the morgue.

"Please, Josephine," I begged. "I'll do anything. I'll help you get Larry behind bars. We can turn him in together. The two of us..."

No answer.

I forced my neck to stretch as far as it could go. My eyes moved wildly around the room.

Josephine was gone. Evil orange flames had taken her place.

"Please!!" I screamed.

I prayed that Josephine was somewhere downstairs, that she hadn't abandoned me, that she'd have a sudden change of heart.

Blood pounded in my ears. Endless streams of tears nearly choked me. I shook my hands and feet as hard as I could, but the ropes seemed to enjoy every ounce of my struggle.

"Adam! Someone! Help!"

The smell of burning fabric and wood came next. I could feel the weight of the smoke as it hovered over me, trying to squelch my struggle, trying to keep me from calling out, which I managed to do one last time: "Adam!" The black smoke swirled around me like a miniature tornado trapped between cement walls.

Maybe it's better to be unconscious instead of wide awake and aware of every terrifying moment.

For the first time ever, I wished for a fainting spell. I held my breath and waited, and thought how strange it was that I would end up in a firehouse at the end, when it was fire that had led me to this very moment.

As my eyes fluttered, the word "ironic" slipped through my lips and entered the smoky room.

***

When I was five, I burned the tip of my finger while secretly lighting a match in my playhouse. For hours after I was drawn to its smell.

My own burned flesh.

Now, as I teetered on the edge of the black hole, that smell was mine again, only this time it was more than a little girl's finger; so much more than a blister that would scab over and heal in a matter of days, barely leaving a scar.

I was slowly suffocating. Smoke covered me like a giant octopus, forcing its tentacles into my nostrils and down my throat; forcing me to give up the last of my air.

Clomping boots again sounded through the room.

Had Josephine had second thoughts? Come to finish what she'd started? Was I imagining things? I tried to open my eyes, but the burning smoke forced them shut.

Something yanked hard on the ropes that held my wrists and ankles. My mind screamed, but the actual words fizzled out somewhere between my brain and throat. I was convinced Josephine was tightening them, making sure they were going to hold. I jerked my head from side to side. The strong hands forced something against my nose and mouth.

She was going to do it herself. In case the fire didn't complete the job. Leave nothing to chance.

A sense of calm came over me as my body sank into the mattress. I would give in to what I knew was inevitable.

This is what it feels like to die.

First, the searing in my wrists was nearly too much to bear, but then the pain abruptly ended. My hands and feet wiggled with freedom. My mind sobbed with relief.

This is what it feels like to leave the earth.

I floated upward. A tiny religious part of my brain assured me I was in the hands of God, lifting me up to heaven. If I gave in to the feeling, there would be no more pain. No more fainting spells. No more counting down to a cure. The fire would melt away all uncertainties of living and dying; all fears that had plagued me up until now.

Once you give in to fire, it becomes your friend; your savior.

Up and up I rose, my body limp, my arms and legs dangling like they were no longer a part of me. Soon, the clouds would be my bed and all pain will have vanished forever.

Chapter Thirty-five

As I moved through the air, a stream of cold rushed over me. At the same time, radiating warmth came from below, like I was being held in a mother's arms. *Maybe God is a woman*, I thought and smiled. Weightlessness wrapped itself around me. I drifted up and out and over, accepting the cool air into my spirit-lungs. My breathing grew loud in my own ears, as though I was breathing outside of myself. I flew and flew, and my smile wouldn't go away—

And then, in an instant, everything changed.

My wrists burned with unimaginable pain. Coughing spasms took hold of my lungs. Soot covered the back of my throat like thick tar. A ringing in my head nearly split it in two. My throat muscles suddenly craved to scream, but could not.

How can this be heaven?

Warm heavy breaths rose and fell in my ear. My neck was jostled until I thought it would snap. I was afraid to open my eyes, but I had to see what God had in store for me. Maybe I wasn't at my final destination yet, floating somewhere between earth and heaven.

What if I get stuck here? Trapped in the in-between place where the body aches and the mind never stops screaming...

My ears remained alert, widening to every sound like they'd been plugged by an unyielding dam for years. I willed my eyes to open into tiny slits.

The black smoke had disappeared. The walls around me had vanished. I floated on my back beneath a nighttime sky, pinpricks of bright white poking through the black. A bitter chill invaded my bones.

But how can a spirit have bones?

As if to answer my question, the cradle beneath me collapsed, and my body tumbled downward, causing my throat muscles to contract instinctively, forming a scream that wouldn't come. I landed on my tailbone and fell onto my back. All air was knocked out of me. The warmth beneath had been replaced by a cold hard surface. Pain like I'd never known attacked me in waves. Each deep breath was met with a coughing fit. My lungs burned like they were bleeding. My wrists felt like someone had cut them with razor blades and poured alcohol into the open wounds.

The thought came to me as unmistakably as the pain itself: *I am not dead.*

Aside from the stars overhead and a streetlamp glow, the world was dark. I rolled onto my side, my cheek making contact with cement. I was lying on a sidewalk. A brick wall stood in front of me. Bright red flames reached out through a broken window a story above me. I rolled onto my other side. Five feet away, a yellow rain jacket lay piled in a heap. A foot away from the jacket, a matching yellow helmet sat near the curb on its side, like someone had casually tossed it there.

As I crawled toward the jacket, my wrists bent. A scream should have followed, but strange grunts fell out of me instead, like I was a feral animal. I lifted my hands before my eyes. Thin, white nylon ropes had melded to my skin like bracelets. From each bracelet, an inch of rope dangled like a frayed charm. But there was no time to think about my wrists as my attention moved to the sooty face among the heap of yellow, a giant black-eyed Susan that had wilted to the ground.

I whispered, "Adam."

The simple word pushed my lungs into a fit. I curled into a ball. When the spasms finally subsided, I pushed myself onto my knees and hobbled along the uneven sidewalk like a confused zombie, trying to keep my balance, fearful that if I put weight on my wrists I'd pass out from the pain. I shuffled along with my arms extended and collapsed beside Adam's unmoving body. With my mind praying for the cold to numb the relentless pain in my wrists and lungs, I turned his head toward me and placed an ear to his mouth. His breath was shallow, his face drained of color. His right eye was swollen shut, his top lip cracked and bloody.

"Fire," Adam whispered.

The entire second floor of old Engine Number Three was engulfed. Sounds of sizzling wood and bending metal filled the cold empty night. Eager flames reached out through the upstairs windows. I was positive those flames were looking for me; that they wouldn't give up until they had finished what Josephine had started.

"Hurt," Adam said, touching the right side of his jacket.

His hand fell away to expose a large rip in the thick yellow material. My own pain dulled as I tore open the coat. A large wet circle of blood stained his T-shirt.

"Adam. What happened?"

"Homeless guy…stabbed me…took wallet…cell phone…but…not this…"

He opened a gloved hand. In the center lay the Swiss Army knife.

"Adam," I said. "You cut me free…"

My sobs turned into another round of coughing spasms. My throat burned like I had swallowed a cup of bleach. "Oh, Adam," I managed.

As I placed my wet cheek against his, I spotted the phone booth across the street. In its center stood an orange shape.

The shape turned. A face peered at me through the dirty glass.

"Come," I told Adam. "Now."

"Can't."

"No choice," I said, slowly standing up, crossing my legs for good luck, the cold seeping through the bottom of my stocking feet. My peripheral vision caught a flicker in the gutter: the flashlight. I grabbed it and forced Adam to stand. His weight leaned into me as we stumbled together like a couple of drunks down the sidewalk.

The fire above us screamed louder, angry that we were getting away. Across the street, the phone booth was now empty. Maybe it always had been. Maybe I'd had a hallucination. Maybe I'd lost my marbles.

But I knew the fire was real. I wondered how far away the rising smoke could be seen. I listened for sirens as we hobbled along but could only hear the lashes of flames, like whips striking the air.

At the truck, I leaned against the passenger door.

"Car keys," I said.

Adam pointed to his side pocket. Carefully, I dug out the keys. I threw the flashlight onto the seat's center. Then I helped Adam into the truck and pulled the seatbelt across him as he drifted into unconsciousness. In the glove compartment, I rummaged through junk until I found a package of travel tissues. I pulled out a wad and pushed it against Adam's wound. After I shut his door, I ran around to the driver's side.

As I climbed inside, a pair of monster-hands entered the cab, seized my arms, and yanked me out of the truck. The edge of the door checked my forehead as I fell to the sidewalk in equal parts of surprise and pain.

Josephine lost her balance and leaned against the truck for support.

I reached for the door to help me stand. Just as I got a hold of the steering wheel, Josephine grabbed the back of my turtleneck and heaved.

"I won't let you do this to me!" she wailed.

I kept my grip on the wheel. The truck rocked. A hand yanked a clump of my hair and I screamed. I took one hand off the wheel and nabbed the bulky flashlight from the seat. My back was toward Josephine as she worked to pull me out of the truck. I whirled around, brought my arm back, and let my loaded fist fly through the air. The flashlight exploded against a cheek. Josephine went down in a blur of shiny orange. The helmet flew from her head as she slammed into the pavement. She howled like rabid dog. While she lay on the sidewalk writhing, I took the flashlight, leaned over, and hit her again, this time against her skull. A thunderous crack filled the night.

Beside Josephine's unmoving hand lay a ring of keys. I nabbed them.

I jumped into the truck, locked the doors, and adjusted the mirrors. Then I froze. Could I really do this? I glanced over at Adam. Out cold, head against the window.

The shakes took over. My head swam. My wrists throbbed.

Okay, okay, okay…you can do this…come on, O'Donnell…

I counted to three and pressed my shoeless foot against the brake. I fumbled for the truck's key, stuck it into the ignition, and turned it. The Dodge roared into life, a dragon that would either fly us to safety or kill us with its otherworldly power. With the knotted pieces of rope still dangling from my screaming wrists, and a prayer lodged in my throat, I slid the stick on the steering column to the letter *D*.

Anguished tears streamed down my cheeks as I glanced in the side-view mirror. Josephine's body lay motionless on the sidewalk, one arm gracefully draped over the curb like a model in a photo shoot.

She would come to, eventually. I always did.

Still, my foot remained frozen against the brake. Even if I got the truck going in the right direction, there was a chance I wouldn't get us anywhere in one piece.

I counted down from ten, sucked in a deep breath, and let it out again. I looked back at Josephine. Her arm was no longer hanging over the curb. Her hand was rubbing a cracked and bleeding cheek. I released my foot from the brake and switched it to the accelerator. The tires squealed as the truck tore from the curb.

As I drove away from the burning building, I glanced in the side-view mirror one last time. Restless flames produced an eerie glow against the dark sky behind me. Beneath the glow, where, only minutes before, the orange jacket had melted to the ground like the Wicked Witch of the West's cape, lay a deserted sidewalk.

Josephine was gone.

I pressed my foot harder against the accelerator. The truck took on a life of its own, shredding the night. I zoomed up the littered streets, each stop light nothing more than a blur of red as I sped underneath.

The highway onramp was just ahead. The green sign pointed me in the right direction, but adrenaline kept an aggressive pace with my speed as it soared through my veins, racing to my heart. The tunnel vision that was always lying in wait wrapped itself around my head. My trembling hands could barely keep the wheel steady. A vicious pulse banged against my skull.

"No!" I shouted. "No, no, no!"

A few yards before the entrance to the highway, I pulled over to the curb and slid the stick to *P*. I turned my head to the right. My eyes peered through the dark. Adam seemed far away, like he was sitting at the bottom of a hole. Blood had soaked through the thin wad of paper.

"Adam," I choked, "I'm going down. I can't do this…"

He whispered, never opening his eyes, "You know what to do."

I know what to do.

Leaving the engine running, I opened my door. A strong gust of wind pushed me against the side of the vehicle as I stepped out of the truck. Blackness slithered in from the shadows, hungry for me. I made my way around to the passenger side and fell to my knees on the cold dirty sidewalk. Shaking uncontrollably, I rolled onto my back and raised my legs vertically against the side of the truck.

A tin can rolled down the street. An abandoned building watched me through its broken windows. Oncoming headlights sent fragments of light through the blackness beneath the truck, as a car drove past in the opposite direction, the driver in too much of a hurry to notice or not curious enough to stop.

My eyes closed. Time means nothing when a person is trapped between worlds. I pictured myself sitting on the sand, watching Adam ride his surfboard over the waves. I saw us sitting on the beach. Holding hands. Hugging. Kissing…

I counted breaths as the cold air moved in and out of my scorched lungs, the pounding of my heartbeat finally slowing. I brought my legs down and got to my knees. Still trembling, I used the top of the truck's tire for leverage and the hood for support as I made my way in front of the headlights.

Back in the driver's seat, I spoke to Adam. "Adam, I'm here. I'm back." I placed my fingers against his neck. His heartbeat was barely noticeable.

I put the truck in *D* and headed toward the highway onramp. As I crawled like a snail into the curve, the poster from Doctor Seymour's office wall suddenly appeared on the windshield, the happy young people sailing over the surge, the words splayed out like the Times Square tickertape: *What would you do if you weren't afraid?*

Nothing else mattered. Only Adam. Either he lived because

of me, or he died because of me. There was nothing in the middle. Stopping along the highway because of a spell was a strong possibility. Driving us headfirst into a ditch was another. But I didn't have time to analyze possible outcomes, refusing to let Fear dictate which way this was going to go. Fear was the enemy.

What would I do if I weren't afraid?

As I merged onto the highway, I announced to the windshield and the universe beyond, "I'd fucking burn rubber."

Chapter Thirty-six

Lindsay pulled her sputtering truck into the semi-circular driveway and let it idle. A robotic Santa Claus with a cheery plastic face stood in front of the revolving door, waiting patiently for a visitor to walk by and trigger its motion detector.

I unbuckled my seatbelt and reached for the door handle.

"Erica, wait," Lindsay said, placing a hand on my arm, careful not to touch my bandaged wrist.

I glanced through the passenger window toward the large block letters across the building's front: COUNTY HOSPITAL. It was my fifth time visiting in two weeks but the first time I'd get to see Adam in person.

"Thanks for letting me drive you," Lindsay said.

I nodded but said nothing. It had taken me until that morning to return her calls and an hour of persuasion for my mother to let Lindsay give me a ride. All the way to the hospital, she had spoken to me like I was a Catholic priest. Now, as we sat in the hospital's driveway, she continued her confession.

"I know you say you forgive me," she said.

"I do."

"I wanted to call you that night to let you know I'd got the truck started…that I was on my way back home…I should have charged my cell before I went down there. Sometimes I'm so stupid."

"We don't need to go over this again," I told her. "What's done is done."

Lindsay sniffled and wiped her tears with a pink bandana. She wore her hair in an unkempt bun, pulling her face tight like a doll's, and no makeup covered the pimples that dotted her jaw line. She said, "The worst part was when the cops made me identify him, and I saw his face, and the way he glared at me. All of a sudden, he looked like a monster."

"Larry always looked like that," I told her. "You just didn't want to see it."

"I should have," she said. "I'm not a child. I knew what I was doing. I just got caught up in everything—"

"I know, Linds."

"—and the thought of what Josephine did to you, and mailing out that video—my mom hasn't stopped crying—and Larry's family being ripped apart…"

"Larry did most of the ripping," I reminded her.

She nodded sadly. "I'm not going back to school."

"You weren't the only girl he did this to."

"I was the only one at Grayson," Lindsay said. "My mom thinks it'll be better if I finish out my final semester home-schooling. I'll still graduate. Then I'll take a gap year, maybe go stay with my grandma in the mountains. I can't go back, Erica. It's too hard. You know that."

I did know that. It took less than a day for the stories to snake their way through the school hallways. I'd heard the kids' cruel whispers behind Lindsay's back the second she left the cafeteria or disappeared around a corner.

The super-brains: "What a freaking dolt."

The Bible beaters: "That Jezebel's gonna rot in hell."

The invisible kids who rarely offered an opinion actually debated the matter: "I'd leave town and change my name" versus "She's gonna need all kinds of therapy."

As we sat in front of the hospital, I changed the subject to legal matters. "I heard Larry didn't make bail."

"They're holding him on statutory rape charges," Lindsay said. "One of the other girls was only fifteen. And because he secretly taped all of us...my attorney says he'll push for the maximum sentence." She shook her head and wiped her cheeks again.

"What about the twins?" I asked.

"They're with Larry's parents up north."

"When's the trial?"

"No one knows. Without Josephine's testimony..."

"I can't believe she abandoned her kids," I said.

"Me neither." Lindsay looked in her rear-view mirror. "There's a car behind me. I should go find a parking spot."

"Could you take your time?"

"I'll hang out in the cafeteria," she said. "Text me when you're ready."

I stepped out of the vehicle and headed into the tall white building, the robotic Santa waving an arm and shouting its automated "Ho, ho, ho!" Inside at the information desk, a tiny blue-haired lady wearing a volunteer name tag asked me where I was headed. The ICU sat on the third floor and only allowed family. But I wasn't going to the third floor today.

"Second floor, please," I told her. "Room 243."

The volunteer handed me a slip of paper with the room number scribbled across the front. In the elevator, I pressed the number two button. When the doors opened again, a happy, peach-colored hallway greeted me. I shuffled down the passageway in my coat and Uggs, read the number printed next to each doorway, took a deep breath outside 243, and entered the room. A television commercial competed with beeping sounds from one of the monitors. The wide window sill displayed get-well cards and flower-filled vases.

Adam lay sleeping upright, a blanket up to his sternum. The remote sat on the swivel table near the bed. I muted the television and placed a hand against his cheek, noting the healthy pink color. His eye was surrounded by a healing pale green.

Adam's eyes opened. He smiled. "Hey, girl."

"Hey, boy. How's it hanging?"

"Dazed and confused." He licked his chapped lips. "They pump drugs into me like I'm a bottomless Pez dispenser. Could you hand me that cup of water?"

I helped him sip, placed the cup back on the table, and leaned against the edge of his bed.

"I'll be released by the end of the week," he said. "Lung nearly healed, ribs still sore. I'll need some rehab for the torn ligaments in my knee, but I'll be shooting hoops in no time. Maybe even get on the surfboard next summer."

"That's awesome, Adam."

"How are you doing?" he asked. "My mom says you got burned pretty bad."

"You don't remember?"

"Not everything."

I slid back my coat sleeves and showed him my bandaged wrists. Hidden beneath the gauze were rings where the ropes had left their imprints. "My mother says they're the coolest tats she's ever seen." The doctors had told me how lucky I was, and I agreed. Getting treated for burns was nothing compared to Adam, who had lost nearly two pints of blood.

He touched my left arm the same gentle way Lindsay had, but not because he thought I'd break. "You saved me," he said.

"I thought *you* saved *me*."

He smiled thinly. "Rumor has it you drove my truck like a bat out of hell."

"I flew like a mother-clucking pterodactyl. Thank God that cop spotted me. Can you believe he thought I was drunk?"

Adam laughed and winced. He placed a hand against his side and let out a long, slow breath.

"I keep thinking of different scenarios," I said. "Like, what if you hadn't gone back to the truck for your fireman's jacket? Or, what if you didn't have the knife with you? What if that homeless guy had—"

"Erica, none of those things happened; only the things that got us here. Let the rest go."

I nodded.

After a moment, Adam said, "I've only caught bits and pieces of news in between my drug highs. What's the latest?"

"Larry's in jail awaiting trial; the kids are with their grandparents."

"And Josephine?"

"Still MIA. But I have some good news," I said, swiftly changing the subject by pulling a folded letter out of my pocketbook and handing it to Adam.

His eyes roamed down the length of the paper. "I got one, too," he said.

"You did?"

"My mom told me a few days ago. She thought the good news might help me recover faster."

When I had shared the Duke acceptance letter with my own mother, she'd whispered, "Eight months isn't so far away." With her eyes welling up, she had stood across from me like the kitchen table was a wide river. Ruthie O'Donnell, always the odd girl out.

Funny how the same trait that divided us was the one we had in common.

"Duke?" I asked Adam with way too much hope in my voice.

"Wilmington," he said. "Duke was a long shot, remember?"

"Oh. Right."

"Yeah."

"That's great, Adam."

"Is it?"

"Isn't it?"

We were silent for a moment.

Adam said, "We still have winter and spring and most of summer…"

An orderly came into the room, picked up some trash, and threw it into a container.

After he left with Adam's breakfast tray, I said, "I have some other news. My parents got me a dog."

"A dog?"

"You know. A service dog." I pulled out my cell phone, clicked on a photo, and turned the screen so Adam could see. "Part German shepherd and part who-knows-what. His name is Buster. He was saved from the gallows."

"He's cool," Adam said.

"I had to get tested for allergies," I explained, "but it was totally worth it. In January, I'll go to the training center and start working with him. He'll be coming with me to Duke. I hope he doesn't join a loser fraternity or fall in love with my roommate."

Adam laughed.

As I started to put away my cell phone, it chimed. "It's probably Lindsay."

"You're speaking to her?"

"She's been ostracized at school," I told him.

"I don't doubt it."

"She feels horrible about what happened."

Adam smirked. "She should."

"She's downstairs. She wants to apologize to you in person."

"Oh, Erica…"

"That night was a perfect storm, Adam."

"Lindsay was the catalyst."

"I know," I said. "But if her truck hadn't started when it did, who knows what Josephine would have done to her? Or maybe that creep who attacked you would have found Lindsay first."

"Those are a lot of maybes."

"I feel sorry for her."

Adam said, "Your heart is bigger than your head."

"Maybe that's why I faint," I said, smiling wanly.

I finally read Lindsay's text. Then I grabbed the remote.

"What are you doing?" Adam asked.

"Lindsay says to put on channel eleven."

The television remained muted as I changed the channel. We watched in silence as a helicopter shot a scene from above a freeway. Down below, three police vehicles had pulled over a red compact car. Small letters rolled across the bottom of the screen: *Video from earlier today.*

"Un-mute it," Adam said.

A male reporter was speaking: "…on the run now for nearly two weeks, was apprehended early this morning just outside Raleigh, North Carolina. Josephine Taggert, police say, gave no struggle while taken into custody for suspected arsons in the River Town area between June and November of this year…"

"There she is," Adam said.

A tiny speck of a woman with frizzy hair stepped out of the red car. Within seconds, four police officers surrounded her, their guns pointed. Her face was pressed against the asphalt. Another cop pulled Josephine's hands behind her back and clicked them into handcuffs.

The reporter went on: "Josephine Taggert is the wife of fireman Lawrence Taggert, arrested earlier for the same crimes. The arson charges against him, however, were subsequently dropped, but he is still being held on statutory rape and acts of videotaping a minor. Mr. Taggert, who has been denied bail, was a fireman with the River Town Fire Department for seven years. Prior to that, he worked with a fire department in the state of New Jersey, where, our sources say, he was asked to leave for having inappropriate relationships with several female high school students. No charges were brought against him at that time, but it is suspected that in lieu of the new charges and New Jersey's laws regarding the statute of limitations, that could change.

"Police say that evidence leading to Josephine Taggert's arrest was found in the couple's home, but they will not comment at this time on what that evidence is. The quiet and family-friendly Great Pines neighborhood is still in shock after hearing that a member of their peaceful community has allegedly committed crimes including arson, kidnapping, and attempted murder, making this one of the most bizarre cases seen in Eastern North Carolina."

The camera zoomed in on Josephine's blurry face peering through the police car window.

"So far," the reporter continued, "a handful of female minors, whose names are being withheld, have agreed to testify against Lawrence Taggert. Another female minor, who was allegedly kidnapped by Josephine Taggert, along with a male minor, who worked as a local volunteer firefighter, will more than likely be called to testify—"

I clicked off the television. "I don't want to hear anymore."

Outside the hospital window, a blue jay landed on the roof and pecked at something in the gutter.

Adam took the remote from my hand and put his own hand in its place. "It's over now."

"No, Adam, it's not."

"We'll testify together. We make a good team, you know."

I whispered, "I'm afraid."

"After what you've been through? This'll be a cake walk."

I didn't respond.

"Look," he said, "before you know it, all this shit will be behind us."

I nodded. Tears tried to reach the surface, but I forced them back.

"And then we'll get on with our lives," Adam went on. "We'll graduate from high school, then college. Get real jobs. I'll work for the Feds and you'll be a famous scientist."

"*Researcher*. And I could care less about being famous."

"Well, get ready, 'cause there's a Nobel Prize out there with your name on it."

Adam handed me my letter from Duke. I refolded it and tucked it back in my pocketbook. I had kept it close by since its arrival, occasionally taking it out and reading it again, focusing on the one noun that stood out among all the others, like it was a magic word I had to convince myself was real: *acceptance...*

Adam suddenly pulled me to him.

"Don't hurt yourself," I said.

"It's worth it."

He kissed me softly on the lips. My heart fluttered, and I didn't care.

My phone chimed again. I read the text. "Lindsay wants to know if you're ready to see her."

"Her timing sucks." Adam's head fell back onto the pillow. "If it makes her feel better, then whatever."

A few minutes later, Lindsay stood in the middle of the room like she wasn't sure where she was or how she got there.

"I'm going to get some tea," I said. "You want something, Adam?"

"Maybe a hot chocolate? The room service around here is *mucho sucko*."

I smiled and walked past Lindsay without a word. I was all out of words for the moment; she could do the talking for a while. I stepped into the maze-like hallway, staring from one end to the other, trying to remember which way to go.

In the room, Lindsay was saying to Adam, "I'm so sorry about all of this."

"I know," he mumbled.

"I don't think you'd be here now if it weren't for Erica. She's my hero."

"Mine, too."

"And just so you know," Lindsay said, "I can't imagine you being with anybody else."

Adam replied, "Neither can I."

Chapter Thirty-seven

A double dose of perfume and hairspray entered my nostrils and rose into my sinuses. The soft leather seats cushioned me as we rolled to a stop in front of the entrance. The limo driver tipped his cap and held the door for us like we were rap stars. As I stepped onto the pavement, my toes tingled, but it was a sweet sensation, standing four inches taller than I ever had before. Live music cascaded from the gymnasium and greeted us in the lobby. My eyes squinted against the bright silver sparkles hanging from the hallway ceiling.

In his white top hat and tails and gloves, Adam's cane was the cherry on top of a very handsome sundae. He had smeared the cane with glue and doused it with silver sparkles to match my dress. I still wore bandages on my wrists, so instead of a wrist corsage, Adam bought me a shimmering tiara to wear in my up-do.

"For the princess of the ball," he had said, positioning it in my hair before my parents took a billion photos.

I kept touching the tiny crown, making sure it wasn't falling off my head, dragging my curls with it. Making sure I wasn't dreaming.

Stepping into the decorated gym was like having one foot in Disney World and the other in Santa's Workshop. Dozens of large silver balls hung from steel girders that stretched across the gym's high ceiling, and expansive white sheets hid the folded bleachers, miles of holly strung across the front. From somewhere hidden, gobos projected floating giant snowflakes against the cinder block walls. Twenty round tables lined either side of the room, the students already nabbing chairs, saving their spots with fancy jackets or glittery purses. Sweet sounds of laughter and intimate conversations swirled around us. The only light in the room besides the spots over the band and the snowflakes was a pale blue that fell across the dance floor where a few brave couples showed off their dance steps. If this had been my first time in the school gym, I'd never have guessed that a thousand pairs of tennis shoes ran across this same floor five days a week.

We double dated with Adam's buddy, Colin, who invited a girl named Tanya from a private school across town. The four of us planned to hang out at the Winter Formal for a while and then head to the Duck Creek Inn, where we had a late dinner reservation.

Classmates came up to Adam and asked to see his cane. Some wanted to sneak a peek at his stitches, but he told them it would take too long to put his cummerbund back on. A few girls who had never given me the time of day before, Cheerleader Captain and Homecoming Queen included, told me how beautiful I was and snapped pictures with me in the middle. The girl who won "Most Likely to Succeed" in our yearbook's *Who's Who* said, "If

I could write my college essay all over again, it would be about you."

They called us heroes, which I thought was ironic, since Adam and I didn't save anyone but each other. Maybe it was because they knew we still had a trial to undergo; that our real heroic work hadn't yet begun.

But I wouldn't mull over any of that tonight.

The four of us sat drinking punch at one of the tables as the five-piece band played country-rock, R&B, and some underground techno stuff.

As soon as the lead singer began his rendition of a romantic John Legend tune, Adam stood and leaned his cane against the table. He took me by the hand. Without words, he led me to the dance floor, walking slowly for his own sake, but also so I wouldn't tumble to the floor, a novice when it came to high heels. He wrapped his arms around my waist, and I wrapped mine around his neck. Dozens of couples joined us, but I still felt like we were the only ones in the center of the universe.

As we held one another, swaying beneath the silver sparkles and blue lights, Adam's warm breath whispered in my ear: "You're going to kick ass next year. I can feel it."

"You'll kick more," I whispered back.

He kissed my earlobe, my neck, my cheek. "I'll totally miss you, Erica O'Donnell."

"I'll totally miss you more, Adam Carchelli."

He took a tiny step back, his serious brown eyes falling into mine. Then he grinned. "We freaking rock, don't we?"

He didn't wait for an answer as he again pulled me close. His lips pressed against mine, the taste of Colgate and punch mingling like honey on my tongue. He held me with equal parts passion and protection. I'd take all the passion I could get. But I didn't need Adam's protection, though I would never tell him that. Once a fireman, always a fireman. For Adam, protecting others was as reflexive as blinking. Or sneezing. Or catching a dropped object.

Or fainting.

The gap between my spells hadn't grown any wider, but, on the flipside, it hadn't become any narrower. Who knew what the future had in store? I could faint twenty minutes from now while reapplying lipstick in the bathroom, or pass out in Adam's arms while making out in the limo. Maybe the spells would lie dormant until graduation day and then surprise me as I walked across the stage to collect my diploma. Perhaps they would hold out until summertime and reappear just as Adam and his long board faded into the surf. There was never a guarantee from doctors or the latest pills that my spells would vanish entirely or that they'd rule my life. There was never a guarantee of anything, ever, that things would be exactly as I wanted.

But there was always hope.

Adam and I kept our arms locked tightly around one another even though my wrists were still tender and his stitches made him itch; even after the pretty song had ended and crazy house music rocked the room. We remained in that pose like a plastic couple standing eternally on top of a fancy cake, not afraid to let go, but brave enough to hold on for as long as we could.

Author's Note:

Erica O'Donnell, the main character in *Rules of Falling*, suffers from a type of syncope which falls somewhere between *vasovagal syncope* and *orthostatic hypotension*. In effect, her doctor is not sure exactly what causes her episodes, a common situation for many real-life chronic fainters.

According to the Mayo Clinic, there are seven types of syncope. All names are related to the cause:

1. *Cardiogenic syncope:* usually related to abnormal heart rhythms and is considered more serious than other types of syncope.
2. *Neurocardiogenic syncope:* also called *vasovagal syncope* (aka "common faint"); related to heart and nervous system problems.
3. *Neurologic syncope:* related to problems with the nervous system, such as seizures.
4. *Metabolic syncope:* caused by disturbances of the chemical functions within the body, such as low blood sugar (*hypoglycemia*) or hyperventilation with or

without perceived anxiety (causing gases in the
bloodstream to become unbalanced).

5.   *Psychogenic syncope:* sometimes triggered by states of
mind, such as panic, anxiety, major depression, or
hysteria.

6.   *Orthostatic hypotension:* characterized by a drop in
blood pressure when standing.

7.   *Syncope of undetermined etiology:* unknown causes.

Because there is a varied scale of severity within each type, I felt
it was more important to show how chronic fainting can affect
daily life rather than focus on one particular type.

If you suffer from undiagnosed syncope, please see your physician.

Book Discussion Questions:

Do not read the following before reading the book!

1. Have you ever fainted? How did you feel afterward? Were you embarrassed? Frightened? Did you share what happened with others?

2. Describe Erica's relationship with her mother. Did you take sides while reading *Rules of Falling*? Explain.

3. Why does Adam keep vying for Lindsay even after she tells him it is over between them?

4. What do you think Lindsay sees in Larry? If it hadn't been Larry, would it have been someone else? Explain.

5. Compare/contrast Lindsay and Erica.

6. Compare/contrast Erica and her mother.

7. Who did you suspect early on was committing arson? Did your suspicions change as you continued reading? Explain.

8. Who do you feel is the antagonist in *Rules of Falling*? Why?

9. Erica is not allowed to do everyday things that other girls her age do. How does this hinder her? How does it make her more mature?

10. Do you have a friend who suffers from a chronic disease? If so, explain how you handle the situation.

11. Do you feel that Erica's choice to pursue Adam is ethical? Why or why not?

12. Were you angry with Lindsay or did you feel sorry for her? Explain using details from the story.

13. How does Erica change from the story's beginning to the end?

14. Do you think Erica is brave? Why or why not?

15. If the story were to continue beyond the last chapter, describe some details of Erica's last summer with Adam. What about her first semester of college?

16. What would you do if your best friend disclosed that she or he was having an affair with a married adult?

17. What kind of punishment do you feel arsonists deserve? What kind of punishment do you feel pedophiles deserve?

18. Continue the story for Lindsay. Has her personal journey changed her for the better or worse? How can she use what she has learned in the future?

19. If you were the parent of a child with syncope, would you have done the same things as Mrs. O'Donnell? What would you have done differently?

20. Keeping all of the characters in mind, explain who you believe lost or gained the most in *Rules of Falling*.

Acknowledgements

Creating a book from vague idea to prewriting to publication is the epitome of the old saying, "It takes a village." There are global editors, copy editors, beta readers, photographers, cover designers, formatters, reviewers, librarians—the list seems infinite—all working in their respective fields to bring a book to life, keep it breathing, and resuscitate it when needed. I will start with my literary agent, Uwe Stender, founder and president of the TriadaUS Literary Agency. Without Uwe's words of wisdom, matchmaking expertise, and perfectly timed pats on the back, *Rules of Falling* would never have evolved into the story it is today. Thank you, Uwe, for keeping an open mind and pushing me further than I knew was possible, especially in an ever-changing publishing industry. This leads me to my next thanks endearingly given to my husband, Jay Kenton Manning, the talented designer of the book's cover. More importantly, he listens as I read aloud every word of each book before it ever hits the stands. My career choice would not be achievable without his unwavering support, constant hugs, and morning laughter. I am forever indebted to the following beta readers, my sweet Street Team: Patty Howard, Deborah G. Lynn, Finola Corbett, Karen Lankton, Lynn Murray, and Linda McDonald. Thank goodness for my authors' Zoom meetings which kept me sane as a pandemic swept across the globe. I am the luckiest writer in the world to have these ladies as the constant wind beneath my tattered wings, and fantastic story tellers in their own right: Tracie Barton-Barrett, Heather Cobham Brewer, Padgett Gerler, and Michelle G. Flye, the most wonderful book store owner in the Southeast. A huge shout out goes to my beast sisters, Sandra Ferguson, Angela Maurer, and Jennifer Argenti, for waiting loyally and patiently as each book is created and gently placed into their hands. Thanks additionally to Amanda Edwards, who has never stopped rooting for me. I'd like to sincerely thank Chase Barden, former volunteer fireman and all-around awesome guy, for teaching me the ins and outs of firefighting procedures, along with sharing his personal stories. Of course, this book would not have been taken seriously if not for the indispensable medical information offered by the Northwest Ohio Cardiology Consultants; Dr. Carlo Oller, MD; and Doctor Alex Kirby, MD, respectively. Their collective cache of knowledge not only helped me but currently helps those suffering from syncope and other medical issues. *Rules of Falling* is available in both digital and printed formats thanks to the expertise of Jason and Marina at Polgarus Studio who make all my books shine from halfway around the globe. Special thanks to the editors at Entangled Publishing for taking the time to offer sage advice way back in the beginning of the book's journey. And finally, I'd like to thank my students, both former and current, for allowing me to dig into the secret parts of their everyday lives and for reminding me what it is to be a teen in today's socially overwrought world. While technology has changed, the heart of a teenager has not. I love each and every one of these amazing humans. Even when they drive me crazy!

About the Author

Leslie Tall Manning is an award-winning novelist who loves writing about grownups craving change and discovering it in ways they never expected (*GAGA, MAGGIE'S DREAM,* and *KNOCK ON WOOD*). She also writes about teenagers who believe in independence, often stumbling into it headfirst (*RULES OF FALLING, UPSIDE DOWN IN A LAURA INGALLS TOWN,* and *I AM ELEPHANT, I AM BUTTERFLY*). As a private English tutor and study skills specialist, Leslie spends her evenings working with students of all ages and her days working on her own writing projects. When she isn't clacking away at the computer keys or conducting research for her books, she loves traveling far and wide with her artist husband and then coming back home to their wonderful North Carolina town.

Book Awards

Sarton Women's Literary Award
North Carolina Author Project Award
Taleflick Pick and Taleflick Finalist
International Book Award Finalist
Self-e Library Journal Selection
Indie BRAG Award
Readers' Choice Award
Story Monsters Certificate of Excellence

Feel free to leave a review for *Rules of Falling* on social media.

To learn more about Leslie, visit her website:
www.leslietallmanning.com

You may also find her on Facebook, Instagram, Twitter, Goodreads, and Pinterest.

What reviewers have to say about the award-winning
Upside Down in a Laura Ingalls Town

"Brooke's voice feels authentic as she struggles to reconnect with her fractured family, and Manning's historical research shows…an entertaining novel with realistic characters readers should find it easy to invest in." ~ **Publishers Weekly**

"This endearing tale will make any young reader realize the importance of family, especially when one of them is no longer there." ~ **Midwest Book Reviews**

"Poignant and funny by turns, *Upside Down in a Laura Ingalls Town* touches the heart through both the tears and laughter." ~ **Hen Scratches Reviews**

"Beautifully written, with fully developed characters and a setting so well-researched I felt I was learning about the time period in the most enjoyable way." ~ **Crossworlds Reviews**

"An eye-opening story for people who think their life is tough and for people who need to appreciate what is right in their lives." ~ **Story Circle Book Reviews**

"Touching, heartwarming, humorous, and inspiring." ~ **Story Monsters Ink**

"Clearly, [Manning] has researched living situations at that time very well…I appreciated how in depth this was when describing the differences in living circumstances…nice twists at the end!" ~ **YA Books Central**

"I laughed, cried, was mortified and scared, any emotion you can think of while reading this gem of a book." ~ **Novel Gossip**

"[A] coming-of-age story with equal parts humor, angst, grit, and charm." ~ **Padgett Gerler, author of** *Invisible Girl*

"Few novels are crafted as creatively as this delightful novel!" ~ **Katherine Sartori, author of** *The Chosen Shell*

Read on for an excerpt of
Upside Down in a Laura Ingalls Town:

An out-of-control sixteen-year-old finds her life turned upside down when she becomes the star of a reality show set in 1861 in the North Carolina Backcountry. But can a young girl's wishful heart surrender to a time and place she believes she can never call home?

"I'm Ricardo Gonzales," said the smiling man behind the desk. He had long dark hair tied in a ponytail, and his hands were folded neatly in front of him like he ran a country. His words held on to the traces of an accent. Next to him sat a large woman with short, curly red hair and a T-shirt that said, *Roll 'Em!*

"Have a seat on the couch over there," Ricardo said, pointing with his head, "and we'll begin the audition."

Why did everyone keep saying that word?

We sat with Dad in the middle, me on his right, Rebecca Lynn on his left.

"So," Ricardo said, "no one has told you anything about the actual show, is that correct, Mr. Decker?"

"Correct."

"What makes you want to be part of a project you know nothing about?"

"Our family could use a little—diversion."

"What's *diversion*?" Rebecca Lynn asked.

Dad explained, "Something to take our minds off what we've been through."

"And what have you all been through?" Ricardo asked.

"Their mother passed away last summer. It's been a long haul."

"Oh," Ricardo said, his smile tipping. "Right. You wrote about that in your letter. I'm sorry for your loss."

He said he was sorry, but I caught a slight twitch in his eye as he glanced at the fat woman next to him.

"So," Ricardo said, "if you were chosen for this venture, you feel, after what you've been through, you'd be able to handle adverse situations?"

"Of course."

"And your girls?"

Rebecca Lynn said, "Daddy showed us how to be strong."

"That's awesome," Ricardo said. Then he turned to me. "And you, Brooke? Do you think adversity makes a person stronger?"

"I don't know." I started to play with the ring in my brow but stopped myself.

"Do you think you could live for a time without certain things?"

"Like what?" I asked.

"Makeup? Hairspray? Jewelry?"

Why was this Ricardo guy asking me such stupid questions? I looked at Dad, but he was staring at the camera.

"And what about the mall?" Ricardo went on. "Your cell phone? Your social media? Could you live without those things for a long period of time?"

"I can," piped Rebecca Lynn.

But Ricardo didn't care about my sister. He was waiting for my answer.

"How long is long?" I asked, the spit in my mouth drying up.

He shrugged, not like he was bored, but like he really didn't care how his answer affected me. "Four months."

I laughed, but it was just a spurt of nervousness, not a LMAO kind of laugh.

Ricardo waited.

"Well, no," I said. I could feel Dad's body stiffen next to me, but I didn't care. "I could never go that long without those things. They're a part of life. Where does this show take place, on an island?"

Ricardo didn't answer my question. "The show would require your family to leave behind the modern accoutrements you have become accustomed to. Like soda, fast-food, television. For four months, you'd have to give up your friends, your social networks, your favorite iTunes, your boyfriends, your weekend slumber parties—"

The large woman next to Ricardo, who had stayed silent up to this point, said, "Your high heels and deodorant. All the creature comforts."

I was beyond nervous now. I didn't know where the television show was going to take place, but I did not want to do it. No freaking way, no freaking how. I would have to make too many sacrifices. Shit. I had already sacrificed my mom. Wasn't that enough?

My dad patted me on the knee again. "Those kinds of things aren't important to us."

"Yes they are," I said.

"No, they're not. We've learned as a family what it means to do without."

He was lying. We hadn't done without. If anything, since Mom had died, Dad was buying more crap than ever. We had every new gadget known to modern man: a Kindle; a Nook; the latest iPhone; iTouch; iPad; i-*Everything*. We had three PCs collecting dust, two laptops, and a 3D television. Last October, on my sixteenth birthday, Dad bought me a brand new Explorer with heated leather seats. We took a trip to the Bahamas for Thanksgiving, Christmas looked like Macy's exploded in our living room, and we spent New Year's skiing in Vail. He never said a word when I added pink to my hair, or when he spotted the panther tattoo on my lower back while swimming at the country club. He never showed any emotion when I went for that dark eyeliner look, almost, but not quite, Goth. I never heard a stink about quitting the track team. And he still gave me money when report cards came out, even though my *A*'s had dropped to *C*'s, except for Gym which was a *D*+. At the end of last semester, as he handed me a fifty, he said, "I know you'll find your way back."

Now, my dad's face seemed desperate. He wanted this. I didn't know why he wanted it, but I wanted it for him. For *him*. But not for *me*. Maybe I could live with relatives while Dad and Rebecca Lynn went off to this strange land where no one used deodorant or checked out Youtube videos.

My stomach rumbled and my heart raced as pictures of a labor camp popped into my head, the three of us dressed in gray coveralls, a six-digit number stamped on our forearms, barbed wire surrounding us.

"Is this a prison reality show?" I licked my chapped lips and waited for the answer.

Ricardo smiled and said, "We can't disclose exactly what it is until you pass the first round. If you make the cut, then you'll be told. For now, we have to keep the details as quiet as possible. Too many ears in Hollywood looking for a good reality show. Know what I mean?"

My head nodded yes even though I had no clue what he was talking about.

Ricardo continued with the questions:

"Okay, then. Do any of you have any habits you can't quit for a few months?"

Like making out with cute boys or pounding Jell-O shots on a Friday night?

I watched with horror as my dad and sister shook their heads.

Ricardo jotted something down on the paper in front of him. "Anyone who makes it through will receive a full physical, but to save us some steps, do any of you require regular medication?"

Like pot brownies?

Again they shook their heads. Dad nudged me until I did the same.

"Any pets that will be difficult to leave for any length of time?"

Rebecca Lynn said, "My goldfish died."

"How did that make you feel?"

"Sad. But I didn't cry. We flushed him down the toilet. He's with Nemo now."

Ricardo leaned forward. "What are your fears?"

My dad spoke first. "Something happening to one of my daughters." He put an arm around each of us and squeezed. "Or something happening to me."

"And you?" he asked Rebecca Lynn. "What scares you?"

"Zombies. And ghosts."

Ricardo nodded. "Me too."

Rebecca Lynn smiled.

"And Brooke," Ricardo said. "What frightens Brooke Decker?"

Well, let me tell you, culo burro *Ricardo. Yesterday it would have been getting caught sleeping in history class, having Dad find out I'd snuck beer onto my school's field trip to Charleston, or getting a speeding ticket out in Greenville. Now, my fears are having a camera in my face, the incessant grin on that woman next to you, and the way you keep staring at me, like I'm going to be the reason we either will or won't make the cut.*

"Nothing," I told him. After seeing my mom suffer through a double mastectomy, watching her wither away from chemo, then floating to her death on morphine, I believed at that moment I was telling the truth. I raised my chin a notch. Dad's pride filled the room. "Nothing frightens me."

"Very good," Ricardo said, nodding slowly, marking a sheet in front of him. "Thank you for your time. We'll be in touch."

We were quickly escorted out of the room, and just as the door was about to close behind me, I saw Ricardo fist bumping the chubby lady beside him, her pudgy smile in the center of that pasty face turning her into a redheaded Pillsbury Dough Boy.

Upside Down in a Laura Ingalls Town is available now

Made in the USA
Coppell, TX
06 May 2022

77488092R10177